GHOSTS OF GRAVEYARDS PAST

Laura Briggs

I0691842

GHOSTS OF GRAVEYARDS PAST

Contact Information: titleadmin@pelicanbookgroup.com

Cover Art by *Nicola Martinez*

White Rose Publishing, a division of Pelican Ventures, LLC
www.pelicanbookgroup.com PO Box 1738 *Aztec, NM * 87410

White Rose Publishing Circle and Rosebud logo is a trademark of Pelican Ventures, LLC

Publishing History
First White Rose Edition, 2014
Electronic Edition ISBN 978-1-61116-450-3
Paperback Edition ISBN 978-1-61116-451-0
Published in the United States of America

Dedication

For Mary, whose love for history has inspired more than one story.

1

It was mid-October, with crimson and yellow leaves curling away from branches on trees that lined the highway. Ignoring the chill in the air, Jenna Cade lowered the rental car's windows. The cool breeze fanned strands of gold hair before her eyes and rustled the map beside her in the passenger seat. Her destination, a rural town in Alabama, had been circled in red.

Three months and four states had slipped past since Jenna first began her journey. Not a pleasure trip, but a tour in search of the Deep South's forgotten burial grounds—cemeteries dating back hundreds of years, somehow lost in the fray of time and property development, their existence little more than lore to those living around them.

Such gravestones were scattered across wooded hollows, remote pastures lands, even the muddy banks of a swamp. Hallowed grounds haunted by nothing and no one, Jenna's feet the first to tread their soil in decades for all she knew.

"Dead Cemeteries," as her agent, Joyce Edel, referred to them.

Jenna preferred the less macabre *Stories Behind the Stones*, a title penciled in the notes of her work portfolio. Its pages bulged with material from visits to sites in Georgia, Tennessee, and Mississippi. Photographs and gravestone rubbings mostly, her observations recorded on a handheld device she kept in her knapsack.

At night, she played back the recordings as she typed a first draft. Her voice sounding tinny and faraway on the machine, a breathless quality as she noted, "There's a face sculpted into this marble—a woman's face. Young features, a wide mouth and oval eyes…"

Other oddities greeted her past the acres of brush and bramble. In one place, the hollowed shell of an old church watched over the monuments, its stone foundation the only part untouched by the flames of a past fire.

"How does this even happen?" her agent asked, reading over the materials Jenna e-mailed from the weeks she spent on the road. "It's like these people just got erased from history, like no one even remembers them. They've just—disappeared."

"I know," said Jenna, the same photos spread before her on the bed. She had never seen anything look so desolate, even when researching a manuscript for the communities rendered ghost towns by the railroad deals. She had dug broken pottery and arrowheads from the dust of former Native American villages, but this was her first time to unearth someone's headstone from a deserted landscape.

She tried to imagine her own grave in some isolated wood someday, thorn plants tangled round the moss-encrusted stone. Unlikely, considering the Cade family's attentive nature for previous generations, with family burial plots and with memorial and decoration days observed every year since she could remember.

But then, hadn't someone cared for these

individuals, as well?

"Most cemeteries aren't on the tax roll," a city official had explained the first time she phoned to report a neglected burial site. "If the legal descendants are dead or untraceable, the city may supervise a grant for maintenance. Otherwise, it's up to the community to find the money and resources."

It was this last option Jenna hoped the book would set in motion. If she could put a story with the stones, then readers might feel a connection to neglected cemeteries in their towns and neighborhoods.

But how did one describe a stranger's heart or capture the tone of a voice long since faded from any ear? The answer evaded her as she crushed carpets of poison ivy to find just a pile of rocks for a marker or sometimes deep impressions in the earth where a grave may or may not be planted.

Babies' graves were the easiest to identify. She knew them by the sight of a lamb's shape etched into the surface, or sometimes a single flower severed from the stem. A broken sword might represent a youth cut down in his prime, a broken branch the same.

Slave cemeteries, she learned, were nearly impossible to document. The few inscriptions were chipped away by harsh elements, the limestone crumbling beneath a green film no amount of scrubbing would ever remove. There had been one in Mississippi—a boggy strip of acreage known among the locals as Angel's Pass—where the tombs were half-swallowed by greedy, spongy brown earth.

Jenna's boots sank, her knees caked with mud as she knelt to examine the damaged markers. Even the ones lacking names bore traces of a design, or maybe a special curve in the stone's shape. Proof that someone, somewhere, had once cared.

Such markers were too fragile to withstand even the gentlest of gravestone rubbings, the stone yielding a hollow sound when she tapped it with a pencil. She photographed them instead, angling mirrors to slant the sunlight so it bathed the carved portions in shadow. That was an old trick, one safer than brushing the cracks with flour, or wrapping the stone in tin foil to make an imprint.

"Believe in ghosts?" more than one person asked whenever she spoke of the project in the towns surrounding the cemeteries. Their mouths would quirk in a sly smile as they waited for her response.

The answer was always the same: a firm "No," a shake of the head, and a faint laugh. Her fingers instinctively moved to the silver cross around her neck, a graduation gift from her parents when she left their family home for the university in Annapolis.

Faith in her Heavenly Father had long ago replaced any childish fears she might have harbored for phantom visitors stealing between this world and the next. These days, her sole fascination lay with how the people lived before the flesh had wasted into bone, and, from there, into dust.

∂∽∞

The cemetery at Sylvan Spring was almost a ghost in its own right.

At least, that was the slant the newspaper story had taken. Filed among Jenna's research papers, the article was dated eight years back, and focused on the stretch of woods that bordered the rural Alabama town.

Hikers who braved its paths in search of the spring had claimed to see old headstones planted among the acres of foliage. None could ever find the cemetery a second time, and accounts of where it had been seen varied so much that the article's writer chose to call it a "ghostly encounter," the stones appearing and vanishing as mysteriously as a phantom.

Her agent was certainly far from convinced, reminding her that the publisher was adamant; the upcoming New Orleans site had to be a prominent feature. "Take a week, maybe ten days, and check this place out," Joyce told her, "but remember—there's no time for detours. No second guesses, especially when the site in Louisiana is a sure thing. "

A graveyard with a confirmed location, and volunteers already on site to help with the genealogical research. This was the silent implication of her agent's words.

"Ten days," Jenna agreed, her gaze falling on the destination circled in red. Less than eighty miles of country road remained between herself and the truth of her latest search.

Dusk arrived ahead of her, bathing the town in a soft glow. She had expected to find a tourist trap after reading about the local spring, but there were no spa centers among the collection of buildings that slid past her windshield. There were churches of different denominations and a prayer chapel with stained glass. Also, a tarot card reader, whose cottage-like building seemed to hunker in the shadows, its porch banisters swathed in kudzu vine.

More businesses caught her eye: a crystal and candle emporium named Moonspell, a custom-design jewelry store, and a pottery shop with local goods on display. The strains of a live folk band echoed from the open door of a pub-themed restaurant on the corner.

Her accommodation for the week, a historic inn, was located at the end of the square. She parked before the white-washed structure her agent had called "old-fashioned and overpriced," when she booked the room on her client's behalf.

Jenna conceded the first part of the statement, her gaze taking in three stories of gables and balconies and the trellis with its mask of purple wisteria. A black-wrought-iron fence hugged the corner, hinting at a possible flower garden in the back.

As she climbed from the car, something else caught her eye: a banner flapping in the breeze between two lampposts. The words, *Ye Old Hallowed Days Festival* had been formed in curving script, a date given for the following weekend.

Painted below was a series of strange shapes. Triple spirals and interlocked circles, an intricate set of knots that formed a shield. A Renaissance festival was her first guess, or something of a medieval nature. Maybe some sort of Halloween celebration, given this time of year.

It was likely to be the last one, yet something about the symbol seemed ancient, almost pagan-like. Her mind flew to the card reader's business and the shop of crystals and mineral rocks. At a glance, this place seemed to offer as much to New Age crowds as it did to the Christian congregation.

Inside, she questioned the clerk about it as they checked her reservation.

"Oh, the Celtic thing," said the girl, scarcely younger than Jenna, hair bleached blond and in short spikes, a piercing in her left nostril. "Yeah, it has to do with the county's heritage society. They thought it up decades ago to keep town history alive, but it's grown since then. Games and booths and stuff like that were added to it."

"Is it supposed to be for Halloween?" Jenna guessed. Perhaps the celebration was only a harmless fall-themed cultural festival with no connection to the hints of occult dabbling she'd seen elsewhere in the town. She was curious to know the truth.

The girl's brow furrowed. "I think it's more of a history thing, maybe something to do with a legend? Anyway, it's something that happened ages ago. A curse or hex on the town."

"Curse?" Jenna echoed. "What—like a drought or a grasshopper infestation or something?" She couldn't help the laugh that escaped as she tried to imagine what kind of old superstition could possibly demand its own celebration, short of the usual one that had people carving pumpkins and donning costumes at this time of year.

"Not sure," the girl answered with a shrug. "I've only lived here a couple years, but someone told me it goes back to stories in the 1800s." She shrugged again as if to emphasize her lack of certainty, and then turned to the computer screen beside her.

This explanation was more bizarre then Jenna imagined, making her wonder how many other legends the town might have.

Shifting her knapsack, she reached for a brochure display on the desk—lots of pictures of quaint shops where workers demonstrated such techniques as candle making and basket weaving.

"Is there someplace I can learn more about the town's history?" she asked, thumbing through the glossy pamphlet. "A university or genealogy center, some place with old records and deeds."

"There used to be a museum, but I heard all its stuff burned in an accident." The girl paused mid-type, thinking. "I've seen a historical society over by the library. An old building with stained glass windows."

"Perfect," said Jenna, pocketing the brochure. She would need help from local researchers to identify the names on the headstones—if there *were* any to identify, that is.

"You're in the Dragonfly Room," said the clerk, sliding a key across the desk. "We serve breakfast at eight, and you'll find the dining hall through that set of accordion doors by the stairs..." she broke off as the phone by the computer rang.

Jenna wanted to ask more, to find out if the festival could somehow tie in with her research for the book.

But the clerk was busy moving a reservation for someone, her fingers stroking over the computer keyboard as she talked.

For now, Jenna would have to be content with unpacking her bags, and the glimpse of the town below through her second story window.

2

The shops were still locked when Jenna made her way outside the next morning. She had skipped breakfast in her eagerness to explore the town, pulling her cellphone out to snap pictures of the old-fashioned buildings in the square. Architecture that was mostly 1920s, though some looked as if it might be Queen Anne period.

She found the historical society next to the library. Its windows were still dark, a sign advertising the hours as 10AM to 1PM, no weekends.

Maybe its volunteers would be eager for a credit in her upcoming manuscript. The other sites had required a genealogist to hasten the process of identifying the graves, some of whom were still at work on the slave cemeteries, the damaged stones threatening to never yield answers beyond what met the eye.

"Morning," said a woman who passed her on the sidewalk, her arms cradling a tray of plant seedlings. She had a stocky build and pleasant face, her auburn hair pulled back in a handkerchief. She unlocked the door to a shop called *Old World Herbs*. Once inside, the woman left the closed sign facing out as she fussed with a window display.

Jenna continued down a series of streets, feet turning where a sign indicated the Sylvan Grove Cemetery would be. She hoped its older stones might give her some clue as to when the wooded cemetery fell out of use—and out of memory. Surprised to find the cemetery gates open when none of the shops were, she peered past the entrance. Rows of cold gray monuments glittered in the morning light. The air was crisp and her denim jacket seemed insufficient as she moved forward.

It was quiet here except for the occasional bird cry and the rustle of dry leaves beneath her boots. The older graves would be somewhere in the back. She glanced over more recent dates on nearby tombs. Her breath hitched as, out of the corner of her eye, she saw something move.

A figure had appeared among the markers on the other side of the graveyard. A man, his hair dark and slightly rumpled. Not the caretaker, and certainly not a spirit, though her heart continued to beat as if he were an apparition.

Dressed in jeans and a green utility jacket, he crouched before a tomb that was sculpted in ivy. One hand rested against the chiseled pattern as the other clutched a bouquet of wild flowers.

They were too far apart to speak, to do anything more than exchange a look, except his face was turned away.

She continued to walk, her steps slow and noiseless, as she stared at the stranger.

As if sensing her gaze, he turned, revealing a profile with features young, but tired, in the morning light.

Another second and he was gone, her glimpse of him obscured by the spread of angelic wings from an elaborate monument. A faint flush covered her cheeks. Shame, perhaps, for disturbing a mourner come to pay their respects.

She didn't see him again, didn't look back to see if his gaze followed her through the paths. Quick steps carried her to a far corner of the yard where a pair of weeping willows stood guard over tombs as old as the 1880s. The slabs of limestone and slate were impressively preserved, sunlight reflecting off the gilded lettering.

The stones changed to the more durable marble and sandstone the further she moved into the 1900s, implying a shift in the town's fortunes. Instinctively, she raised her camera, focusing the lens on hand-carved designs that seemed far more varied than those of modern tombs made by machines.

Winged skulls with gap-toothed smiles. An angel with a scroll and another with a trumpet; a hand that reached to snuff a candle. Lambs, butterflies, and hands folded in prayer. Her finger traced the beveled edges, lips forming a sad smile. Angling the camera lens so that no sunlight obscured the carvings, she snapped a picture.

Footsteps crunched behind her, and she turned, half-expecting to see the stranger with the wildflowers.

Instead, an older gentleman strolled, a trash sack in one hand as he collected withered bouquets and pieces of ribbon shredded by the wind. "Good morning," he said, one hand doffing his cap in a gentlemanly manner.

Jenna smiled, hoisting her camera as she said, "These headstone engravings are beautiful. I couldn't resist a few pictures."

"Yes, they are impressive," the man agreed, his voice pleasant as he studied the ones she had just photographed. "Taking care of them is an honor, though my knees are getting a bit weak for the job."

This was said with a chuckle as he patted the worn patch in his corduroy trousers.

"You work here, then?" Jenna asked. She wondered if he had an inkling of the wooded burial ground or if those rumors were mostly for the tourists.

"Robert Kendrick," he said, extending a hand. "I look after the place during the week. My retirement job, I call it."

Shaking his hand, she said, "Jenna Cade. I'm here researching a book—a history narrative about cemeteries in the Deep South."

"A young lass interested in history." Humor sparked in the gentle gaze that studied her beneath the cap. "That is a rare thing these days." With some difficulty, he bent to yank the stray weeds from the base of the stone with the lamb engraving.

Stowing her camera back in the knapsack, Jenna crouched beside him. "Do you know how far back the stones date? I noticed some from the 1880s and wondered if there were any older than that."

"The oldest I know of are about ten years before that," he said. "Some of them my own family. My great-great-uncle, Lucas Kendrick, traveled here from Georgia to make a homestead in the 1850s."

"Did he fight in the Civil War?" she asked, realizing she hadn't seen any military emblems among the rows, although some men from the town must have enlisted.

"Ah, not Lucas, A farming accident mangled one of his legs as a boy. Others served, though, and were killed in battle. Their resting place became a mass grave, with those who shared their fate that day."

Her fingers stopped plucking the weeds with the somber thought. The image was not a new one; she had learned of the battle conditions from text books and the history documentaries she viewed obsessively as a college student. It never failed to impress her with its sense of loneliness, the wounded and dying, stranded so far from a home they would never return to, even in burial.

Her companion rose to his feet, extending a hand. "Don't trouble yourself on my account, dear. The youngsters from the high school volunteer on the weekends and catch the odd weeds these blurry old eyes miss."

She dusted her hands, remembering the question she should have asked before. "I wonder if you could tell me...if you've ever heard stories of another cemetery in this place. An old one that hasn't been taken care of by anybody in the town. Somewhere in the woods, I think, near the spring. "

His look of confusion told her that he hadn't, even before he answered. Though he did have some advice to offer as they moved slowly back through the stones. "I do believe there's a local fellow around who does some gravestone carving by hand. If anyone could tell you about local gravesites, it might be him."

"I thought carving stones by hand was a lost art," Jenna said. She had developed a special fondness for the craft in her recent travels, learning to distinguish the skill of the expert from the amateur. The beauty of the former could still amaze even beneath the thickest layers of grime.

"It is a dying trade," Robert agreed with a sad smile. "But I've seen this fellow's work advertised in the paper sometimes. What's his name again? I haven't spoken to him in some time, but then, I don't get around much." He patted his stiff limb and gave a faint chuckle. "You might ask the funeral home—I'm sure they could give you his business address."

"I will," she said, with a small wave of thanks as their paths parted near the cemetery's entrance gate.

There was no sign of the other man, the one she'd glimpsed when she first arrived that morning.

A bouquet of wild flowers was draped across the stone with the ivy vine chiseled around its edges.

∽•∾

The director at the funeral home knew of only one stone carver who worked in the town, a Mr. Sawyer. He worked in Sylvan Spring as a freelance craftsman for some fifty odd years, and he may have once restored some stones that were shattered in the old section of the town's cemetery. But Mr. Sawyer died some ten years ago, a sudden stroke felling him as he carved in his workshop that was now a garage at the east end of town. "Hand-carved tombstones are an expensive venture," explained Mr. Stroud, the funeral director. "It has been our practice here for many years to order stones from a company in Mobile."

Tall and thin with hair that swept his temples, he resembled the kind of mortician children sometimes made up stories about. His accent, soft and precise, might have charmed, if not for a slight hiss at the back of the throat. His smile was intended to soothe customers, she perceived, although it seemed out of place at this moment, as if he was practicing for future grieving visitors.

"Sylvan Spring is already rich with history," he informed her. "A lost cemetery—that would be a fine contribution to its legacy. If you can find it out in those overgrown woods."

"Are you certain there's no other stone carver in the town?" Jenna asked, her fingers toying with the strap of her knapsack. "Or maybe Mr. Sawyer had a child or grandchild, someone who might remember his work."

"Mr. Sawyer was a widower, I believe. As for children, I'm not sure." He offered a look of sympathy. "I'm truly sorry, Miss—"

"Cade," she supplied. "And I could really use any information you can give me on the stone carver. Anyone who knew him, worked with him…"

"There may have been an assistant," he said. "A young man who worked at the shop." He looked uncertain now, as if trying to recall something beyond his reach. "I don't know if he continued in the trade, but if we ever commissioned a piece from him, it would be in our records." He moved towards a narrow hall, motioning for her to follow. "I may be of little help concerning the stones themselves, but ask me anything else regarding the dead in Sylvan Spring. I can tell you the traditions, from coffin bells to covering mirrors and wearing veils to ward off the spirits."

"They aren't still practiced, I hope," she said, her boots soundless against the carpet.

The hall seemed oppressive with its odor of musty drapes.

"No, indeed." Mr. Stroud's chuckle sounded more natural as he pushed open the door to a small office, the walls adorned with a series of framed photographs and newspaper clippings. "But you'll find the old traditions are still very much alive in our stories and legends. The festivals bring many of the former practices to light, especially those of a spiritual nature." Sitting at the desk, he opened a business ledger and began to scan the list of dates and names in search of a local mason.

Jenna's glance wandered to the wall where the framed images paid homage to the town's celebrations. Christmas in the square with a lighted tree and patriotic floats for the Independence Day parade. There was also a Scottish-type fair with costumed men and women dancing to a bagpiper's tune.

"Can you tell me about the Hallowed Days Festival?" she asked, turning back to face him at the desk. "I heard something about a curse on the town. Is it a ghost story of some kind?"

"Not a ghost story," he said, glancing up from the ledger. "The trouble back then was real enough, though its cause may have been embellished a little from one generation to the next. After all, it was in the 1800s. Those kinds of stories get changed every few decades."

"What sort of trouble?" She took the seat across from him, unable to help the journalist-like stance after weeks of interviewing historians on similar subjects. Though none of those stories had puzzled her as much as this one, with its allusions to past lore.

He laughed, another soft chuckle of amusement. "Depends on who you ask. There's some who believe it was a sickness that caused a series of deaths. Others say it was a possession of sorts or a haunting. There were legends that a Celtic curse had been levied on the town for the wrongdoings of its people—probably the old folks' idea of things back then."

"No one knows for sure what it was?" She was surprised, given how proud the community seemed of its past. Surely, someone had researched the strange event, combing through whatever documents were preserved in the town's historical society.

The funeral director offered an apologetic smile. "I'm afraid the answer is pretty much a mystery, even to our ancestors. All we really know is that people were dying, terror had a grip on the community in general, and many feared a judgment was upon mankind for the bloodshed in the fighting."

She nodded, feeling foolish as she posed yet another question. One that had stayed on her mind since she first arrived last night. "The banner for the festival has some interesting symbols," she began, unsure how to describe the scrawls that seemed so primitive. "Someone told me they were —"

"Celtic," he answered, finishing her sentence. "And Druid, I suppose. Symbols for harmony, energy, mortality...any number of things. Many of our native families trace their roots back to the Celtic culture with all its legend and lore, and to Scotland, in particular. You'll find that both have influenced our stories and arts. It's very much a part of us as a town, even with our Southern pride."

Pulling a ring from his right hand, he held it up to reflect the light. "A Scottish thistle ring, passed down from my father's side of the family," he said. "The local jeweler produces similar designs, as well as the knots of the Celtic region. Just one of the ways our town reflects the ancient customs."

"And the old superstitions," she wondered aloud, "did those carry over, too? I mean, nobody believes it was a Druid curse that struck the town, do they?"

He frowned. "These days, we see the festival as more of a celebration of history or as a cultural memorial. To those who suffered the trouble and those who survived. It was a dark time in so many ways, with the war going on, and the town was lucky to survive so much turmoil."

Jenna stayed silent as the funeral director scanned the rest of the ledger. Her thoughts were focused on this strange piece of the past, and the way it seemed to be etched into the lives of the modern-day citizens.

A curse. Rumors of ghosts and malicious spirits wreaking havoc at home while a battle raged miles away. Nothing about the legend made sense to her, but every new facet flamed her curiosity as much as the possibility of a lost burial site from the same era.

Sylvan Spring seemed laden with secrets. Like a time capsule buried in the earth, the remnants of its previous civilization were lingering somewhere just beneath the surface.

"I'm sorry," Mr. Stroud told her a moment later, flipping the folder's cover closed. "But we have no records of business with a local craftsman. It appears your friend was wrong."

Disappointed, she shouldered her knapsack. The caretaker must have confused his memory of the stone carver as being more recent then was actually possible. Not a surprise, really, considering he seemed to know of the man mostly through word of mouth or old newspaper advertisements.

"Thanks so much for checking," she said. "Sorry to have bothered you."

"It was no trouble." He rose to see her to the door. "You know, if it's old gravesites you're looking for, you might try the Lesley homestead. It's a half mile south of the spring, a favorite spot for hikers to visit. A few have mentioned seeing some family headstones behind the house's burned remains."

Family headstones—not a community burial ground. It would do for a start, though, and she scribbled the directions down for lack of a better clue.

3

The stretch of wilderness known as Crooked Wood must have become a popular hangout for the local youth. Jenna guessed this from the numerous cigarette stubs and rocks that were arranged in a campfire circle. Plastic bottles littered the ground, a pile of coals nearby from a recent campfire.

She had parked her car in a clearing off the main road, striking off down the footpath with only a vague sense of where she was going.

Thunder trilled overhead and Jenna hoisted her knapsack higher as she wished for a compass like the one her father used to carry on family camping trips. It would have to be guesswork and the satellite maps from her cellphone's on-again-off-again wireless coverage.

The path before her was defined by a mat of golden-brown needles from pines that towered overhead. She could still hear the sound of car motors passing over the main road. Emboldened with this sense of direction, she moved deeper into the woods, glancing back to see the path's opening gradually shrink and disappear in the changing foliage.

She walked in the same direction for as long as she dared, ignoring the trails that seemed to fork in a more promising route than the one advised by the funeral home director. The homestead might not be connected to the burial ground she sought, but it was her only current location for markers in the dense growth of the forest.

A half mile or so slipped past as she trudged on with nothing to break the landscape of hardwood, the trees growing thicker the further she went. The urge to turn back was increasing with the clouds in the sky, despite her need to confirm at least one lead before the day's end.

Climbing a small embankment where a stream snaked between stones, Jenna lifted her gaze to find something unexpected on the other side. Smoke billowed somewhere on the horizon, a thick gray cloud rolling across the tree tops.

A wildfire was the first possibility to enter her mind, remembering the burned remains of the church in Georgia, the tombstones nearby damaged in the flames.

Her steps quickened, a mixture of urgency and curiosity carrying her towards the scene ahead. Skirting thorn plants and sagging tree limbs, she made her way to a crest in the path where the ground below turned abruptly steep. At the end of this slope, a farmhouse, rustic and somewhat shabby in appearance but not abandoned by any stretch of the imagination, was visible. The smoke curled upwards from its red brick chimney. White paint was flecked in places, a tangle of ivy stretching from the roof to the picket fence below. Old garden tools leaned there as if forgotten mid-project, the weeds grown tall enough to twine around the wooden handles. It took her a moment to register what else leaned there.

Gravestones. Old ones, judging from the condition, most broken or cracked. Others were simply tarnished beyond reading beneath the layers of grime and rust, the lichen and moss she had learned to dread when searching for an inscription.

Confused, her gaze moved beyond the house to a smaller structure that was even more battered in appearance. Cement blocks were stacked beside a storm door, a sign hung from the rafters above with the words *'Monumental Masonry'* stenciled in letters that peeled away. A name and phone number appeared below, too faded and far away for Jenna to make out from this distance.

So there *was* a stone carver still working in Sylvan Spring. One of her sources must have been mistaken then, leaving her to wonder if Mr. Sawyer still lived, or if this was someone else. The apprentice mentioned by the funeral director, or maybe a member of the Sawyer family in the same trade.

Her instinct to move down the sloped path and find out was checked by the sound of a door slamming somewhere nearby. The figure which emerged from the back of the farmhouse was instantly familiar, with dark hair and a faded green jacket. Instead of flowers, though, he cradled a postage box, resting it against the hood of the truck as he unlocked its door.

Jenna was close enough to call out this time, but stayed silent, speechless from surprise, or maybe excitement at the thought of someone who might hold the answers to the cemetery's location. Although, neither reason could explain the intent way she studied his face.

He was no more than thirty, but with a haggard expression that lined otherwise appealing features, a jaw shaded with stubble; a lean-muscled build evident beneath the work clothes. All this was registered as quickly as it took him to climb in the vehicle, sliding the box into its passenger seat as he started the engine.

For the second time that day, Jenna was an intruder.

He guided the truck down a narrow dirt lane that was flanked on its other side by a field.

Thunder rumbled overhead, a drop of moisture landing on her face. She brushed it away as another fell, and then another, followed by a steady sprinkle of rain against her clothes and boots. She continued to stand there without reason, staring after the vehicle as it disappeared around the bend. Why hadn't she called down to him? Now it seemed pointless to linger, with the storm gathering strength at a fast pace. She would come back in the morning, she decided, with one last glance at the display of crumbling monuments.

~∞~

By the time Jenna realized she was lost, it was too late to turn back. How it happened she couldn't say, except that somewhere in the growing downpour she lost track of the scenery. The path diverged in places that caused her to backtrack more than once, and even the stone carver's house was lost to her, its chimney smoke dissipating in the rain.

Pausing beneath a canopy of oaks, she pulled her cellphone from her pocket only to find a no signal bar. Her heart lurched at the sight, a sense of panic at the thought of being stranded here as twilight grew closer. There was a flashlight in her knapsack, but she wouldn't need it for some time yet. Her fingers curled around it for comfort more than anything.

Would there be bears in such a place? She had never lived in the country, or anywhere with forestry, her experience limited to picnics and camping trips. And those were so long ago that she could scarcely recall her father's advice on avoiding dangerous wildlife.

Help me, she prayed brokenly, her thoughts circling in a loop of worry. *Tell me what to do, where to go...keep me safe.*

Broken branches and tree tops littered this part of the woods, where it seemed wind or ice had felled some of the timber at one time.

She wondered if there were other residents within walking distance or if the masonry shop was the solitary inhabitant of this wild place. It seemed a strange location for a business, so isolated from the bustle of the town. His work must come from elsewhere, she supposed, remembering the lack of records at the funeral home.

Something about the craftsman drew her thoughts, even in her current predicament. Crouched beneath the shelter of bowed branches, she pictured again his ramshackle farmhouse and workshop. He seemed young for such an old-fashioned occupation, a trade that men twice his age would have seen as archaic in their day.

Did he possess a strong love for the past? She believed he must have a sense of protection for history to make his living in a lost art form. Like museum curators who dusted off relics and made them seem new and inspiring to the modern world. Or maybe she just imagined as much because of her need to preserve the things others had forgotten.

By now, the downpour of rain had slackened to a drizzle pattering softly against the tree leaves. As it grew quiet, another sound became audible in the distance. The drone of a motor, followed by a car horn that blared long and loud in the afternoon air. *The main road*, she realized, with a surge of relief and elation. Now she had a way to pinpoint where she was in this tangled mess that seemed less friendly the darker the skies grew.

She stood hastily, forgetting the branches overhead until they showered her with droplets. This was a small annoyance compared with her excitement, and she brushed them aside without caring. Her knapsack flapped as she picked up the pace, moving in the direction of the motor sounds. Dodging another low hanging branch, she failed to see the shape that jutted up from the path, until her knees hit it, sending her forward with a gasp of surprise.

Pain shot through her as she landed, hands shielding her face from the impact. Damp earth clung to her skin, mud streaking the front of her jacket. She scrambled to a sitting position, her breath coming in short, hard gasps. "It's OK," she told herself, eyes fluttering closed in an attempt to calm down. There was no damage done, no sprains or broken bones. Tentatively, she shifted position, testing weight against the injured leg. At the same moment, her hand brushed something buried in the leaves. Debris from the thing she had tripped over.

A wall of stone, packed together with sand. Parts of it had collapsed, fragments still visible running in an L-shape among the trees. The remains of a building's foundation? No, it was the wrong shape, more like a fence. Meaning there must have been a yard for it to protect at one time.

Her pain already forgotten, Jenna scrambled past the stone barrier. She searched the ground, hurriedly pushing aside leaves and soil with a sense of anticipation. Moving from one spot to another, her efforts were finally rewarded. Layers of dead foliage gave way to a piece of stone, flat with carvings that were more easily felt than seen.

Jenna stared, heart pounding with disbelief. There were more, a cursory check of the yard revealing graves that were leaning or broken off at the base. Limestone and slate were filled with cracks, the flat stones faring better than ones that stood upright beneath the piles of fallen tree limbs.

It seemed the phantom cemetery was real after all.

4

"You could've been killed! What if there were wolves out there? Or a coyote, at least." Jenna's agent was using her "mother" voice, or maybe it was more like an older sibling, considering only twelve years separated them. Whatever the case, there was a definite scolding in her tone as she learned of the nocturnal adventure.

"It was fine," Jenna said. Her sore leg was propped on a pillow, and her mud-spattered clothes and boots had been exchanged for a camisole and pajama pants as she rested on the hotel's four poster bed—although part of her wished to be back in the woods, a flashlight in one hand as the other parted thick branches to find a gravestone hiding beneath. "I just lost track of time after I spotted the first grave. And get this—there are a dozen at least. Probably a lot more hidden beneath the storm damage, as well."

"It's hard to make out anything from these pictures you e-mailed," Joyce said. "Except that most of them have been smashed into about a hundred pieces."

Her tone was skeptical, her expression easy for Jenna to picture after two-and-a-half manuscripts together. A trim, orderly figure in business clothes, Joyce Edel disliked surprises as a general rule, but especially those involving a client's manuscript. No doubt, she envisioned this discovery as interfering with the New Orleans site the editors were so keen on having featured.

"I know the markers are in rough shape," Jenna began, a defensive note creeping into her voice, "but it's amazing that anything could survive those conditions. Especially something so fragile. Some of them could have a Civil War connection," she added, thinking of the dates on the stones in the town.

"Un-huh," Joyce murmured noncommittally. "The lighting is really dim in these pictures. Please tell me you won't go tramping through any more unfamiliar woods. Not at night, at least."

"I won't," Jenna promised. She had marked tonight's path with some rolls of flagging tape from among her knapsack's supplies. There would be no trouble locating it from the main trail next time.

"Any special engravings?" her agent prompted. "All I can see is what looks like an arched doorway."

"I think it's a half moon, actually." Jenna glanced at the picture gallery on her computer screen, double clicking to enlarge the image of stone that bore the name, *CHARLEY*.

"Yeah, it's definitely a crescent, but it's inverted. And it's got another shape laced through it..." She trailed off, frowning. "There's a lot of rust covering it, but I can probably clean that off." She expected such gravestones to be simple in their designs, given the time and condition from which they came. Yet this basic carving was equally interesting to her mind as she tried to fathom its meaning for Charley, whoever he may have been among the town's early citizens.

"I may have stumbled on a good interview source," she told Joyce before they hung up for the night. "A mason who actually lives pretty close to the gravesites. Apparently, he keeps up the old method of carving stones by hand."

"Interesting," said Joyce, sounding as if she actually meant it this time. "Maybe he can tell you if there's a story behind the place. Something to make up for the lack of photographic material."

Of course, there was a story worth telling behind every gravesite she investigated. The problem was finding someone who could remember it. In this case, the stone carver seemed the most likely candidate for the job, though she couldn't say why exactly.

If he did know something of the old burial ground, he must be indifferent to its fate. Why else would it still be abandoned when someone so qualified to salvage it lived but a half mile away?

She couldn't get the idea out of her head, even as she tried to sleep. Moonlight threw shadows on the floor in the form of long branches waving outside her window. As a girl, Jenna pretended such shapes were the bony fingers of a wandering spirit, reaching out in a desperate bid for human contact.

At this moment, a very different—and very real—image haunted her mind. The memory of a figure crouched before a stone engraved with an exquisite ivy pattern. The sculpted vine had seemed almost life-like as it crept across the stone's surface, the detail as vivid as the colorful bouquet of wildflowers clutched in the man's hand.

It was assuming too much to think the grave's occupant might be the cause of the man's weary expression. She knew almost nothing about him, after all, not even his name. Just an occupation listed on a battered sign she'd found in the wilderness.

❧

Jenna clicked the recorder on, holding the device close to her mouth. Her breath formed small clouds in the morning air as she noted the layout of the burial ground.

"Twenty-three possible gravesites located so far. I've unearthed several half-stones with broken pieces still lodged in the earth. These could go several inches deep, so I'll need a spade and a metal probe for further investigation."

She brushed a strand of hair from her eyes, strolling among the rows to examine the recovered monuments. There was something here that puzzled her, something she hadn't seen at any of the other locations she'd unearthed across her travels. It was the kind of angle Joyce would appreciate, especially if she could find out the reason behind it.

She continued speaking into the recorder. "Seven of these markers bear identical half-moon engravings. There's another image laid over the crescent— something like a capital letter V, though it's hard to tell, given the amount of dirt and damage." It was a strange design, unlike any she had seen among the common grave symbols that dominated most cemeteries. She supposed it must be a regional thing. "There are few dates given for birth or death," she continued, "and no obvious connection between the stones that bear the symbol."

Could they be slaves? It might explain why they had been buried in the north section of the yard, a part sometimes reserved for outcasts and so-called "inferior" citizens. The area seemed too poor to have so many servants, though. Plus, no slave would have been given the honor of a decorative memorial, unless they were unusually close to their master's family.

"Whatever the reason, these stones have been set apart—isolated."

All except one, she learned. The only marker with the cryptic half-moon engraving to appear elsewhere in the yard, its carving had escaped her notice the first time. Nestled beneath the shade of an old sycamore, it kept company with two stones that bore entirely different carvings.

Crouching beside it, she let her gaze roam across its faded limestone surface. "Looks like her name was Mariah. It's hard to be sure," she said, scrapping her fingernail along the letters that were caked with rust. "Last name appears to be Moore." Surprisingly, there were only a few cracks in the stone's surface, making her certain it could be cleaned at some point to reveal the owner's full identity.

"Doesn't look as if there's a date anywhere," she continued, moving on to other details. "It's a flat marker, placed beside two stones that stand upright. These monuments are..." She paused in a moment of surprise, her fingers reaching for the stones as she murmured, "Wow," in a voice too low to reach the recorder.

She couldn't explain it. The stone with the moon carving had somehow ended up next to a pair of graves that were much newer in appearance, marble monuments that seemed extravagant compared to the slate and limestone of the other graves.

"This is weird," she admitted, speaking into the machine again. "Every other marker I've examined in this yard bears characteristics that point to pre-1870. Meaning the cemetery probably fell out of use sometime after that. So why are these two stones—which are clearly from the 1890s, maybe early 1900s—buried here instead of in town?"

And why were they next to the stone with the moon carving? This was the part that puzzled her most, as if there had to be some reason for these three monuments to be together, just as there was for the tombs that were isolated in the back part of the yard.

It was a question she left hanging as she examined the newer markers. "A. D. Widlow," Jenna read aloud from the first one. "There's a carving of a sword and shield at the stone's base. Could mean he's a veteran," she added, thinking his birth date would have made him a young man at the time of the Civil War. Goosebumps raised on her skin when she touched the military style insignia, still visible beneath the grime.

The stone beside it bore a simple carving of a violet blossom. "Another Widlow grave, probably a spouse. Maybe a sibling. First name is Nell. "

But who was this Mariah Moore, then? A relative, perhaps, or a close friend. It struck her as odd, the possibly married couple and a woman who died years before, judging from the appearance of her headstone.

No inscription graced any of the tombs, making her sigh with frustration. The more personal she could make this the better, for both her readers and the poor souls forgotten among the wilderness. No doubt, there would be a mountain of paper sorting ahead, once the names and dates were catalogued and the photographs taken from every possible good angle.

She checked her watch, frowning at the time that remained between now and the historical society's opening hour. There was little else she could do here, until she had reported the cemetery to the local authorities and secured the tools she needed for further recovery. Overhead, leaves rustled, drawing her gaze upwards, where a cloud of smoke rose along the skyline.

"Time to seek professional advice," she told the recorder, switching it off as she moved in the direction of the masonry shop.

5

The chisel slipped, leaving a gash on the stone carver's left hand. He grimaced, biting back the urge to swear. Cursing was never the best form of expression, but somehow it seemed worse when one was in the process of fashioning a large, cross-shaped stone.

Blood trickled down his hand, a few drops spattering the work table. He grabbed the least dingy rag from his supplies and carried it to the sink in the corner of the room. A quick splash of water to clean the wound and he was already wrapping the rag in place. It formed a makeshift bandage that was flexible enough to let him continue working, which was all he really cared about at this moment.

Colleen would never approve. Somehow, this was the first thought to enter his mind anytime he did something slipshod or semi-reckless. He would think of her gentle tsking sound, her dark, slender eyebrows raised in feigned scolding.

He would remember her smooth hands tracing his skin, gently dabbing the injury with crushed herbs to ward off infection. That spicy scent was like a perfume to him, its faint aura never leaving Colleen's fingers from her time spent working in the garden or the shop downtown.

Her lips, warm and soft, would press against the skin just above the bandage, dark eyes rising to meet his with a look that ghosted right through him. Always the same, always a need between them that never seemed to quench despite their time together.

Just like that, an ache swelled in his chest. The pain expanded, traveling up his throat to stop just short of a groan. How this was still possible after nearly two years never failed to depress him, or make him wonder at the intensity that accompanied these moments.

"Grief is like any deep wound," Pastor Brin had assured him, in one of those rare times he'd actually stirred himself to seek spiritual counsel. "It scabs over and eventually leaves a scar. That scar may not hurt as much as the wound did, but it's always there, nonetheless."

Resting his forehead against the cool porcelain sink, he let his breath come in deep huffs. It didn't help that he was on his second day in a row without a decent meal or any real rest. Just cups of coffee and the occasional doze on the couch before he was back to the grindstone, literally.

There was never much reason for him to leave this place, beyond the necessity of groceries and supplies for his work. But lately, he had found himself avoiding the outside world even more, aware that festival preparations had consumed the town, the superstitions of old rising to the surface like scum floating on a pond.

Mischief Night, All Hallows Eve, Halloween. It didn't matter what they called it, since there was darker history behind the event than children playing make-believe. The songs and stories the festival dredged up and the ghoulish decorations they used to fill the square were a little too sinister for his tastes, given the grim legend behind the town's celebration. A tribute to the dead, everyone claimed, though it felt more like an offering to whatever spirits had supposedly plagued their ancestors.

The cracked mirror above the sink showed him a face that might have belonged to a phantom, if such things did exist. Tired, heavy eyes and rumpled hair, his jaw shaded with stubble. He nudged the tap on, splashing water over his face in an effort to erase the grim expression that seemed almost permanent at times.

Another work cloth served to pat his face dry. He left it crumpled on the nearest counter, where a series of framed photographs were busy collecting dust. A picture of his parents taken during his school days; an image of Colleen digging in the earth behind their farmhouse. The two of them on the porch swing, her dark braids nestled against his shoulder as she flashed the camera a girlish smile. His own face seemed serious beside hers, not quite trusting the lens with his shuttered blue gaze.

A bitter reminder that even then he was far from tranquil, his mood a see-saw between the scales of gray and normal, his natural reserve causing feelings to build beneath the surface. Colleen had called it his "brooding artist mode"—a name that made it sound more appealing than it actually was, at least to him.

Back at the work table, he ran his fingers over the chiseled slab of marble. The shape of rose petals had begun to take form in the corners of the cross. There would be another blossom in the center and a basket weave pattern to fill the spaces between.

This project was a little more challenging than most he received—a duplicate of a marker from a Savannah cemetery. The 1782 original had been damaged irreparably in an act of vandalism that left it more dust than stone, the criminals blasting it apart with a chainsaw that sent bits flying in every direction.

"Just *awful*," the deceased woman's descendant had confided over the phone, her Southern accent infused with a drawl that belonged in a Tennessee Williams play. A member of the Daughters of the American Revolution, his newest customer was more conscious than most of the importance of preserving monuments for one's forebears.

She had mailed him the remnants of the stone, along with a series of photographs taken before it was hacked apart. "Those young men should be in jail," she had told him forcefully. "Disrespecting the dead like that."

"Absolutely," he agreed, hoping nothing resembling guilt had crept into his tone, the memory of a youthful indiscretion that rose every now and again to cause him discomfort despite the passage of time. In a way, carving this stone was like an act of penance for that long-ago mistake, as was every other project that entered his shop over the years.

He had scraped and chiseled so many stones since that fateful night that it seemed almost to wipe the transgression completely away. Each project was like a clean slate, enabling him to start anew, until the error faded to a shadow in the back of his mind.

Surely that was the sort of scar Father Brin had meant, the kind that stayed with one, but somehow lost the power to make one bleed. He tried to imagine a similar means of purging his grief for Colleen, but the two scenarios didn't compare.

Prayer and time—that was his only solution at the moment. Not a quick one, but slow, like sand flowing piece by piece through an hourglass.

Leaning over the stone, he studied the damage. A small bruise had appeared where his chisel bit too deep moments before. He would need to file it, removing the blemish far more easily than the one he dressed on his own hand.

He unwound the nearby canvas belt to study a selection of steel files, tools far older than himself that were well preserved by their meticulous former owner. The largest was diamond-tipped, and he began to pull it from the compartment, when a knock sounded on the door.

Was he expecting a delivery? He tried to remember ordering supplies from anywhere besides the local hardware store. There were no future commissions scheduled to arrive, no packets of photographs and gravestone rubbings to guide him in replicating an antique headstone.

Another rap sounded against the storm door that framed the heavier wooden one. It had an urgent sound, making him release the tool and cross the room to confront the visitor.

☙❧

It was not a deliveryman, but a woman. Young, with a pale complexion and gold hair that curled past her shoulders. Her jeans and boots were crusted with mud, her gloved hands clutching a notebook that looked as if it had seen better days.

Before either of them spoke, her gaze fell to where his bandaged hand rested on the door knob. Blood had seeped through the fabric, leaving a dark, rust-colored stain. He automatically moved it out of sight. "May I help you?"

"I hope so." Green eyes met his gaze with a force that left him unsettled. There was excitement buried in their depths and also a sense of eagerness that he found puzzling. "Are you"—she glanced quickly at the sign above the door—"Con Taggart? The stone carver," she added, as if to be extra clear, eyes re-meeting his with another rush of concentration.

"Yes," he said. So she was a customer, then. The notebook, he presumed, would contain sketches of whatever stone she was wanting commissioned or restored. It was strange she hadn't phoned first, considering the remote location. Most who drove back here needed a vehicle capable of off-road navigation, but he didn't even see a car in the drive.

"At last," she said, as if starting in the middle of a conversation. A relieved laugh escaped. "I had to find you by accident. You should really find a better way of advertising such a rare skill, Mr. Taggart."

He nodded, trying to follow this stream of logic. Before he could form a reply, though, she was talking again.

"I need your advice about something," she said. "A book I'm researching that involves abandoned cemeteries. I've been documenting a site all morning and found some unusual engravings—" She broke off for a moment, ruffling the pages in the notebook. Only a breath's pause passed before she continued. "I took some rubbings from the stones, which were pretty rough, considering a storm seems to have ravaged the whole area in the past. Most of them were too fragile to copy, but I do have one here that is fairly detailed. Where is it now..."

A sense of confusion enveloped him, along with

fatigue from the late night work sessions. Running a hand through his already mussed hair, he finally managed to break into the conversation. "I don't understand. What are you talking about?" It was so blunt that he almost winced the moment the words left his mouth.

The woman didn't seem offended, though. She continued to page through her notebook, finally holding it up to reveal a crayon copy of something that resembled a half-moon. Another shape was laid over it, the detail hard to discern in the coarse shading.

"I keep finding this design," she explained. "And I hoped that you might be able to tell me something about it." She glanced past him to the interior of the workshop. "Is it possible for me to come in for a minute?"

Con's face grew warm with the realization he was using the door like a shield, his foot propped against it in a defensive stance. It was as if he were trying to form a barrier between him and this person with her unexpected train of questions.

With a brief nod, he pulled the door open wide, letting her pass into the small shop. Dust and chalk layered the counters and floor along with bits of stone that chipped off during the sculpting sessions. He hadn't swept the place in days, and the area seemed as neglected as his own scruffy appearance.

The woman glanced around, taking in the general untidiness. Her gaze wandered over the pictures on his counters, the sketches of gravestone designs pinned to the cork board beside the window. The only semblance of order was in the tools that he kept hung from the wall or rolled inside canvas to prevent the edges from growing dull. He shoved aside a pile of tangled extension cords with his foot. "You'll have to overlook the mess," he said in a voice somewhat gruff with apology. "Manly arts tend to generate a hazardous work environment."

This statement elicited a small smile from the stranger, who glanced back at him.

He toyed with the bandage, twisting the frayed bits of fabric on the end. Why this was making him nervous, he couldn't explain. The isolation must be getting to him, the only reprieve from it having been yesterday's visit to Colleen's grave. That had been his only conversation for the week. A one-sided one, filled with allusions to events long past, which was the only means of keeping his old self alive. It kept that self from chipping away like the stones he glued and pieced back together on a weekly basis. *Not now.* The possibility of slipping into a darker mood threatened.

Across from him, the woman was leaning against the work bench to examine the rose-festooned cross. "Beautiful," she said, looking up at him with genuine admiration. For the stone, of course, though part of him couldn't help the flush that scorched his face, his gaze cutting awkwardly to the side. "So Miss—"

"Jenna Cade," she told him, spreading her notebook across the only cleared space on the work bench. "I'm a non-fiction writer—well, a history writer, to be specific. Sylvan Spring is part of my research for a manuscript."

"Right," he said, crossing to the bench. He braced his hands against it, wincing at the pressure against the injured one. She probably thought he was some kind of eccentric, holing himself up with his work, barely taking the time to shower, eat, or sleep. Lately, that wasn't far from the truth.

She tapped the notebook with its strange drawing. "I really need you to look at this and tell me what it might symbolize. I know that certain carvings have universal meanings—faith, salvation, resurrection. But I've never seen one like this before."

There was a hopeful edge in the request as she angled the book in his direction. He leaned past her shoulder to study it, careful not to brush even the fabric of her coat. It surprised him that she didn't move away, as most people would when placed so close to a stranger. Instead, he felt her gaze scanning his face with an interest that caused him to glance away when he stepped back again.

"You're saying this was on a grave you found in the woods?" he asked, pretending to assess the possible significance of the symbol. In fact, he had no clue what the engraving might mean. It was unlikely to be religious, with the moon being a favorite sign among folklore and agriculture. Beyond that, he was helpless to form an opinion.

"Not just one grave," she answered, flipping the notebook's pages.

More gravestone rubbings whizzed past, some with only dates and names from what he could glimpse.

"There's a burial ground with at least twenty-three stones a half mile south of here, with markers that are dated hundreds of years back."

"A burial ground," he repeated, his voice somewhat hollow. It was hard to believe, and his initial reaction told him to doubt it. His exploration of the woods had revealed nothing more than a handful of markers scattered throughout the abandoned homestead sites. But that was a far cry from twenty stones, or however many she had claimed to find.

"Are you sure?" he asked. "Because when a stone ruptures, it may look like more than one marker but actually—"

She cut him off with a shake of the head. "I've already matched several of the headstone pieces together. Believe me; this is a cemetery, not a few family graves."

Con considered this for a moment, thinking how strange it would be if she was right. A forgotten cemetery within walking distance of his shop, its stones crushed beneath the debris of a powerful ice storm that tore through the landscape years before, knocking down trees all over town.

"You've never heard of it?" she asked, surprise in her tone as she attempted to catch his eye. "The man I spoke with in town—a caretaker at the cemetery—thought you would be an authority on the subject. He said you knew about the local gravesites."

"Only the ones at the homesteads," he explained. "I have an arrangement with some of the property owners. They let me use stone from the old foundations in some of my projects. I've seen family graves but never more than two or three at each place."

"I see," she murmured.

She looked disappointed, making guilt ripple through him. He felt the need to justify his ignorance. "I've only lived here—as in this part of town—for a few years. My, uh, wife and I...we moved here after she finished college."

A subtle change flickered over her expression with the words. Her gaze went to the hand where his ring finger was currently hidden by the bandage. He knew it was empty beneath the fabric, a faint impression of where the band used to sit visible amidst his tanned skin. He cleared his throat, moving away from the subject he least wished to discuss. "I used to live in a neighborhood just past the town high school. My family moved there from Kansas City when I was fifteen."

"So you're not fully a native," she said. "I should have known—the accent's a little different."

This seemed to count against him, making Con wonder what she expected to find. A local expert, probably, with all the answers to the town's long-lost graveyard.

"You worked with the former mason, though," she said, brightening a little with this important piece of information. "Mr. Sawyer, right?"

"He taught me," he admitted, wondering how that could matter. Unless she thought his instructor possessed some knowledge of this place that he had since passed down to his apprentice or left behind in old paperwork.

"I'm sorry," he began, seeing the hope fade from her face again, "but there's nothing I can tell you about this cemetery. I've never heard of it, from Mr. Sawyer, or anyone else." Handing her the notebook, he added, "As for the moon, it can symbolize different things— rebirth, cycles of life, victory even. Probably it's not a faith symbol, though. More of a cultural thing."

She considered his words, staring at the image with a blank look. After a moment, she pulled a pencil from her knapsack and scribbled something in the corner of the headstone rubbing. Tearing it from the notebook, she held it out to him with quiet pleading in her green eyes. "My cell number—in case you think of anything." Her hand brushed his bandage, urging him to take it, waiting until his fingers curved around it before she turned towards the door. Halfway there, she turned back and offered him a smile. "Thanks, by the way. For what you do, I mean. It's really nice to see someone keeping up the old traditions, putting the time and detail into these old monuments."

He didn't know what to say, especially considering he'd practically dismissed her a moment ago. He managed a mumbled "Thanks," before crossing the room to hold the door open. She walked down the path, her hair ruffled in the breeze.

How did she even find the cemetery? He wondered this, now that it was too late to ask. She was more of a stranger to this place than he was, yet somehow she uncovered a piece of history lost to it for who knows how many decades.

Alone again, he contemplated the gravestone rubbing. He had never duplicated this pattern in any of his restoration work. There were none like it in the old section of the town cemetery, either.

A crescent moon turned on its side. The symbol laid over it was harder to guess, though he felt it could be an arrow, bent or broken. Such a symbol was often used to represent something about mortality or danger.

As he turned it towards the light, something stirred faintly in his memory. Had he seen the combination somewhere before? In a book or photograph, maybe a newspaper clipping from his former employer's records.

He shook his head. It was useless to try and remember. Especially when it might be a false memory or just a design that was somewhat similar. The moon was a common enough pattern to see, along with the stars and sun and other celestial wonders.

Pinning the sketch to the cork board, he watched it flutter in the breeze from the open window. His thoughts wandered again to the woman with the green eyes who pleaded for his advice, his help, really. And he had sent her away with a piece of knowledge she could have obtained from a simple Internet search.

A fresh wave of guilt coursed through him, a sense of regret for treating her request so lightly. If he wasn't knee deep in this current project, or overwhelmed by one of his bouts of weariness, he might have offered to go with her and view the site. It was the sort of thing a person in his line of work would do, something she clearly expected when she showed up this morning.

Well, she would find another source of information. Someone capable of the energy and enthusiasm required for resurrecting a forgotten cemetery. That was what he told himself, anyway, as he turned back to the unfinished stone on the work bench.

6

Sunlight filtered through the stained glass window, throwing patches of color across the documents Jenna studied. The window's design, an elaborate piecing of violets on a hillside, seemed too vibrant for the musty-smelling historical society.

The manager had sent her upstairs after checking the list of names from the cemetery against a computer database. "You're looking for a part of our collection that spans the 1860s. Most of these artifacts are extremely fragile, so I'm afraid no photo copies or scans will be possible."

"What about a checkout policy?" Jenna asked.

"I'm afraid we don't have one," he admitted. "All research takes place on site."

He scribbled down the shelf's location number. "It's the first door on the second story. Ask one of the volunteers to retrieve the items and a pair of gloves for handling them."

This request earned her a blank look from the two university students sorting boxes upstairs. The girl, whose nametag identified her as Paige, was perched atop a ladder, her gloved hands easing a garment box back in its place. A boy with spiky brown hair lounged on a stool down below, his fingers scrolling through something on a cellphone.

Neither was happy to see her, though the girl did a better job of hiding it. Pulling earbuds free, she hopped down from the ladder and rolled it towards another aisle in the back. "Here for the festival?" she asked Jenna as she glanced over the labels on the requested items.

"Sort of. That is, I'll definitely be attending. This is everything?" Jenna shifted her weight beneath the armful of notebooks and documents handed down, hearing the disappointment in her question. Somehow, she expected a town this obsessed with its Civil War past to be overrun with priceless relics. Hadn't the clerk at the hotel mentioned a museum being open at one time?

"There's some uniforms and revolvers and stuff. But the festival workers will be using those for displays this weekend."

"No more papers, though," Jenna said.

"I think there used to be more," the girl replied. "Documents down at the courthouse, but most of it was damaged in the fire. The same one that burned the museum."

"Of course," Jenna said. With a sigh, she spread the contents over a nearby table, as the volunteer disappeared into the rows of shelves once more.

There was an album of tintype photographs, most taken of town businesses and landmarks that she suspected no longer existed. She glanced over sepia images of a dry goods store, a post office, and many more buildings that were not as readily identifiable.

A snort of laughter echoed from among the shelves, followed by a shushing sound.

Jenna glanced up, a frown tugging her mouth. In truth, it wasn't the students' hushed chatter that distracted her but something else. Something she was almost ashamed of, given the circumstances.

Her encounter with the stone carver had left her feeling restless. Seeing him up close, catching hold of his guarded expression...there was a sadness behind it she wanted to understand. His manner, though awkward at times, had seemed to pull her towards him, like the force from an invisible string.

"He's a little different, isn't he?" Those were the words of the county clerk she had phoned to report the cemetery's neglected state. A reference to the stone carver had prompted a tsking sound. "Almost never leaves his shop, or has visitors. Sad, especially when you consider he's still young."

"What about his family?" Jenna asked, remembering the mention of a wife.

"He's alone, as far as I know," the woman replied.

A call on another line had prevented further speculation, leaving Jenna to wonder even more about the craftsman's strange habits and her own fascination for someone she had only just met that morning.

Yes, he was good-looking—almost in a haunting way, if she could bring herself to use such romanticized language. But the pull she felt was something deeper than a chemical reaction. More like the same urgency that drove her to uncover the cemetery, as if she hoped to piece his secret self together the way she did the bits of jagged stone.

But why? He hadn't shown any enthusiasm for the recovered headstones. Which made her think his skill was for business reasons only and not enough to make him feel a connection to the lost and damaged monuments.

So that was that—best to forget the whole thing, and cross him off her list for potential research sources. Her agent would be disappointed, but hopefully something else would turn up to make the graveyard come alive, so to speak. One of the objects on this table, perhaps.

Placing aside the collection of tin types, she reached for a stack of documents grown brown and crumbly with age beneath their plastic shields. Most were newspaper fragments, articles with topics that ranged from the war to the weather. No obituaries or marriage announcements, though, to her great disappointment.

The bottom of the stack contained papers salvaged from the museum rubble. Among them, sheets of stationary, penned with a feminine script. Singed in places and too fragile to touch, they had been labeled as "Two Letters to Soldier from Sister." The dates were from 1862, making her bend closer for a look at the contents.

My Dear Brother,

I pray this letter finds you, and all from your camp, in good health and spirits. The training sessions you described sound most arduous, though you seem to be managing them well. I know you are eager for marching orders, but I cannot help hoping it is still some time before that day occurs.

You would laugh, Henry, to think how often I worry about your uniform. My poor sewing skills were all that could be found, with both Mama and Granny Clare suffering rheumatism of the fingers. I fear my fortune will never be made by the needle, though, and once dreamed that all the stitches began to burst, leaving you as raggedy as the toy soldier doll you played with as a boy.

Do you remember the time his poor jacket was torn by the dog? It was I who sewed it up back then, and what a mess my clumsy fingers made of it! Poor little Jack (for I believe that is what you called him) was nothing but a mass of frayed threads around the arms and shoulders. I would hate to think your own coat should suffer such a tragedy, so please put my mind at ease by writing that it is quite sturdy thus far.

I can scarcely believe you have been gone from us these many weeks. Sometimes, I will hear a sound from your old room—some faint creaking as the doctor arranges a trunk or medicine cabinet say—and for a moment, I will think it is you. How strange the mind is to play such tricks on the heart!

Forgetting that she came only for documents that matched names from the cemetery, Jenna let herself sink into the letter writer's old-fashioned narrative. Her gaze following the curve of the script to another place and time, where a young woman composed her thoughts to a brother called away to battle.

❧

Nell Darrow was almost twenty when the war that tore the states apart finally made its way to Sylvan Spring.

It came in the form of a newspaper advertisement. Her brother, Henry, folding back the *County Times*, showed her where a recruitment meeting was being held two towns over, a call for all able-bodied men between the ages of eighteen and thirty-five to pledge their service to God and homeland.

"You won't be eighteen 'til March." Nell's voice held a note of panic, her hands buried inside the dough she was kneading for that night's dinner. The worried remark had earned her a sigh of exasperation from the youth who shared her suntanned complexion and tawny-colored hair.

"Yes, but *they* won't know that," he said. "All they're looking for is someone to handle a rifle and pull their weight on the trail." He spoke matter-of-factly, though neither of them knew anyone from the soldier camps. Until recently, the war had been just a rumor, a story brought by the tradesman passing through from other territories.

"What will Papa say?" she asked, knowing full well he would tell the boy to do as he wished. That was the luxury of a blacksmith, whose harvest was small and livestock holdings even smaller. Her father could spare a son's help easier than his neighbors, whose crops and cattle were a livelihood that demanded the strength of youth to run smoothly.

Later, she had watched as Henry squeezed into a cart with six other boys. Others from the town were riding horses and taking turns with those who traveled on foot for lack of better options. All were laughing as they sang snatches of a war song she had heard played at the last community dance. As if they were going off to a picnic, she thought, heart sinking with the carefree sounds.

It was her small hands that sewed his uniform a week later, and pieced together a kepi hat in the fashion of Johnny Reb from the newspaper cartoons. She stitched the brass buttons in place with a mixture of pride and nervousness, the idea it might become his burial garb causing her needle to slip more than it normally would, pricking little dots of blood along her fingers.

She cried when he tried it on for size and then

again when he packed it inside a haversack with his other scant belongings. Squeezing her arm reassuringly, he said, "It's not as if I wouldn't have gone eventually. This way it will be over and done with. Besides," he added, "the war can hardly last much longer. Everyone says as much. I want my part of the fuss before it's over."

Glory, excitement, adventure—these were things enrollment in the Confederacy promised to bring. Compared to this, Sylvan Spring was just a sprinkle of homesteads along a wooded stream, gradually expanding to include a church and school, a post office and general store. The blacksmith's stand and mercantile shop were the last obvious signs of civilization before dirt lanes gave way to fields of cotton and corn, a few farmhouses visible here and there to break apart the acres of crops.

Planting and gathering the harvest was the main past time of the local youth, even more so than the subjects taught in their one-room schoolhouse. Perhaps this was why so many of them chose to don the uniform of a private. Boys who once used rifles for hunting wild game talked excitedly of driving Yanks from their native territory. Others spoke of marching into places they had only seen on the pages of a school atlas, tracing the battle sites they read about in the newspapers with a sense of awe.

Wives and sweethearts were left to worry and to send their love in letters to the camp where newly signed soldiers underwent training. Nell had only her brother to write to, her heart unsought by any among their small community. Which wasn't to say it had no secret admiration of its own—for Nell was hard-pressed to conceal her girlhood crush, now turned to something deeper with the passage of time.

The object of this quiet affection had not been among the figures she saw bound for the recruitment meeting that day. Instead, he fought a different kind of battle, one he seemed to be losing as the days slipped by.

Our friend, Arthur, does no better since you left. The sickness that came upon him these past weeks refuses still to leave, a remitting fever as many says it must be. I see little of him in the family's fields, and last week he did not attend church, which ought to tell you how severe he suffers with it. Such attacks leave him no choice, though he says nothing will stop him from being among you all when marching orders are finally given.

Dark, serious Arthur. His face flashed before her with astonishing clarity, causing her to break partway through her narrative. Those features, still so boyish, yet full of understanding, were as familiar as her own shabby reflection in the mirror.

She knew them from years of glances stolen across a schoolhouse aisle, where Arthur's head was always more inclined to the lesson than those of his friends. The same was true in church. When others had passed tic-tac-toe on scraps of paper or hid magazine stories between the pages of a Bible, always, he kept his eye upon the pulpit, an action that Nell would try to mimic, as thoughts of him drew her away from the sermon.

He was handsome, but not with the bold air that made his friend Wray Camden such a favorite among the local girls and envious boys. The two were inseparable and the natural leaders for the group of boys who trailed through the woods after school each day.

Eight year-old Nell would try to tag along after them, bare feet and braids getting caught in the thick foliage that grew among the woods.

"Go on," called the oldest Stroud boy, as he spotted her in the thicket. "Leave us be, why don't you?" He was perched on a log above the spring, where the youth had been daring each other to walk a balancing act.

Tears sprang in Nell's eyes, her hands clenching the fabric of her worn pinafore. She wanted only to watch, but their laughter forced her to turn back most times before the fun even started. One day, she followed them to a part of the wood where violets grew in thick clusters among the roots of the trees. Collecting a handful, she strung the blossoms together for a crown that quickly tangled in the coarse head of hair. She tugged at it desperately in an attempt to make it more pleasing, hearing the guffaws of a classmate as they cried, "Look there—Nell is trying to be a girl."

"I didn't think she knew how," teased Preston Cray, whose sisters were called the prettiest in the county by those who knew.

Blushing, Nell had ripped the flowers off and run back through the path. When she stopped to catch her breath, there was a rustling sound on the trail behind her. She gasped as a hand rested against her shoulder, dark eyes meeting hers with a look of apology when she turned around.

"They don't mean it, you know. It is only talk to them." Arthur spoke with reassurance, twining the purple flowers around her wrist, a friendly grin forming at her look of surprise before he ran back to join the friends who called his name impatiently.

The chain of blossoms had lain on her bedside table until just a sprinkle of dust remained to blow away in the breeze of an open window. She thought of it whenever the flowers came back into bloom, sprouting in rich, velvet hues with the change of the seasons.

This season had not been kind to any but nature, it seemed. Already a poor farming community, Sylvan Spring had only grown poorer in the absence of its young men. The work was harder than before, slower as well, with children and elderly folk alike shouldering the burden.

Arthur, meanwhile, could take part in neither world. The illness that kept him from the regiment made it equally difficult to work his father's fields. A fevered look haunted the dark eyes, and more than one began to speculate that a grave waited for him in the cemetery in the woods.

❧

There was no physician in Sylvan Spring at that time, and the apothecary was buried several summer's back, from an illness beyond the aid of his medicine cabinet. Healers would sometimes pass through, and traveling men boasted of miracles in a bottle from displays in the town square.

The town's reverend was among those who cast a wary eye at such claims. He had not always been among them. His younger days were passed in Mobile, where a relative's illness brought him in contact with a doctor's more refined practice. Anxious to provide for his flock—most of whom suffered the effects of old age—he was the one who sent a letter to that same clinic, inquiring if any who trained there might fill the position of doctor for a small farming community.

He shared its reply from the pulpit, a sheet of stationary in one hand as the other adjusted the spectacles balanced on his nose. "I regret to inform you of Dr. Moore's recent death," he read from the paper, "and the subsequent closing of his clinic. However, I can promise to fulfill the request for a qualified physician set to begin practice in your community within the month."

Signed M.R. Moore, it would seem the doctor's son had followed in his footsteps and would soon be among them to continue his medical trade.

It was Nell's family who would board the physician, a decision that gave her unease as she pictured a stranger moving into Henry's old room. Her discomfort grew when she learned the reason why, her mother's voice carrying through the window to the kitchen where Nell scrubbed the family's breakfast dishes.

"He is likely to be older, you know," she said, crouched in the herb garden beside Nell's grandmother. "A man with no family but a skill to keep him busy when even the crops are bad. It may be he will take a shine to Nell, since no one else has spoken for her these past years. "

Her granny sounded less certain. "There can be no hurry to lose Nell. I would miss her terribly, and with her brother gone, you would find it hard to manage the house and farm both."

"What else can she do, though?" her mother wondered. "I have urged her to think of teaching, but she will have no part of it."

Mortified, Nell had almost dropped the plate she cleaned. Leaving it half-washed in the basin, she retreated quickly to her room, burying her face in a pillow as she prayed, *God, please don't let this be my future. A marriage made out of no other choice—I would rather be alone, or to teach at the school, as Mama so wants me to do.*

The same thoughts ran through her head as she drove the family's cart to meet the stagecoach over in Woolwich. Her mother had insisted she be the one to go, since Mr. Darrow's smithy work kept him in town, and her hands were too stiff for guiding the reins. Really, though, it was just an excuse to push her daughter in the doctor's path as soon as might be.

At the station, Nell's voice shook when she asked for the passenger who came from Mobile, only for the clerk to point where a woman scarcely older than herself waited, a trunk and bag piled beside her on the bench. Seeing Nell, she rose with an expectant look on her face while the girl struggled to grasp the scene before her.

"We assumed the doctor was alone—unmarried," Nell stammered, remembering her mother's words on this subject with fresh shame. How bitter that woman's disappointment would be upon learning the physician had a wife. Nell quickly banished the thought for one even more startling.

"I *am* alone," the young woman replied, drawing her shoulders further back as she spoke. "My father, Dr. Moore, was the recipient of your minister's letter. I have answered the post in his stead."

A woman doctor. The notion was unfamiliar to her. Nell stole glances at the figure beside her as the wagon bounced over narrow lanes. She was nothing like the herb women who peddled their plants in the square, or the diviner who dangled a wedding band over women's palms to tell whether it was boy or girl who formed inside their growing stomach.

The doctor's skin was untouched by harsh weather. Auburn tresses wound into a crown of neatly pinned braids. Nell brushed the strands of dingy yellow from her face, seeing dirt lodged beneath her fingernails from helping in the garden earlier. Dr. Moore—or Mariah as she was called—showed hands that were smooth and clean folded atop her medical bag.

"She's got no grit," had been the estimate of Nell's father. Shaking his head in a wry motion, he watched the doctor set off on foot for a house in need of her skills as a midwife.

She had brought no money with her for buying a horse, the boots she wore broke down quickly under the rocky paths in the nearby wood.

Their neighbors viewed her with begrudging acceptance, coming to her for medicines that were sold by the former apothecary. Broken bones and gaping wounds—some of them belonging to livestock—made up the bulk of her work, among the few early patients who would trust a woman doctor. In between, she struggled to fill her time, and Nell wished fervently her talent might be applied to another case, as Arthur struggled even to plant the seed for his family's barley crop.

She heard the cough that stole his breath, felt the clammy nature of his skin when he offered her a carriage ride back from a neighbor's house one day. As they neared the Darrow homestead, the doctor passed them on one of the family's horses, saddlebag bulging with supplies for customers who lived in the stretch of woods beyond the spring.

"Have you seen the physician at work yet?" Arthur asked, his gaze following the woman with curiosity.

Her beauty was unmistakable, even in the plain clothes she wore to navigate the landscape's rough terrain. She had not returned his glance, posture ramrod straight as she followed the path that would take her to Crooked Wood.

"Miss Moore seems a good hand at medicine," Nell told him, "though I have not seen her skill so much as heard about it. She receives few visits at the house, though anyone is welcome to call on her in the parlor."

This was a hint, one she put forth timidly. To contradict his parents was something Nell would never dream of, though she feared they might be his undoing. She pressed his hand affectionately as he lowered her from the cart. "You are welcome to come inside for a cup of Granny Clare's tea."

"Another day," he promised, thoughts elsewhere as he released her fingers. Where, she did not have to guess, as he gazed back down the road where Mariah's horse had long since disappeared from sight.

At last, he sought the doctor's advice. Mr. Widlow gave him permission, since he was beginning to feel the loss of his son's strength in tending the crops. His arrival caught the family by surprise, Nell and her mother patching garments, while Mariah conducted inventory of her medicine cabinet.

Both women stayed present for the exam, although Mrs. Darrow's mouth formed a line of disapproval, and Nell tried in vain to concentrate on the shawl she was repairing for her grandmother.

"This illness has been upon you for some time," Mariah guessed once the exam had commenced. Her stethoscope tested his chest and lungs as they sat on the bench by the parlor door. She kept her voice low, though not a word escaped the audience seated by the stone hearth.

"Weeks," he agreed. "More than a month, I believe. I've lost track of the time, though it passes so slowly here at home."

She put her stethoscope aside to make notes in the daybook she always carried. "You compare it to the regiment, I suppose. That is where you wish to be, if not for this affliction?"

"Of course. It is all anyone talks of and all I think about."

Without glancing up, she told him, "I have not corresponded with anyone from the camps, but heard many letters from those who do. There seems an equally restless spirit among those in the regiment as there is here."

"They spend much time waiting for their orders," he admitted. "And there is illness among their quarters far worse than what I suffer now. Still, I can't help envying their sense of purpose."

A look of sympathy flitted across the doctor's face. "To be helpless is unbearable," she agreed. Raising a hand, she felt his forehead, saying, "You are not feverish at present. Have you suffered any confusion when the chill comes over you?"

"It troubles my dreams," he admitted.

She rose and went to the medicine cabinet with its collection of glass vials. "I wish to start you on a quinine dosage for the bronchial inflammation," she told him, selecting a bottle from the upper shelf. "It will help with the cough and the fever both and has proven itself many times for my father's patients."

"Then I will take it right away if you will tell me the proper dosage."

"Such faith." A smile stirred the doctor's lips. "You have benefited from a physician's care before, Mr. Widlow?"

"No—that is, never a qualified one. When I was a boy, a traveling man beseeched the audience members to provide him a lock of their hair. In exchange, he mixed a special elixir to cure their woes."

"And this worked?" Mariah raised her brows at the story.

"For a time." He leaned closer. "I suspect the chief ingredient was rum, you see."

Jealousy rippled through Nell as she witnessed their playful exchange. Never had she seen anyone threaten the doctor's taciturn demeanor so effortlessly. Every smile, every blush he drew from the other woman's reserved exterior was like a stab to her own carefully concealed feelings.

With mixed emotions, she listened as they arranged to meet again within the week. "This illness has been allowed to take firm root," Mariah explained, seeing her patient to the door. "It may be many weeks before the medicine dissolves its hold on you."

Consultations like this one in the parlor were beginning to cause anxiety among the Darrows for fear of gossip. As a result, Nell was quietly appointed as chaperone. Placed in the background, she performed such household tasks as hanging the wash or scrubbing the plank floor that never came clean while trying to be as unnoticed and unobvious as possible.

How painful this became—watching the boy she loved grow to love another—was not to be thought of in comparison with the relief of seeing his strength return. His spirit improved even before the quinine and other treatments took their miraculous effect on his body. Obviously caught by the doctor's beauty, he showed even greater admiration for her knowledge.

Their conversations, which spanned everything from politics to science, fell on Nell's unwilling ears with a sting. She could hear the undertones that laced their voices, the things left unsaid as they traded looks and ideas. Emotions pushed their way to the surface when the doctor's touch lingered too long, her patient reaching to brush her hand in return.

One day, looking up to dust the mirror above the mantel, she saw the couple reflected past her own plain features, standing in the hall, their heads bent close together, as Arthur pressed a kiss to the doctor's upturned mouth.

It was not their first, judging by the way it lingered. Mariah's hand reached to trace his jaw, a smile forming as she told him something in a whisper.

Nell quickly moved out of sight, hands clutching the rag close to her chest. Her heart beat wildly, her mind reeling from the image in the glass. She had not meant to see it, but soon learned it was hardly being kept a secret.

The couple was seen together in town and sometimes walking by the spring on a Sunday afternoon. Mariah never attended church, else word of their courtship might have spread faster.

As it was, the doctor showed no sign of relinquishing her agnostic beliefs, though Arthur's staunchly devout family would surely approve less of this practice than of the medical one she ran from the Darrow's parlor.

But they continued to plan for a future that was uncertain in more ways than one. With Arthur's improved health came also his chance to enlist. Six weeks after his first visit to the doctor, he came to see her wearing the coat and trousers his mother had dyed a dark gray with the help of walnut oil. He left with his hat in his hands, eyes full of regret as they met with Nell's ahead on the path.

She had been to the neighboring wood and carried back with her a handful of violets. Her fingers crushed the stems when she saw his uniform, heart aching with the knowledge of where he went.

"I will tell Henry how you get on," he promised, taking her hand in farewell. "Pray for me Nell—that I will do my duty as the others have and come through it to see you all again."

"I will," she said, reluctant to let him go as he moved further down the path. Before he reached the gate, she caught up with him. "Wait. Take one of these. For remembering home." With a shy smile as she tucked a blossom through his jacket's buttonhole.

The violet face peeked back at her with a friendlier gaze than that of somber, wistful Arthur when he looked back one last time.

8

November 1, 1862

Dearest Henry,

The rowdy doings of Mischief Night have left their mark on our town once again. Maple syrup was smeared on door handles, and Mr. Cray's gate was taken off its hinges so that all his cattle escaped. Our house was among those spared, with Granny setting out the broken buckets from the garden to let the children take for burning.

Amidst all the trouble, the Hinkle's youngest boy, Charley, received a painful wound to his leg. He bears it bravely and says it must be nothing compared with the danger a soldier faces.

"Nell? Are you there, dear?"

The girl stopped writing at the sound of her grandmother calling. The rattle of saucers and spoons told her the older woman was preparing tea for the doctor's guests. Hastily, she laid her pen on the desk, her plain skirt rustling as she moved towards the family's kitchen.

Pine planks creaked beneath her boots, the knots in the wood creating a pattern that was almost ornamental. The Darrow farmhouse was a rustic one, fashioned by her grandfather when the family migrated from Scotland years before. His craftsmanship—though not exquisite by any means—was all that Nell could associate with the man, since he died while she was still in the cradle.

"You should have called for me earlier," Nell scolded the figure that was stooped over the table. "I thought Mama was with you," she added, wondering what new task had called Mrs. Darrow away.

"She went with your papa into town," her grandmother explained, shaky hands arranging a pot and tea cups on a metal tray.

Though nearly blind, Clare Darrow was sharp in every other sense. Her memory of the house's layout was enough to aid her in this daily task as she insisted on brewing tea from the well water Nell fetched each morning. She preferred it even to water fresh from the spring, and the rest of the family had grown used to drinking it.

"Be a good girl and carry this tray in for the Hinkles," she said, patting Nell's hand. "I may be fit to stew it, but I dare not trust myself with the serving." This was said with a wink. Her voice was still infused with the native accent of her birthplace in the Scottish Highlands. A strange thing, considering Sylvan Spring had been her home for almost thirty years now. Strands of white hair were knotted at the back of her neck, hands gnarled with age and a life of labor on the Darrow's homestead.

At times, Nell fancied something of her grandmother's quiet strength in her features—though none of the woman's famous girlhood beauty had carried over if the reflection in her mirror was anything to judge by. Limp yellow tresses framed eyes that were set close together, her complexion made tan from the sun in her father's crop field.

She could see the same image distorted in the silverware balanced on the tray she carried now. Glancing quickly away, she formed a smile of welcome for the figures gathered in the family's parlor. "Morning, Mrs. Hinkle," she greeted the farm wife, whose homestead lay within walking distance of their own.

The Hinkles were better off when it came to farmhands than some of their neighbors, having so many helping hands in the form of their children. Though, of course, that meant having more mouths to feed, giving everyone reason enough to pity them.

"Nell has brought us some tea," her grandmother told them, settling into the rocking chair beside the unlit fireplace. Her hand grasped the shawl she kept there for fending off the morning chill, wrapping it tightly around her thin shoulders.

Mrs. Hinkle merely nodded in reply, her attention demanded by the infant fussing in her arms. Gathered round her on the sofa were children in various stages of growth. They all had the same shade of straw-colored hair and a complexion as tan and uncared for as Nell's.

The patient, a boy of roughly ten years, was seated on a wooden chair, a deep gash visible below his left knee. Beside him, the doctor knelt to gently clean the wound, squeezing the sides together to bind it with a needle and thread

"I hope it leaves a scar," Charley announced, fingers gripping the chair as the needle pierced his flesh. Like his siblings, he was lanky and rail thin. He was paler, though, his eyes a shade of pastel gray that reminded Nell of storm clouds.

At the sound of his voice, a dog's bark had echoed

from the farmhouse porch. Nails scraped against the front door, followed by a low whining sound, as the faithful pet begged for entrance.

"Go home, Rufus," Mrs. Hinkle ordered sternly from the sofa. She shifted the complaining baby in her arms. "There won't be any scar for showing off. Will there, Miss Moore?"

"There will be a mark," the doctor confessed, securing the bandage. "No doubt it shall fade in time. You must be more careful in the future, Charley," she added. Her gaze softened as she studied the boy's gaunt frame, smaller than that of even his younger siblings.

"Boys collect scars and scrapes the way girls collect butterfly wings," Nell's grandmother chuckled, cradling her tea cup between knotted fingers. "It is their nature. Your papa can attest to that," she confided to Nell, who seated herself in a nearby chair. "Once he fell down a drinking well, poor lad."

"Ah, but this one is always finding trouble," Mrs. Hinkle insisted, casting a glare in her son's direction. "Guess how he came by this scrape? I'll tell you how," she said, not giving them time to answer. "By climbing over the Roans' gate, that's how."

Sneaking onto the Roan property was practically a rite of passage for the children of Sylvan Spring and had been since Nell was a child. Ellis Roan, the heir to the family property, was a hermit of sorts, never seen in the town shops, or the church. He preferred his privacy for whatever reason and survived off the hares and other wildlife he trapped in the woods around the spring.

"That old fence had sharp edges," Charley boasted. "Rufus got his fur caught in it, great big tufts coming out."

At the sound of its name, the dog began barking again, the woofs deep and insistent with its growing desperation. Wishing to spare the animal another scolding, Nell told them, "My brother once had a dog with that same devoted temperament. I remember it slept outside his window at night, and sometimes he would sneak it inside and let it sleep on his bed."

"Don't go filling his head with ideas," Mrs. Hinkle said, as Charley's eyes lit up with the story. "That dog's so big and clumsy he'd soon break every bit of furniture in the cabin."

"He's not so big," the dog's owner protested. "Not compared with the dog Billy Cray saw t'other night. The size of a mare and all shaggy with black fur—"

Laughter greeted the wild statement, everyone but the doctor joining in the mirth.

Her expression was one of confusion and mild concern.

Charley's mother demanded, "What nonsense are you talking now, child?"

"The plat-eye," he insisted. "Billy and his pa saw it twice down by the Crooked Wood spring. It had eyes like fire."

Plat-eyes were the spirits conjured by the dead in the form of menacing, oversized animals, according to old folk tales. Nell had heard plenty of tales of it, and shivered through them, as a girl.

"Oh, hush now," his mother said, embarrassed by the smiles of amusement the story was drawing. "Billy Cray is not to be trusted anyhow. Were it not his fingers left such an ugly mark on our door the other night?" She spoke of a recent prank the children had played in the Mischief Night tradition, the scrawling of a mysterious symbol on various doors in the community.

Nell's family had been spared this indignity, but the Hinkles, among several others, had woken the next day to find their homes marked with a blood-red dye, streaks of it trailing down the wood from the painted symbol above.

A death symbol some claimed, though Nell wasn't sure why. When she went to borrow a volume from her former instructor's shelves, Nell had seen the one left on the schoolhouse door. A half-moon with an arrow bent through it. The teacher, Miss Mitchell, had studied it with pursed lips and a cold eye, muttering something about "heathen youngins" under her breath.

"Mr. Roan's door has the same mark," Charley insisted, revealing his reason for braving the hermit's fence. "That makes eight I've heard of, besides ours. Reckon I will have to see them all to be sure."

"Not until your wound is healed," the doctor cautioned. "You must take care not to loosen these stitches. I will be extremely disappointed if I hear otherwise." She had begun to repack her bag, a battered leather one said to belong to her father in his early days of practice. She rarely mentioned her family, or anything of a personal nature, but Nell had seen text books on her shelves that bore the former physician's name.

"Billy says the plat-eye's the spirit of a convict," a shy voice offered, the only Hinkle girl, her hair twisted in a long braid that she toyed with nervously. "Hung back in granddaddy's day. That is why no one's seen it outside the woods—'cause its spirit is trapped there."

Nell squirmed to hear such talk. The story of the

convict had inspired more than one nightmare for her as a child. Suspected of thieving from his neighbors, he was said to have hanged for his crimes on the big, twisted oak from which Crooked Wood took its name. No burial for the body, only a rope to slowly fray, and birds to pick the bones.

The doctor snapped her case shut, her expression unreadable. What must she think of their superstitious talk? A woman of science and education, her love for reason excluded even the possibility of a higher power, something Nell's family had learned the first Sunday she refused their invitation to church.

"Could be that's what marked up the doors," Charley said, an idea coming to him. "Vengeance in blood for the hanging—"

"Enough of such talk," his mother said, waving away the boy's excitement. "You will be scaring the young ones," she added, with a glance at the other Hinkle children. None of them looked remotely frightened as they sat forward, eager gazes trained on their brother for more of this wondrous knowledge.

Relief flooded through Nell as the subject changed to the crops and eventually to Henry's last letter. She read part of it aloud, as their neighbor made tsking sounds at the regiment's shortage on food and supplies.

"We expect to move camp at any moment," she read, fumbling the words as she thought of delayed communication and her brother and the other soldiers trudging through the autumn weather. "Some of the fellows' boots have been pulled apart in the mud along these banks we now occupy. Mine have held true, as have Arthur's, though his feet swell so, he can hardly get them on..." She trailed off, her gaze drawn to where the doctor slipped from the parlor, her skirts rustling quietly down the hall. Guessing the reason for her withdrawal was not hard, though Nell couldn't help feeling a pang of discomfort. Miss Moore's letters from the battlefield were not ones to be read aloud, or so she suspected.

Envy flickered through her, a faint spark that threatened quickly to grow to a flame. Part of her longed to know what lay inside those envelopes which disappeared to the doctor's desk and bedside table. The other part prayed to overcome this weakness that haunted her since childhood, an infatuation for a man who would never return her affection.

"There now," Mrs. Hinkle said, pressing her hand with a look of sympathy. "How you must miss your brother, dear."

"Yes, ma'am" she replied, a flush creeping over her face at the woman's misunderstanding. For as much as she missed Henry, this other burden weighed on her heart with a force equally stunning and far more hopeless.

Tucking the letter away, she offered a grateful smile to the older woman. "Henry is in our prayers and thoughts at all times. He and—and all our friends who face this difficulty."

Her grandmother murmured her assent, the atmosphere in the parlor growing somber and silent until the only sounds were the ticking of a clock and the Hinkle daughter sipping loudly from a teacup.

ॐ

Young Charley's story should cost you a blush, Henry, along with certain of our friends who know of what I write.

For, do you not recall a different Mischief Night some ten years ago, when you helped to play a prank on that same unsuspecting neighbor?

You will no doubt say this event has escaped your memory, the same as that time you snipped off my braids during a spelling lesson. I shall gladly recount the whole event, as I am sure it would earn more than one laugh when shared by the campfire some quiet evening.

How innocent it began as we blackened our faces with the soot from the hearth. Granny Clare let us take the old broken stool and barrel for the bonfire, and you generously let me throw both into the blaze. I do believe your plan was to sneak away unnoticed and leave me there as you and the other boys carried out that dreadful scheme with the snuff pinched from Wray's father.

Yes, if Wray Camden is sitting beside you, he will recall it was his idea to "smoke out" Mr. Roan from his hiding place. There were four of you eager to share in the guilt, clambering over that rusty old gate in the moonlight. I witnessed it all from the blackberry hedge where you made me hide out of the way. You did not want a girl to tattle on you, but it was not my voice that protested when Wray's bold fingers struck the match.

Crouched in the bushes beside Roan's shack, Nell had watched, breathless as her brother's friends prepared to carry out their prank. No one had expected Arthur to show up since he already condemned the scheme when they hatched it over school recess. But it was his figure that came beside her in the hedge, placing a finger to her mouth before he slipped out to confront the mischief makers.

"We will be caught," he reasoned, "and the punishment severe." He spoke chiefly to Wray, whose match was snuffed before it could touch the line of powder.

The warning brought a scowl to the other youth's handsome features, though his father's anger was known to have blackened eyes and broken farm equipment in drunken rages. In hushed tones, they argued the danger with Wray ignoring his friend's advice to light the trail before the hermit's steps.

The powder crackled, smoke pouring out just as they hoped. It caught fast, Nell stifling a scream as the popping sound was accompanied by a bright flash. Flames shot high, licking at the porch banisters. A small fire, one that was easily put out, thought it left its scorch marks on the weathered timber.

Arthur had been lined up for punishment with the others despite having taken no part in the deed. To defend him was her first instinct, but he put his hand gentle on her arm. "Don't tell. I have to cast my lot with the others. They would do it for me."

Keeping his secret had been a privilege, making her feel as if they shared something deeper than the connection of schoolmates and neighbors. It wasn't true, of course. Arthur, though kind, had never showed any partiality for his friend's little sister. And now his heart belonged to another, their love carried out in the letters the doctor posted each week.

Seated before her dresser that night, Nell finished the communication she had begun that afternoon, before the Hinkles' visit and other tasks demanded her attention. A candle's flame illuminated the page before her, its glow reflecting in the mirror to show her tired, drab features.

I finish this letter by candlelight, in place of my usual

diary entry. Although, what I record in that tiny leather volume is not so different than what I write here. You must know, brother, that I am consumed with thoughts of this war, and all who suffer from it daily.

If only I could be of more use, perhaps these fears would not plague me so. There's work enough for me at home, helping our dear parents and Granny Clare, yet it seems trivial compared to what you and the others must sacrifice.

Perhaps I will try for a teaching certificate next year as Mama has often suggested. I believe she sees little else for me in this place we call home. Everyone says Miss Mitchell will give up the school house soon as her rheumatism grows worse (though she has not said as much herself).

Let me hear from you soon, Henry. I will hope that your regiment does not move camp before this reaches it, as I cannot bear to think of such a long delay in your response. Believe me when I write that the suspense of your reply is continuously in my thoughts as much as any of my daily chores or pleasures. There will be no rest for my heart until you and all our dear friends have safely returned home.

As ever, you are in my prayers.

Your Loving Sister

⇛⇘

Jenna placed the letter aside with a wistful feeling, wishing to know more of the letter writer and her family, the fate of her brother and their friends.

There were no more letters from the unknown girl, though, or from anyone. All that remained from the scant collection was a series of Confederate Army regulation documents and a battered ledger stored in a plastic bag. Probably a local business's records pictured in the tin type photos that emphasized the dry goods store and bank.

Disappointment crept over her, along with a sense of fatigue. If she was lucky, the Internet would yield some birth and marriage certificates from genealogy sites. She envisioned tracing family members via phone or e-mail, ones who might or might not be able to divulge the details of their ancestors' lives. Often people were uninterested, even with the promise of an acknowledgment in a soon-to-be-published story.

Reluctant to begin, she reached instead for the ledger. Her gloved fingers rustled the pages gently, opening them to a random section. Hand-written entries filled a page faded to brown, dated for the year 1862. Paragraphs were written journal style, instead of the bullet type lists one usually found in a record of sales or inventory.

She glanced over one of these, catching its meaning as she read.

"Mrs. Morgan, one o'clock. Patient split her left foot open while chopping firewood, nearly severing one toe. Have cleaned and stitched the wounds and advised her to return as soon as Monday to see how it does."

A physician's daybook, not business inventory. One from 1862, the same year as the letter she just read. Which meant…yes, it had to be. This item belonged to the doctor, the one mentioned in the girl's letter.

Jenna had to stop herself from turning the fragile pages too hastily as she made her way back to the front of the ledger. There, inscribed on the leaf insert, was the name Mariah Moore, MD.

Moore—wasn't that name among the stones at the abandoned cemetery?

Yanking her notebook free, she flipped its pages until she found the one she wanted. The one with the moon engraving that was mysteriously placed beneath the sycamore, two marble headstones beside it.

A woman doctor? Jenna raised her brows at this unexpected development. A female doctor in the Civil War era rural South was not something she would have imagined.

Already trembling a little from excitement, she jumped when someone laid a hand on her shoulder.

"Ma'am?" the voice was apologetic, belonging to the male volunteer. He gestured to the clock that hung above the stained glass window. "It's uh...almost time to close."

Unconsciously, Jenna tightened her grip on the artifact, remembering the manager's warning about no scanned copies. "Could I have this put on reserve at the desk? I'll need to see it a few more times," she explained, thinking how valuable it might prove for providing background on the town as well as the cemetery. The little details were what her readers looked for and what she desperately needed to make this feature come to life for them.

The boy looked uncertain, his fellow volunteer, Paige, reappearing from one of the aisles with a rolling cart. "No problem," she told Jenna. "You'll need to fill out a card for it. That's all." Rummaging among her supplies, she located one and handed it over. "Write the serial number from the tag on this bottom line," she added.

"Thanks." Jenna filled out the necessary information. "Any chance there's a genealogist in the area? I'm looking for someone who might have copies of those papers that burned in the fire."

The students exchanged a meaningful glance. With a smirk, the boy told her, "Old Lady Maudell. She has everything from the last hundred years—which is about as long as she's lived."

"This...Maudell," Jenna said, uncertainly. "Is she a local historian?"

He snorted. "Hardly. She has all this rare stuff she's bought up from auctions that no one's allowed to see. It makes her feel important or something."

"She used to work here," Paige supplied, "but that was years ago. Everyone says she's the town's oldest citizen, but I think she's only ninety or so."

"I had to interview her for an essay last year," the boy said, tossing a can of furniture polish between his hands. "You would have thought I was asking her to reveal nuclear codes or something. Got me a 'B' on the paper, actually."

This all sounded a little daunting, but Jenna was willing to do some wheedling if it meant learning the secrets to the town's past. And if anyone knew them, why not the oldest citizen? Especially one locked away with a collection of priceless relics.

Placing the pen against her notebook, she asked them, "What's her address?"

9

A coincidence—it had to be.

That's what Con told himself when he found the gravestone rubbings. Chalk shading, a little bit crinkled. Made by his wife a few years after they moved near the spring, all three bore the same design.

A half-moon turned on its side; a cryptic V-shape laid over it.

Considering how often he visited the old Lesley homestead, Con should have noticed sooner. Maybe he had seen the markers too many times, had grown so used to them he didn't think about the weird design carved into all three. When he held the chalk copies of the Lesley stones next to Jenna Cade's crayon one from the cemetery, there was no mistaking the connection between the symbols.

Should he call her, then?

It hardly seemed worth it, to tell her something that only raised more questions. But the paper with her cell number continued to flutter on his corkboard, catching his eye every time he fetched a tool or answered the wall phone.

His conscience tugged at him, along with the memory of the young woman's persistent gaze. There had been no resentment in her manner, only disappointment and a kind of hurt. Part of him wished she had chewed him out, accused him of being unprofessional—anything to make him feel justified in letting this go instead of calling the number she gave him.

Being in the middle of a project hardly seemed the right excuse, but he would take it for now. He looked at the cross-shaped monument that still lacked its most dominant pattern. The roses were finished. The basket weave would come next.

Air-powered tools created the three-dimensional effect, while special-made rubber stencils would help to shape the lettering. Keeping things old-fashioned was difficult, but necessary, for preserving the art. At this moment, he was thankful for the marble's soft surface, letting his tools carve more easily than the granite he was often commissioned to use.

He preferred these symbols of faith to the secular ones requested by most customers. They seemed to endow his work with more meaning, giving the fragile creations an almost eternal significance. Death was part of his trade, but the life afterward concerned him just as much, especially in light of his recent grief.

The writer had worn a cross, he remembered. A silver one around her neck, catching the light as she leaned to study this same memorial. Did it represent faith? Or was it just a pretty ornament? Instinct said it was faith, though, he knew for countless people that a cross was just a necklace, its symbol no relation at all to the soul within the person it adorned.

Why she kept returning to his mind was hard to say. Guilt was one explanation but curiosity was another. As if his interest extended beyond her work and their shared link to the world of forgotten monuments.

He shoved the thought aside, along with a cardboard box that clinked noisily as it moved.

Glancing inside, he saw the remains of the marker he was currently duplicating, broken beyond repair, the chips and bits of jagged stone unrecognizable as the work of an eighteenth-century artisan.

Trashing it would be difficult as he knew its original glory through photographs. His fingers cradled a few of the pieces, coating his skin in layers of dust. As he held the fragments, the rough edges brushing his palm, he thought of another occasion involving shattered gravestones.

Like this one, they were torn apart by vandals. Kids seeking an outlet for the boredom found in a small rural town as they wielded baseball bats in a darkened cemetery. And he, Con Taggart, had been one of them.

⮞⮜

It had been Marcus Gradley's idea to smash the headstones that summer night fifteen years ago. A rebel by the standards of most adults in the community, Marcus was the only boy in Con's tenth grade class to own a car, and more importantly, a motorbike. This had given him an edge over the older high school boys and even the athletes, none of whom could match him for sheer daring, despite their brawn.

Why he chose to include the transfer student from Kansas among his circle of friends was a mystery to most of Sylvan High, Con included. Not that Con was complaining—he was simply relieved to belong somewhere amidst the crowd of strangers, where it proved dangerous and a little painful to draw the eye of a resident bully.

It wasn't until later that he realized he had aligned

himself with a force just as destructive.

Marcus and his friends spent their weekends straddling the line between unruly and unlawful, snitching booze from their parents' kitchen cabinets, breaking curfew hours, and lobbing rocks through windows on abandoned buildings.

Con went along with most of these, as he reasoned it didn't hurt anyone but himself. His parents knew only that he stayed out later than they preferred, but since neither his homework nor his church attendance suffered, there were no repercussions.

Until the cemetery.

"There's no caretaker, so all we have to worry about is Deputy Vic's patrol," Marcus instructed, handing out steel bats and cans of spray paint to the group of five gathered by Sylvan Grove Cemetery's fence. "We'll start with the rows in the back, the old stuff. Most of its already half-broke, so we're just finishing the job."

A few snickers met this comment.

Con fumbled the bat another kid tossed him. He might have argued or thought of some excuse to leave, except that Marcus' girlfriend, Liane, had come with them. Small, with fierce features and strawberry curls she kept bundled in a ponytail, she was the only girl to infiltrate the group.

She surveyed Con with narrowed eyes as they waited their turn to scale the fence. "Scared?" she asked, one brow flicking upward in a question. She seldom spoke to him, but he had sensed her watching him before, in class and the cafeteria, her gaze sliding away before he could read whether disdain or admiration lay in its depths.

"No," he answered. He wasn't scared—not of the

graveyard, anyway. It was his father's wrath, should the man ever find out about this or any of their activities, which caused a slight breathlessness in his reply. He climbed over the fence before he could lose courage, his jacket tearing on one of the iron spokes as he dropped to the ground.

They didn't start defacing the stones right away but instead leaned against them smoking the cigarettes Marcus had bribed from his college age brother.

Noticing Con's was unlit, Liane passed him hers. "Try it." A playful edge warmed her voice as she urged him.

He pressed it between his lips, aware it had been against hers moments before. A taste of mint was followed by smoke scorching the back of his throat, a cough escaping before he could bury it.

She didn't laugh but continued watching as he practiced taking drags. Her hand gradually crept through the grass to touch his, sending surprised shivers up his spine. "Good, isn't it?" she said.

"It is." He didn't say which he meant—the cigarette or this new connection between them. Instead, he let his fingers twine with hers, confusion rivaling the warmth he felt from her hand.

Across from them, Marcus stubbed his cigarette's orange glow against one of the monuments. There was an edge of darkness in his expression as he gripped the handle to his bat, telling the group, "Let's do this, all right?" Had he seen them?

Stone cracked beneath the impact of metal, shards of rock mixing with dust to litter the grass below. Con's arm swung to shatter a small stone engraved with a lamb. His hands froze at the sight of its severed body, jagged rock replacing the curve of the neck. A blow from someone else's bat filled the tomb with cracks that snaked from the base to its top.

"Don't start something you can't finish," Marcus warned with a smirk. His heavy boot kicked the remains to the ground, where he crushed them repeatedly with his heel.

The youngest of the group, a kid named Bradley, spray painted a hexagram over the Bible verse on another tomb. The paint stained his fingers and the ground around them a lurid red that nauseated Con.

"Help me with this one," Liane shouted, tugging his sleeve in the direction of a couple's shared memorial. Her flashlight revealed a simple scroll design, the words of John 3:16 etched upon it.

The air around them rang with the others' yells of excitement, the sound of stone splitting apart beneath heavy blows. Con touched the couple's monument, its surface cool despite the summer heat. He could feel Liane's expectant gaze, his fingers tracing the promise carved into the stone. This was wrong, a sin even...but turning back seemed pointless now.

Until another voice joined the shouting. One deep and angry in its timbre as it told them, "Stop right there—don't move a muscle!" A local deputy, his flashlight beam sweeping across the scene of destruction. He was upon them in what seemed no time, the guilty teenagers vaulting over tombstones as they fled.

Only Con hesitated to move, one hand still clutching the baseball bat, the other resting against the monument.

By the time he decided to follow the others it was too late. A hand clamped onto his shoulder. He didn't resist as he was pinned to the ground, a pair of cuffs fastened over his wrists. The scuffle of the other kids' shoes had died away, metal clanging in the distance as they jumped a back fence somewhere.

A long night had followed, first at the police station where he managed to protect his friends' identities for reasons even he couldn't explain. Then at home, where his parents were enraged by both the vandalism and the thousands of dollars it was likely to cost them.

"What if we can't afford it?" his mother worried, her voice drifting from his parents' closed bedroom door.

Con lay fully clothed on his bed, restless and sore from the night's events. Was it the girl that made him shoulder all the blame—or was she just the reason he participated in the first place? No answer came as he turned on his side, staring into the darkness.

Waking at noon, he heard voices conversing downstairs, his parents and a man, one whose gruff tones seemed vaguely familiar in his sleep blurred state.

Still dressed in his rumpled clothes from yesterday, he trailed down the stairs to find them seated in the dining room. Con had seen him before.

The town's stone mason, an older man whose business shared a gravel lot with the tire store. Dark skin was faintly lined with age and silver hair was cropped short beneath the flat wool cap he often wore. He offered Con a short nod from the other side of the table, busy showing Con's father something on a piece of paper.

"There you are." Con's mother rose, her expression less tense than last night. Taking his arm, she gave it a firm squeeze as she steered him around the table. "Conrad, you know William Sawyer. He works for the county sometimes."

"Sure," he said, a sense of foreboding creeping over him with the words.

"Mr. Sawyer will be repairing the headstones," his father explained. Pulling the reading glasses from his face, he offered his son a pointed look. "You'll be helping him."

"Wait—what?" Con's eyes widened, glancing between his parents and Sawyer's calm expression. "But I don't...couldn't I just pay for it?" he finished, hand clenching the frayed material of his shirt in a frustrated gesture.

"Never be able to afford it," the stone carver said, shaking his head. "You'll have to work it off."

His whole summer had just been commandeered. After all, it would take more than a few days to repair however many stones they had smashed. Eight? Ten? He couldn't remember, though the details had been repeated many times at the police station.

"Shop opens at seven every day, 'cept on Sundays," Sawyer told him, ignoring the despair that must have been written on his face. "Bring your lunch if you can—break lasts half an hour."

"I just—" he rubbed the back of his neck, at a loss for how quickly this was moving "This doesn't seem right." He glanced at his parents again. "It wasn't even my idea. There were five of us."

"Then turn them in," his mother pleaded, voice dropping slightly.

"I can't." He felt trapped, his thoughts spinning faster than he could keep up. "You can't expect me to betray friends."

"Should've run faster then," Sawyer advised,

thumping him on the shoulder.

Resentment coursed through the teenager, though he recognized a glimmer of good humor in the mason's face.

"See you Monday," the older man told him, lifting his cap in parting.

Sawyer's shop smelled of concrete and chalk, the odor reaching him as he wheeled his bike up to the doorway. The floors were freshly swept, the tools carefully organized on the walls and benches. Blocks of stone formed a wall, along with crates that looked ready for shipping.

"Ever worked with tools before, Taggart?" the stone carver asked, emerging from the back room with a coffee mug in hand. He wore the same faded cap as before, a navy apron covering his khakis and button-down shirt.

"Shop class," Con shrugged, wondering if that counted. "I made a canoe." Not a working one, he failed to add. Or so the teacher's marks led him to believe, discouraging any test runs for the finished project.

"Close enough," the mason chuckled. "We'll see how you get on with the basics first."

The basics turned out to be mending some of the broken headstones with screws and a can of carpenter's glue. One of them—the sculpted lamb his bat collided with—was beyond saving and would have to be duplicated from scratch.

For the other nine, Sawyer held out hope for repair. "Those friends of yours have a mighty powerful swing," the mason observed dryly. They were reassembling a headstone with a memento mori in the form of a grinning, winged skull. "Don't suppose they're on the baseball team?" he guessed with a side glance at his new apprentice.

"No sports," Con answered. "We try to avoid clichés." Something Marcus had said once, that sounded much less impressive coming from Con's stilted tone.

"Rebels, then." If Sawyer was making fun of him, it was hard to tell. The craftsman's expression was inscrutable as he joined cracks together, seamlessly forming a set of initials. "Had my own wild streak as a boy back in North Dakota. Stole a car once." A grin cracked his features at the sight of Con's shock. "Well, could be joyriding is more like it. My cousin's old jalopy was part mine on account I handled all its maintenance. That said, he didn't want no one else driving it without his supervision." He paused a moment, coating the edge of his brush in glue. "Christmas of '56 came a freeze like you wouldn't believe. Whole county was a layer of ice and snow. Me and the other boys, we sneaked that car outta the garage and spun donuts with it on the pond."

"You could have crashed through," Con said, amazed anyone would try it.

But then, winter freezes in Sylvan Spring were seldom enough to yield ice skating, much less a stunt like the one Sawyer described.

"Sure could have. Guess the Lord had my back that day." Sawyer stepped away to examine their work thus far, whistling under his breath. "Good job, Taggart. You'll pull your weight around here yet."

And he did, though for a while it was more piecing and gluing, along with such tasks as sweeping up and cleaning the tools.

Sawyer was precise in the care for his carving

equipment. "You can judge a craftsman by the condition of his tools. A serious one, he'll never let the rust take hold or dull the blades with bad storage."

He learned to clean the steel files with special brushes, to wrap them spaced apart in canvas rolls. Sometimes he would pick up supplies from the hardware store or arrange the shipping for one of Sawyer's out-of-state commissions. In between all this, he practiced sketching the lamb engraving, an exercise meant to prepare him for the carving stage.

"Gotta get to know it, think about it from all the angles," Sawyer told him, tacking the photographs of the original monument to a cork board on the wall. It was a plain enough tomb, the only inscription being *OUR LETTIE*. No last name and no clue as to when its occupant might have lived, a common trait for nineteenth-century stones, apparently.

Leafing through manuals on gravestone carving became as routine as studying for an exam. In one of these, in a section concerning gravestone symbolism, Con made a discovery that caused his stomach to lurch.

"Children's graves," he said, his tone semi-accusing as he glanced up. "That's what the books says the lamb carving is used for—infants mostly."

The mason was quiet, contemplating the slab of stone in front of him. After a moment, he said, "Could be right. No way to know for sure, without the proper dates and all."

Con was stunned, staring at the manual with a sense of regret stronger than the moment he first shattered the monument. With a sigh, his instructor placed a hand on his shoulder. "Don't matter whose it was, son," he urged gently. "Not so long as we do our best to honor them with a new marker."

Words that weighed heavy on his conscience as he began to practice shaping the stone, soaking it down with a spray bottle to search for cracks and fissures and then taking his first tentative *ping! ping!* with the chisel and mallet. It was difficult with only the air-powered hammer to aid him, modern machinery and lasers being foreign objects to Sawyer's shop. He was too eager with the mallet as well, his chisel digging deep and leaving blemishes that made his instructor shake his head with disapproval.

"Remember, you're making art, not pounding nails," Sawyer told him as they used a file to smooth the flaws away.

"When did you learn to carve?" he asked the older man, thinking some allowance might be made for both age and inexperience.

"About your age, I guess. My dad and granddad were both in the trade, and it just seemed natural I carry on the tradition. Looks like it'll stop with me, though." The carver rarely mentioned family, though it was common knowledge that he was a widower. No children were referenced, only nephews and nieces. He still wore a wedding band. His wife's picture remained in the leather wallet he sometimes pulled bills from to send Con for supplies at the hardware store. He showed Con her headstone when they began to reset some of the repaired markers at the cemetery.

A simple dove in flight was etched into the marble, the epitaph reading, *'Long did she suffer in sickness on earth; now her gentle soul rises to meet the Redeemer.'*

"Cancer," he explained, one hand resting against the stone. "Harriet weren't the kind to complain, though. Just not in her nature." Those were his only words on the subject, undoubtedly a painful one. Instead, he talked about his boyhood in North Dakota, of his first time to carve a tombstone on his own. "Didn't know the fella it was for," he admitted as they packed gravel around the newly entrenched stone. "But I heard he wasn't a Christian and felt a sadness for it. Carving the lost soul's monument is a different matter altogether from carving the believer's."

Con knew nothing about the owner of the lamb stone, other than the symbolism listed in the book. Frustrating at first, the project began to consume his thoughts until he found himself sketching or making notes on it even when he wasn't at the workshop. For someone who slept through art class, it was suddenly his chief interest, and he even stopped caring that Marcus's group had abandoned him after that night in the cemetery.

His fingers grew slowly attuned to the craft as if he were learning to play an instrument. Chisel and mallet traced the ridges and curves in the stone like a bow running over violin strings. He felt as if the tools were an extension of himself, shaping his thoughts into reality on the blank canvas of the stone.

"Not bad, Taggart," the carver told him, examining the lamb's raised outline, the letters engraved boldly below.

Con thought he detected a stronger emotion beneath the concession, something akin to the pride of a teacher reviewing his pupil's progress.

When he had polished and sealed it, they set its foundation among the other rows in the burial ground. Sunlight bathed the etchings to show a skill that surprised its creator, whose accomplishment was tinged with a sense of emptiness now that it was finally done.

It was August by then, roughly a week before classes were scheduled to start.

Returning to the shop, Con began the ritual of sweeping and tool care when Sawyer told him, "Reckon your debts been paid, then. You'll, uh, not be needing to come in tomorrow." His voice was gruff as usual, but the tone one of calm as he stowed a sack of gravel in the corner.

Con stood still, fingers gripping the broom handle. "I could stay," he said after a moment, sounding more like a question than an offer. Muscles tensed as he waited for the answer.

"Can't afford a full-time assistant," the older man said, wiping his hands on a rag from the work bench. "You'd earn more sacking stuff down at the grocery store."

Con's glance roamed the shop with its collection of archaic tools and gravestone patterns pinned to the walls like a collage. Some were his—the sketches of the lamb design and the rubbings he'd taken of the original stone's lettering to make stencils. "I'm not really interested in the grocery business. You know, as a career."

Sawyer's lined features cracked slowly into a smile of understanding. "All right then," he said. "Come in after school next week."

Con reached to seal the bargain with a handshake.

❧❧

The Lesley headstones might be a coincidence; the photograph in the newspaper was a sign. Con saw it almost as soon as he fetched his morning mail. A thank you card from a customer in Birmingham, an inquiry from a potential client somewhere much further away. And the latest issue of *The County Times*, the headline story devoted to the upcoming festival.

Images from last year's event were spread across the front page. Game booths and vendor's tents filled the town square, as a garish-looking banner danced overhead like something from a Renaissance fair married to a Scottish Games celebration.

He started to turn the page and then paused as an idea came to him. Pulling open a drawer in the work bench, he fished a magnifying glass from its jumbled contents. When he placed it over the photograph, a murmur of interest escaped his lips.

Slowly, his gaze traveled to the paper fastened to the corkboard, to the crayon rubbing made by the writer, her strokes bold and sure compared to his wife's gentler chalk ones. Instinct had told him to throw it away, that he would never call the number scrawled at the bottom.

But instinct, it seemed, had been wrong.

10

"My granddaddy used to say it was weeds that grew on the graves of the wicked, and flowers on those of the good. That's the kind of superstitious talk folks learn as children and forget to leave behind as they grow." The woman who spoke these words was closer to a hundred than ninety in terms of appearance. Lipstick smudged the puckered mouth, a vintage shade that hinted at a time before lines had creased her face. Gray hair was kept in a tidy knot, a strand of pearls visible above the collar of a silk blouse. Bony fingers tugged the necklace, her eyes fixed on Jenna with a shrewd gleam from across the patio table. "Folklore's in our blood here," she said. "Faith, too, though some might argue it's not always the right balance."

They had been talking for nearly an hour, Jenna finding the Maudell residence as soon as she left the historical society. A big Victorian house on a lot just off Main Street, it bore a touch of the gothic in its ornamental turret and steeple. The paint was flecking away in places, a crack visible in the trim above the bay window.

The door was answered by an ample figure in nurse's scrubs, her features lined with middle-age and a sense of authority. She heard Jenna's explanation with a surprised smile, her accent a strong Southern flavor when she spoke.

"Is Mrs. Maudell expecting you?" she asked, waving Jenna through a dark foyer into a living space that was crowded with antique furniture and oil paintings. Mahogany stairs led to the upper story, where faded wallpaper was peeling away from the hall.

"We've never met," Jenna admitted. "I was hoping to speak with her about some research I'm doing for a manuscript. It concerns forgotten cemeteries—"

"Pour her some tea, Mollie," a quivering voice instructed from somewhere close by.

Glancing in its direction, the nurse had hesitated only a second before she motioned for Jenna to follow her through a set of open double doors. There, on the flower garden's patio, Josephine Maudell waited expectantly.

"You are someone from the newspaper," the older woman surmised, looking Jenna over with vague interest. "They called last week, wanting to send someone about the festival." Before her was spread a tea service, bone white china with tiny pink roses to decorate the rims.

"Miss Cade is an author," the secretary corrected, filling one of the cups to set before Jenna. "She's researching a book about cemeteries."

A raised eyebrow greeted this news. "And wonders that I'm not yet part of one, no doubt." The woman chuckled, leaning forward. "I may be the oldest native of this town, Miss Cade, but that's not what makes me special. It's my habit of saving pieces from the past that sets me apart from any of my neighbors. "

"Yes, I know," Jenna said. She took a sip from the steaming brew, finding it bitter. "They told me about you at the historical society. I was hoping you could tell me about the town's Civil War history."

Josephine nodded, a faint jerk of the head. "I used to be chairwoman there. Did they tell you that? Oh, I suppose most have forgotten, but I did quite a bit for them." Without warning, she changed the subject. "What do you think of my flower garden? It's as old as most things I have, older than some. The roses were cultivated by my husband's ancestor back in the 1880s."

"It's a beautiful arrangement," Jenna told her, recognizing some of the varieties from gardens she toured in Annapolis. Most of the plants were dormant in the fall chill, but the section of asters blossomed in glorious shades of red, pink, purple, and blue. There were toad lilies that resembled orchids and a vine-like clematis snaked around the trellis.

"Prize-winning peonies," Josephine continued, stretching a shaky hand towards plants clustered beside the porch railing. "My husband bred them especially. His hobby, once he retired from banking." She fell silent with this mention of her spouse, fingers stroking the china cup by her hand. Her thoughts were now somewhere else entirely, a blankness haunting her expression.

Behind them, the nurse gave a tiny cough and a nod in Jenna's direction, as if giving permission to move things back on track.

"Mrs. Maudell," Jenna began as she set aside her cup. "I wanted to ask you about the old cemetery. The one in the woods."

Something akin to interest dawned in the green gaze that flicked back in her direction. "The wooded cemetery—I saw it once as a child. Back then, the

Sanders owned the property; they were from down East, a little aloof and unfriendly. No one went there anymore."

"Well, it's public property, now," Jenna told her, "and the county has given me permission to recover its damaged headstones. Over twenty, so far."

The woman leaned suddenly forward, clutching at her arm. "Tell me, have you found any Widlows among them?"

Jenna thought of the marble headstones beside the doctor's grave, one engraved with the sword and shield motif. "There are two Widlows," she admitted. "One with a military symbol—"

"You've found him." Josephine sucked in a ragged breath, a hand pressing against her mouth. Her eyes grew brighter. "You found Arthur," she said, voice raspy in her throat.

Jenna's pen hastily scratched the name alongside her original notes on the headstone. "Mr. Widlow is part of your family tree?" she guessed.

"Arthur Widlow was my great-great-grandfather on my mother's side and the last of the Widlow name in this county. I have his papers, his uniform—where is Arthur's uniform?" She twisted around to address the nurse, who was looking alarmed by this sudden display of emotion in her employer.

Josephine continued to babble excitedly. "I have copies of his enlistment papers somewhere. There are letters he wrote, as well, from the campsites. And the uniform, of course; we must find the uniform and let you see for yourself..." She gripped her chair, as if planning to rise and perform the task that very instant.

Worried, Jenna touched her hand. "I would love to see Mr. Widlow's uniform and the other belongings.

But for now, why don't you just tell me about him? Everything you know of him, from the stories in your family and the town. It would be a great help, believe me."

Josephine began to speak. There was much reverence for Arthur's war service, the fact he fought in many skirmishes and sustained terrible injury. Such scars were thought to have influenced his support for a county hospital in later years, though he was known as well for having invested in the town's grist mill.

"He was a farmer," Josephine said, "farmed his father's land all his life. But there were dreams from his youth, I think, that made him imagine other possibilities."

"Do you know anything about his wife? Your great-great grandmother?" Jenna asked, thinking of the matching marble headstone, with its simple engraving of a violet.

"His wife." The woman across from her blinked, looking confused by the question. "I have heard something of her, some stories, but can't recall. They knew each other before the war, I believe."

"Then she was also a native," Jenna guessed. "Maybe I can trace her story, as well."

Josephine frowned. "There wer stories of something—a tragedy. An illness."

"You mean that Mrs. Widlow was ill?" Jenna's pen grew still with the question.

"No, no." She shook her head impatiently. "Other people were, all through the town. There were wild stories about it being a punishment for something to do with the war."

"A curse," said Jenna, making a connection to the town's upcoming festival. She was beginning to understand the origins for that commemoration, though its finer details continued to prove elusive.

"That was the old ways, you know—to blame the spirits for trouble in the mortal world. All this time, and still no one can say what truly caused their suffering. It was a mystery, what happened to make the town believe dark forces plagued it." Josephine recalled only stories of children falling ill, and general misfortunes that were taken as a bad omen. "So much fear," she said mournfully. "And not enough faith to water it down, I suppose."

When the clock inside chimed three, the nurse rose and placed a hand on her employer's shoulder. "Time for your medicine, Mrs. Maudell. Remember what the doctor said—you shouldn't excite yourself so much."

"You must come and see me again," Josephine ordered Jenna. "Come this same time tomorrow. No, the next day—Mollie will need time to find the uniform and other things. They're to be used for the festival this year, anyway, borrowed by the historical society. See Miss Cade to the door, Mollie."

The nurse was apologetic for the invalid's blunt ways. "She used to be real important in the town, heading committees and all. It's been hard on her adjusting to this condition."

"Has she been ill very long?" Jenna asked, presuming she referred to something other than age.

"A few years. Tumors, slow growing, but painful at times. The doctor says it may be soon, though." Her voice caught, betraying a fondness for the town matriarch. "Used to, she could tell you every name in her family tree, and those in her husband's, too. Lately, though, the illness has taken its toll on her thinking."

"I'm grateful to her," said Jenna. "Her stories will

help to bring my book alive. People will want to read about this. Believe me."

Discomfort stole briefly across the other woman's face. "I'm awful glad you feel that way," she said, "but don't expect too much from her. Even on her good days, Mrs. Maudell's a little careful what she shares about the town. It's her only real care these days, you know."

"Of course," said Jenna. Though she doubted very much that anything would deter Josephine Maudell from helping her learn the truth about the past, especially when her ancestor might turn out to be the hero of the story.

❧❧

Jenna left her agent a voicemail and two texts before she drove away from the Maudell residence. *This* was the twist in the story that she felt certain would win over Joyce. A soldier's romance set against the backdrop of a town consumed by tragedy and fear. Her skin tingled just thinking about it, fingers itching to type the words into the first draft on her laptop.

She pulled into a parking space at the inn, shutting off the car engine in time to remove the ringing cellphone from her purse. Without even glancing at the number, she flipped it open and said, "Joyce, you are gonna love me for this. I mean it; this will blow you away."

"Guess again," said the voice on the other end.

Not her agent, but someone decidedly masculine and with a gravelly tone. Young though, she felt certain. Checking the screen, she saw the number was both local and unfamiliar. "Mr. Taggart?" she asked.

"I remembered something," he explained. "About that gravestone symbol you showed me."

"That's great." She slid from the car seat, its fabric cool from the windows being cracked. "Do you mind if we talk about it in person? I just got back to my room in town, but I can meet you somewhere. Your workshop, even."

"How about the town square?" he suggested, surprising her with the location mere blocks away.

Jenna hesitated, remembering their awkward exchange the day before. "I don't want to inconvenience you. Since your work must keep you busy."

After a short pause he spoke. "It's not a problem. I can be there if you can."

"Well, great," she said, her bag jostling against her side as she moved down the sidewalk. She could wait for him on one of the benches in the square, using the extra time to go over her notes from the Maudell interview.

"Sorry I wasn't Joyce," he added, referencing their mix-up.

"Don't be. It's better for me if we talk before I speak with my agent again. The more information I have on this project, the more likely it is to get the attention it deserves."

"Then your agent isn't a fan of the book?" He sounded confused by the notion, perhaps wondering how the project made it past the idea phase if this was true.

"She isn't convinced that Sylvan Spring should be a part of it," Jenna explained. "But I think she will be after today." Her fingers gave a loving pat to her knapsack as she said this, imagining the new material stowed inside. Tonight she would transfer the notes to electronic files, along with her initial thoughts and questions.

As she rounded the corner, the town square came into view. There was only one figure seated among its benches—a man whose face was angled towards the ground. Glancing up, he waved a cellphone in greeting.

Jenna's steps slowed, her eyes widening in disbelief. She lowered her phone. "You already planned to meet me. Before we spoke."

"That's true." A spark of humor surfaced in the blue depths. "Being a headstone carver doesn't ban me from the land of the living, you know. Though some might argue I've got more in common with the other side."

He's a little different. The county clerk's words echoed through her mind, making her wonder how much he knew of the gossip surrounding his habits.

She sat beside him and tucked her cellphone into her bag. "I didn't mean it that way. It's just…you didn't seem very interested in this project yesterday."

"That's partly why I came," he said. "To apologize for being so short with you. It was rude and unprofessional." He had taken more care with his appearance this time. Dressed in jeans and a dark blazer, he had exchanged the rag on his hand for a real bandage. He had shaved as well, though he seemed to be one of those men who wore a permanent shadow on their jaw.

"You had the right not to get involved," she told him. "Besides, I have a habit of expecting everyone to share my passions. It can make me come on too strong, sometimes."

He said nothing, his fingers gripping the edge of the bench. There was a quiet intensity about him that made her worried of frightening him away. Like a bird perched in a tree, wary of human approach.

She pulled her latest notes from her bag. "I really do appreciate your meeting me here. We could have spoken at your business, though."

He didn't answer, but instead retrieved a square of paper from his back pocket. Unfolding it, he revealed another gravestone rubbing of the moon symbol. Except, this one was done in chalk rather than the crayon Jenna preferred to use.

"Where did you get this?" She was breathless as she stared at it. Accepting the page from his hand, she smoothed its creases to study the block lettering from the headstone that spelled out the name *L. R. Lesley*.

"My wife made it. She, uh, used to visit the family graves at the old Lesley homestead. She took flowers, sometimes. There were two more rubbings like this one—a mother, father, and child."

She registered his use of past tense, the hitch in his voice. "Your wife—" she began.

"Died," he answered, quickly. "Two years ago. It was rather sudden."

Jenna lowered the piece of paper to catch his gaze. She gentled her voice. "I'm sorry."

He rubbed the bandage on his hand, a habit she had noticed when they first spoke at his shop. Feeling for the ring beneath, she guessed, or else its absence.

"What was she like?" A bold question. It didn't seem to offend him, though, judging from the way his features softened.

"She was…one of those naturally cheerful people. Kind to everyone, liked by everyone."

Sympathy coursed through her, along with a sense of admiration for the person described. "She sounds lovely," Jenna told him. "I think she must have appreciated history to make this stone rubbing. And to take the flowers to those graves."

"She did." His gaze shifted to study the shops across the street, eyes heavy with some emotion she couldn't identify. Grief, bitterness—maybe both. Clearing his throat, he said, "I found something else— or rather, guessed it. The symbol on the gravestones is Celtic."

She followed his gaze to the festival banner that waved in the wind. The ancient signs did bear a strong resemblance to the ones from the cemetery. Impressed, she asked, "How did you think of it?"

"The newspaper," he admitted. "There was a picture of school children painting the symbols for the heritage society. The Lesley family immigrated from that part of the world, so it just kind of fell into place." Cleary, he'd been thinking about this, despite his initial disinterest.

She searched his face for the reason why, finding the same closed expression as before. "Care to walk?" He asked in a causal tone as he rose from the bench.

They passed beneath striped awnings, pausing here and there to study a window display.

The people who walked by would sometimes offer Taggart a brief nod while glancing curiously at Jenna.

Con didn't seem to notice this, even when a group of kids snickered at them from a patio table by the ice cream shop. Did he always draw this much attention? The town must resent his habits, or else they believed him to have a secret worth hiding in his secluded workshop.

When they reached the jewelry store, the rings Mr. Stroud had mentioned were in the window, their intricate knots fashioned from silver and brass.

She paused to admire them, noticing the similarity between some of these designs and the one from the gravestone rubbings. "So the moon engraving on the stones must have a special meaning," she said, hands stuffed in the pockets of her suede jacket. "The local funeral director told me the festival is connected to the old beliefs from the mother country. Sort of a cultural tribute to the founding families."

"I called the society in charge of the festival," Con told her as they resumed walking. "They told me it was an ancient and fairly famous Pictish symbol—that's a Celtic tribe, apparently. The symbol's known as a Crescent V-Rod."

"V-Rod," she repeated. "So that *is* a letter superimposed over the half moon."

"Yes and no. It's actually an arrow, bent in the shape of a 'V'. Or so they said."

A group of shoppers passed by, forcing Jenna closer to Con. Her hand brushed his arm as she asked, "And the symbol's meaning? They must have said if it stands for something."

"There's a dispute about that. From what I understand, it's been found on numerous old stones in Scotland and Ireland, graves and other types of monuments. But there's no definitive source for its meaning." Somewhat sheepishly, he added, "It's sometimes viewed as a death symbol."

"Makes sense, I guess. Since it's on a headstone."

They had drifted apart again, the sidewalk empty before them. Jenna frowned, thinking of the questions that still remained. "But why do so many of the stones have the same symbol—but not all of them, for instance? Especially the ones at the Lesley homestead, which aren't part of the cemetery."

"I think the Lesley markers were made by a different carver," Con said. "They were fieldstones, and the carvings were shallower than the rubbings you took from the cemetery. Most likely, it was the work of a friend or family member, rather than a local craftsman. Whoever carved the rest, I mean."

She paused again, their reflections mirrored in the windows of the Moonspell shop. "Were there dates of death listed for the Lesley graves?"

"I'm afraid not. Just names and the V-Rod."

In the store's display window, crystal rocks winked in the afternoon sun. Cards were propped in front of each one, identifying its properties and purpose in swirling letters. Energy conductors to destroy negativity or create harmony in the living space.

They moved on, passing advertisements for special sales at the bookstore and the Potter's Shed. After cutting some tentative glances in her direction, Con spoke again. "Your necklace—does it have a personal meaning? If you don't mind my asking."

"My faith," she answered, catching the cross-shaped ornament between her fingers. "I've been a Christian over half my life. This was a gift from my parents when I finished high school."

The ghost of a smile tugged his mouth, the first she had really seen from him. "Then we have something in common," he said. "Or, I should say, something else. Since we both make a living from the past."

Encouraged by this second glimpse into his

personal life, she returned a smile that was warmer and fuller than his. "That's true." she admitted. "Our jobs are similar. Except that yours is harder and a little more rare. Not just anyone can create something so beautiful."

The compliment seemed to embarrass him, though. He glanced away from her, seemingly admiring the window display they were passing. "It's not exactly in demand. Lasers and computers can duplicate an image so perfectly on a headstone that hand carving seems flawed by comparison."

"But unique," she said.

"Expensive, too. A few thousand, depending on the detail and type of stone."

Was he arguing as a way to put more distance between them? Maybe he was uncomfortable when he realized how close he'd come to sharing personal details with a stranger. First about his wife, then his faith, with his work as the tipping point.

Determined to close the gap again, Jenna slowed her steps.

It forced his to do the same, until they stood face to face beneath a sign that creaked in the wind.

"You must know how special the craft is," she insisted. "Especially as someone who's fighting to preserve it. What you're doing is important to so many people, not just historians."

Some of the tension disappeared from his expression with the words.

She seized the advantage. "Hand carved stones are—well, like a story. The surface is fascinating, but the hidden details are the ones we want to understand. They tell us something about the person who died, as well as the craftsman who made the memorial."

She was thinking of the slave headstones, with their simple but loving gestures of remembrance. "It's the only reason I can write this book," she said. "The stones are the stories—I'm just trying to flesh out the hidden details."

Agreement crept slowly into his eyes, their gaze meeting hers more deeply than before. "That was...persuasive. Your readers may find themselves drawn to old, crumbling monuments when this is done. Taking pictures of stranger's graves at their local churchyard." Teasing seemed as uncharacteristic for the mason as a smile.

Caught by surprise, she didn't answer right away, taking in this new facet of his personality, until the silence was filled by a bell's jingle, the door to the nearby shop opening.

The woman who emerged was middle-aged and somewhat stocky, with auburn tresses pinned beneath a handkerchief.

"Afternoon," she greeted Jenna, her gaze lighting with recognition when it fell on the craftsman. Going up to him, she squeezed his shoulder in a half hug as she asked, "How are you, dear? Haven't seen you for some time, not since you brought the white sage by."

The herb shop must be hers then. Jenna vaguely recalled seeing her with a tray of plants her first morning in town.

Returning the hug, Con asked, "Were they good for business? They look sort of stunted this year."

"Very popular. They're rare, you know—takes a special touch to get them established." Her voice dropped, as if sharing a secret. Taking notice of Jenna again, her lips formed a puzzled smile. "Who's your friend, then?" she asked.

"Miss Cade needed some advice on headstone symbols," he replied, gaze flicking apologetically in Jenna's direction. "She's doing research for a book."

"How exciting." The woman looked more closely, as if deciding whether she recognized her from a book jacket. Of course, most people abandoned this activity once the word *non-fiction* was mentioned. No one but college students and history buffs were likely to recognize her name, the glamour of fame left to novelists.

Extending a hand, the woman said, "Amelia Girvin. Known as the herb lady to my customers."

"I like your shop," Jenna said as she nodded to the display of exotic colored jars. "My grandmother grew herbs in a window box, I remember. She taught me how to crush them for potpourri."

"Makes for a strong fragrance," the woman agreed. "I'll be selling my own special blends at the festival this weekend. Come by the booth if you're still in town. "

"I will," she said.

Checking her watch, the herbalist made an exasperated sound. "I'm almost late. You know how I am," she told Con. "Always late when I have a lunch appointment."

"I know," he said. "Better get going." He squeezed her hand in quiet farewell.

Halfway across the street, she turned back and called, "I'll keep an eye out for that book."

Jenna waved, wondering how she knew Con Taggart when no one else bothered to speak to him. Glancing round, she saw he was already walking ahead of her, following the sidewalk to where it turned at the corner.

"You grow herbs," she said, catching up with him. It was a question as much as a statement, the surprise evident to her own ears. She knew he worked with his hands, but the yard around his farmhouse had seemed almost as neglected as the wooded cemetery.

"They're some Colleen planted, actually. I don't have a green thumb, as they say." His expression was shuttered; he clearly disliked the subject. Or anything that referenced his loss, which ruled out most of the questions she most wanted to ask.

"I guess you'll be at the festival. I mean, it seems like the whole town turns out for it."

"Not me," he answered. "But then, I don't have roots here, so maybe I can't understand it."

"So you think it's strange?" She looked at the banner waving from the lampposts ahead, remembering Josephine's words on the community's darker traditions.

"I think it's mostly harmless. There's the potential for harm in the right circumstances—but that's true of a lot of things in life."

By this time, the inn had come into view. He was seeing her back to her lodgings, a chivalrous gesture that seemed fitting in their quaint surroundings. It also signaled the end of their meeting. Their steps lagged as they reached the gated entrance.

"You've been really helpful to me today," she told him, handing back the chalk gravestone rubbing as she spoke. "Another piece of the puzzle, so to speak."

"What happens next?" A casual question, his tone implying he wouldn't be present to witness the proceedings.

"I check some more sources," she said, meaning the physician's daybook and the letters Josephine promised to show her. "I'll clean the graves, of course. Then comes genealogy and contacting the living descendants…" She trailed off, sensing his thoughts were somewhere else, the distance between them already returning. "Thank you, again," she said, extending a hand. "I'll be crediting you in the manuscript—"

"No need," he interrupted. "I was glad to help." He pressed her fingers then turned and strode towards the square again. He didn't glance back or give a final wave.

"Goodbye—I guess." Jenna spoke too softly for anyone to hear. Her fingers were still warm from his touch as she watched him disappear around the corner.

11

February 3rd 1862: Have heard enough of the former apothecary's remedies as to be thoroughly mystified. If cutting and burying a lock of one's hair relieves a headache, I can only imagine what is required to eliminate abdominal pain. It is a wonder more graves do not populate the community burial ground.

Jenna glanced up as rain drummed the window panes of the historical society. She was not the only patron this morning; a handful of other researchers were scattered throughout the reading area. Seated at a corner table, she struggled to concentrate on the doctor's long-ago narrative.

No word from her agent combined with the morning rain had left her feeling listless. A troubling question echoed persistently through her mind: if she couldn't interest a professional stone carver in the cemetery's fate, what hope was there for the average citizen to care?

One stranger's ambivalence had touched the underlying fear that no one shared her passion for restoring these old monuments. That Sylvan Spring's wooded graveyard, and other places like it, would stay hidden, their beauty languishing in secret like the garden from the beloved children's book.

"Sorry," another patron mumbled, as they bumped her table on their way past, a young girl with glasses and a heavy-looking spiral notebook.

Jarred from her thoughts, Jenna forced them back to the ledger in her hands. There was a lot of ground to cover, the doctor's narrative spanning a series of months, if not a year. Sighing, she huddled over it, with an eye for the more personal details jotted in between the lines of medical jargon.

৯৩৫৯

February 8ᵗ, 1862: Did not expect my first patient here to be one of a different species. The Hinkle's milk cow was most cooperative, attempting only one half-hearted kick as I stitched its wound. Afterward, the fee was met by a jar of preserves rather than the usual currency. I wonder what other oddities to expect as I settle into these new surroundings...

The letter had come at a time that some would have deemed as providential. To Mariah Moore, who retained only a distant memory of faith in a higher power, it was merely the only choice left after her father failed to wake from his nap one harsh winter afternoon.

Addressed to Dr. Barnaby Moore, it came from a minister claiming to have known him long ago, through a relative who underwent consumption treatments at the clinic. If it wasn't asking too much—and begging his pardon for the irregular nature of this request—would the doctor care to recommend any from among his medical students to oversee the needs of a community numbering roughly forty-eight households?

Room and board would be provided by a local

family so long as the physician was unencumbered by wife or children. There was a post office for handling supply orders, and of course, an account would be registered to them at the dry goods store for everyday necessities.

Mariah had read the letter twice then looked up the postmark on a set of old county maps in her father's study. Unrolling large sheets of Northern Alabama territory, she found the place to be a few miles of farmland and outlying homesteads, the body of water for which it was named appearing as a gray squiggle through a stretch of woods.

She scrawled the same address on an envelope the next morning, a single sheet tucked inside that bore her response. It was signed with only her initials, an act of deception she knew could backfire once the truth was known. A risk, to be sure, but one she had to take as she paid the postage to send it northward.

Two weeks later, she followed in person, a single trunk and her father's old medical bag all that rode with her on the stage coach that made its stop at a trading post in a bigger town. There, she waited on a bench, wondering if the blacksmith might withdraw his offer of room and board once he saw the doctor wore a skirt instead of men's trousers and work boots.

Only it wasn't the smithy who came for her. A girl about Mariah's age, plain but neatly dressed, her eyes wide with uncertainty, was the one who greeted her. She helped Mariah load the heavy trunk into the back of the cart, seeming nervous rather than angry at the discovery. Afterwards, her gaze was clamped on the narrow dirt lane as the cart she drove rattled past acres of farmland and crops.

"Your room is upstairs," the girl said, speaking for

only the third time as they neared a small, two-story farmhouse of the white clapboard variety. Timidly, she added, "My brother—he is in the regiment now—has no need of it at the moment. We packed up some of his things, but more can be put away if you want."

Mariah nodded, fingers laced through the handle of the medical bag in her lap. "There is not much to unpack, you see. Just a few personal items and then some additional medical supplies I am having sent by post from my former home."

These would need to be stored in a cabinet, preferably in the room where her consultations would take place. She hesitated to bring this up, unsure it would even be allowed once the community discovered the trick she had played on them. Women doctors were a rarity—more than once she had encountered patients who would rather be left untreated if her father was unavailable.

The couple waiting inside was certainly astonished by her introduction. She couldn't help but notice the wife, Mrs. Darrow, in particular seemed displeased and disappointed when the woman ushered her into the parlor of threadbare furnishings, with a pretty, but inexpensive china tea service on its curio shelf and pile of firewood before its stone hearth. Her husband, the local blacksmith, lowered his clay pipe to offer a curt greeting and then rose to carry Mariah's trunk up the stairs.

"My grandmother is asleep already for the evening," said the girl, whose name was Nell, as she recalled from their brief exchange at the trading post. "With my brother away, there are only the four of us living here. Except, of course, you will be here to make it five again. "

Her room was the second door on the left, a bed and small table arranged against the far wall. Across from these was a dresser and mirror, a writing desk, and shelves that held a collection of dog-eared paperbacks. The blacksmith deposited her trunk at the foot of the bed, a slight nod his only parting sign before he turned to go.

"Your journey must have been tiring," Nell said, studying her in the light of the hall's oil lamp. She couldn't possibly guess Mariah's reasons for being here, since Mariah's letter had communicated only the barest facts of her life, including her father's death. Yet she spoke as if she somehow knew, offering, "Is there anything I can get for you? A plate from the kitchen, a cup of Granny's tea—"

"I think I'll rest, actually," Mariah said, stepping past the threshold to set her medical bag on the desk. "The journey was a long one, as you said, and there is still so much to be arranged." *Such as where I shall go once your family sends me packing,* she thought, biting her lip unconsciously.

"Good night, then. We take our breakfast at six," the girl called over her shoulder, the timid appearance returning to her features.

Alone and surrounded by a stranger's possessions, Mariah sank onto the trunk she had brought. Her fingers played with the brass latch, her thoughts wandering to the items she knew were packed inside. Dresses sewn from a fabric more practical than what she usually wore, and boots sturdy enough for walking long distances. The textbooks from the shelf above her father's writing desk, a tintype photo from his younger days tucked between one of the covers. In a separate stack, a faded Bible, its pages untouched by any hand for nearly fifteen years.

She stiffened at the sound of conversation taking place below, the blacksmith's gruff tones rumbling slightly above the high pitch of his wife's voice. Only their tone was audible, the meaning of the words lost to the grains in the pine boards. Not that it was hard to guess what they spoke of, considering the looks on their faces when she stepped into the parlor that night.

Would they tell her to board the next stage or even hire a cart to take her elsewhere? She imagined they were as confused as she was about what happened next, yet she felt comforted by the daughter's small gesture of kindness. Words spoken softly, if a little less formal than the ones used by her father's more well-to-do patients in Mobile.

Buttoning her nightgown, Mariah let amber curls tumble past her face and shoulders. Without turning back the covers, she curled herself onto the worn mattress, a single breath all that was needed to snuff the candle flickering on the table.

February 10th 1862: It would seem a female doctor is not cut from the same cloth as a midwife, or even a yarb woman. They seem to believe that only superstitious 'gifts' can make a woman any sort of medical consultant and think that medical training is for men alone. I can only hope that circumstances will temper some of this dislike, since my work is badly needed in a place where the aged work long hours in the field, and children strain their strength beyond its capabilities.

The remedies of their forefathers were still greatly favored, and it appeared only special cases would require Mariah's attention. A widow who split her foot chopping firewood; a schoolgirl who broke her collarbone falling from a tree on the playground. Before either of these came a farm wife, frantic over the second best milk cow tearing its udder while her husband was away to another town's market.

"It's me fault for latching the gate poorly," she explained, hovering over Mariah's shoulder in the musty barn. "She never would have gotten into the Cray's fencing if I had checked it like he said to. Whatever will I tell 'im?"

Mariah had no idea what to say, pretending to be absorbed in the task of stitching layers of skin back together. Her father's patients had never spoken so freely of their troubles, society ladies in gloves and hats, their hands folded primly in their laps as they waited to consult the doctor.

She received a jar of preserves in exchange for stitching the cow's udder, the first of many such payments in a place where Confederate notes were rare as a diamond pendant. Soldier's wives had yet to receive any of their husband's military pay, most of them compiling the last of their resources into a care package for the absent loved ones.

The doctor felt the pinch of hard times in ways different from her neighbors. Back home, she had taken a bath once a week, in water that was heated and poured in the cast iron tub by a hired girl. Here, a wash basin and sponge on the bedroom dresser were all she could expect, at least in the winter months. The water was cold, drawn from the well at the town square, which had a brackish taste compared to the pump a few miles away in Crooked Wood.

"Only tolerable when it's stewed for tea," the family's grandmother had explained, pouring her a cup with hands that spilled a fair amount into the saucer. "But tea's the healthiest draught for a body, as I always have said, better than cold spring water, even. Braces you for troubled times and fair weather alike." Her tongue bore traces of an accent that was wholly unfamiliar, her eyes gazing somewhere past the doctor when she nudged the cup gently in her direction.

"How long since your sight began to trouble you?" Mariah wondered, forgetting for a moment that this was her hostess, so to speak, and not a patient from her father's clinic.

"Too long," the woman replied, with a soft chuckle. "Naught to do about it now, if ever there was in the first place." She seemed content despite her loss, busying herself with the herb garden planted just outside the family's kitchen. Her joints were too stiff most of the time for bending among the rows of plants, but the granddaughter would gather baskets of clippings for her to sort and dry on the scrubbed pine table. Little jars of spices lined the cupboard shelves, fresh bundles of rosemary and sassafras strung to dry above the kitchen window.

The rest of the family labored in the field of crops adjacent to the small yard, as well as tending the livestock that were penned behind the house. Mr. Darrow's smithy work took him away by mid-morning until six o'clock, when he returned for the supper prepared by his wife's hands in between the day's worth of sewing and housework.

As part of the household, Mariah was expected to perform some of these chores. She learned first to clean ash from the hearth then to scrub laundry with the washboard kept on the porch. All the while, she felt as if she were an unwanted guest, her appearance at the dinner table and later, the evening fire, causing most conversations to dwindle to near silence.

An outsider, strange in her habits as well as her beliefs—or rather, her lack of them. Her absence from Sunday worship proved uncomfortable for the blacksmith's family. Mrs. Darrow's jaw was grimly set on Sundays, a familiar sight to Mariah whenever the family piled into the cart for weekly services. Her face wore the same expression whenever she found Mariah reading a scientific book in the parlor or buying a pamphlet on abolitionism from a traveling man, for instance.

"You must hate it here," Nell observed, her smile one of sympathy across the chicken they plucked for a winter stew. She had wrung the bird's neck herself, a swift motion that spoke of compassion for the creature's life. "I hope you will not always find things so hard with us," she added, wiping her hands on a soiled apron. "Life can still bring its joys to those of us here, even with just the dirt under our feet."

A child-like view of things, Mariah told herself, lying in the bed she still expected to be her old one each morning she woke. To share her thoughts with someone as freely as she once did with her father was all the joy she looked for now. Except nothing seemed less likely in these surroundings. She did sometimes speak aloud to the darkness but with no real hope that anyone listened.

In fact, she knew they didn't. If they had, she would never have found herself alone and unloved, with her mother taken to the grave before she was even the same age Mariah was now. That poor woman's faith had done her no good, her final days of pain a startling contrast to her agnostic husband's peaceful slumber.

Mariah would never unburden her worries through prayer, not if she could find any other means of sharing her heart's deepest sentiments. But how she would do this—and who would be her confidant among a group of strangers—remained as much a mystery to her as the spiritual being her mother prayed to all those years ago.

☙❧

February 23rd, 1862: Suffering from inflammation of the bronchi, Mr. Arthur Widlow is a young man of gentle demeanor and pleasant looks. The long duration of his illness has recently prevented Mr. Widlow from enlisting in the regiment, and I very much fear the infection will become chronic or even turn to pneumonia. His strength has been greatly affected, though I believe his spirit is more than equal to the challenge.

She had seen him before on the road to town, a tall figure with dark curls tumbled across his forehead. A boyish smile and eyes that looked thoughtful beneath the brim of a straw hat when he tipped it in passing.

Young men were a rare sight following the outbreak of war, the reason Mariah supposed she had noticed him in the first place. They had never spoken, her steps always taking her another direction to some patient's house in the town's scattering of homesteads.

It wasn't until he called at the Darrow's house one frosty morning, his hat crushed nervously between his hands, that she learned the reason Arthur Widlow had stayed home while so many others enlisted. "It never went away, you see. First the coughing, then the fever."

He was seated across from her in the Darrow's parlor, where the blacksmith's wife and daughter continued their mending by the fire. They pretended not to listen, but Mariah could sense their interest, especially on the part of the daughter.

Nell's gaze was upon the farmer's son more than once during the visit, her ear inclined to his voice instead of Mariah's, curiosity at work instead of the needle.

"I kept to my bed for three weeks," Arthur continued, "but even now it is difficult to perform my chores without sitting for long moments in between. The coughing makes it impossible to sleep at times, as well."

He seemed breathless even now, although Mariah suspected this was from nervousness as much as the illness he described. The flush in his cheeks might be for the same reason, his pulse stumbling a little beneath her stethoscope.

If she were to be honest, her heart was racing in anxious beats. This was her first male patient, making her wary of giving offense with every simple touch required for the proper examination. Her patient seemed perfectly trusting, however, his glance open and expectant whenever it happened to meet her own.

They spoke for mere minutes, Mariah pausing here and there to note some important symptom in the daybook she always carried. When she had instructed him on the correct dosage of medicine, she saw him to the door. Lingering on the porch, she spoke to him out of earshot from the women in the parlor.

"These recurring bouts of fever concern me," she told him, her breath forming clouds in the morning air.

"It is unusual for a bronchial infection to linger so long. I'm afraid a more aggressive form of treatment may be necessary to keep further danger at bay."

This meant visiting his home and possibly sitting up with him on nights when the fever was upon him. Swathing his throat and chest in poultice cloths and even withdrawing blood from his veins as a means of purging the infection. She had done this many times for pneumonia patients, something she feared he might become if the sickness continued much longer.

"I would only do what is necessary," she explained, aware they had stood in silence while she thought. "The same as any physician properly trained in their work would do, which I can assure you that I am."

His answer was slow to come, his gaze reflecting the struggle taking place inside. *Eyes the color of coal*, she thought, studying the pools of dark liquid beneath the furrowed brow. A lively mind behind them but one that was also cautious in its decisions.

"I will do whatever you advise," he said finally, fingers pressing hers briefly in agreement. "My life is in your hands, Miss Moore." With a smile to show he was only partly serious, he tipped the frayed straw hat and moved down the stairs. He moved out of sight.

Her fingers absently twined a ringlet of hair as she recalled their brief conversation, until goose bumps cropped over her arms, the cold stinging through the thin fabric of her work dress.

She saw him again two days later, his figure clad in the same worn coat and trousers from before as he sat in the family's parlor.

This time only Nell was present for their consultation, quietly knitting a scarf for her brother who was still undergoing his soldier training at a camp in Huntsville.

"Tell Henry in your next letter that I'll be joining his regiment yet," Arthur told her, the teasing in his voice evidence of a long acquaintance between them.

The girl blushed in response to being noticed, though Arthur seemed not to see it as he continued, "Tell him I'm on the mend already, with the doctor's advice to keep me from a spot in the cemetery we used to fear so as boys."

To Mariah, hearing herself referred to as a doctor—by a man, no less—was a strange experience after weeks of being ignored or spoken of in disapproving tones behind her back. She couldn't help the faint blush that spread across her features or, worse yet, the smile that twitched the corner of her mouth.

A woman doctor must be careful at all times when overseeing a male patient, with no look or touch unguarded by the strictest sense of propriety. Mariah knew this even without being told, emphatically, in the days when her father's clients had found her presence an unwelcome addition to the exam room.

"Give no one even the whisper of an excuse to slander your name," Dr. Moore had cautioned, with a look that told her such a thing was not only possible, but inevitable. "If they're determined to hurt you, be certain it's their falsehood that deals the blow and not some misstep on your part."

She had supposed this advice would be easy enough to follow, given the nature of her father's usual patients. Men well past the prime of their life, with silver hair and sagging skin that bore the marks of age. Such men spoke to her only of weather conditions and common gossip when they chose to speak to her at all.

Arthur, once his initial shyness had passed, spoke to her as a friend might. He talked with enthusiasm of the railroads and other industrial strides that were changing the face of the nation. The battlefield was often in his mind but so were topics of a more personal nature.

Noticing a book that was left among her papers on the desk, he wondered, "You are fond of spiritual writings, Miss Moore? Unless I am mistaken, the author's name is that of a minister whose sermons are printed in the newspaper."

"It is the same," she said, glancing up from a poultice she mixed to send home with him. "Although I read it for his political views, rather than spiritual enlightenment. He writes of the slavery institute, and how it might be abolished."

"I have read before of the abolitionist's cause," he said. "And find much to agree with. My grandfather earned his way from Scotland through servitude and spoke often of the cruel treatment from his employer. It must be far worse for those with no means of earning their way to freedom."

"By enlisting, you fight against their cause." Inwardly, she scolded herself for speaking so boldly to a patient.

He didn't seem to mind. "I wish only to defend my home, and the right to manage this land as we see fit. It is a duty I feel bound to meet, for my family's sake as much as mine."

She could find no quarrel with the words despite their differences, for his initial statement was more open-minded than any she had expected to hear from a local farmer.

But Arthur had proved soft spoken on most issues,

with the exception of one. Having discovered she laid claim to no religion and had not set foot in a church since childhood, he became adamant to know the reasons why. "Medicine relies partly on faith, does it not?" he challenged, barely flinching as a knife's blade flicked his forearm. Blood trickled into a bowl Mariah held in her lap, the patient more concerned with matters of the soul, as he told her, "The simple belief a tonic will work is sometimes enough to help the sick recover, I've heard."

"There is science involved, too," she said. "Some things can be proven beyond a doubt with studies conducted in laboratories. There is no such method for testing Divine influence, as I am sure you would agree."

"Still," he persisted, "you must have seen miracles in your profession. Recoveries that were not possible, except for the aid of a higher power."

Pulling a bandage from her supplies, Mariah answered, "I have seen…nothing like what you describe. Only the senseless pain of many who did believe in He you speak of so fondly. Take that, if you will, as proof of a God who hears but does not care for their suffering." A harsh reply, tempered only by the gentle way she bound his wounded arm.

Mariah's first taste of romance had come the summer she turned fifteen. A curly-haired youth of lively disposition named Clive, he came to her father's clinic as an apprentice from a family in Louisiana. Clive prided himself on the knowledge of a man twice his age, debating her father for hours on theories dismissed by the larger part of the medical community.

"The spread of disease through insects—it is something I have come back to again and again, while observing the swamps near my home. The concept as a whole makes sense, and I am sure it could account for some of the rare blood diseases you described to me this morning." Smoke curled from the pipe he waved for emphasis in her father's direction.

On the settee, Mariah listened with one hand propped beneath her chin, the sewing in her lap all but forgotten. She felt too shy to contribute her opinion to any of these discussions, but her interest did not go unnoticed by the boy who was just three years older than herself.

One afternoon, he approached her as she sat reading on the front porch swing. After standing awkwardly for a moment, he held out a journal that was folded open to an article near the middle. "It is the theory your father and I discussed last night," he explained. "About the water that was linked to the cholera outbreak. I saw how closely you were listening and thought you might enjoy reading it for yourself."

"Thank you," she said, taking the journal with genuine gratitude. She expected him to return to the house, since Sunday afternoons were generally the time when her father required his students to inventory the medical supplies. Instead, he sank into the swing beside her, hands awkwardly clasping his knees. "The doctor who wrote that—he has a very modern way of thinking," Clive said, with a nod to the journal. "I admire that kind of trait. It is so rare to find, especially in the medical field." With a cough, he added, "You have some of that in your nature, I think."

Mariah gave him a brief smile and turned back to

the essay whose writer reminded her of a police inspector in his quest to track the source of an illness. Absorbed in the article, she failed to notice how close her companion had grown until the warmth of his breath fanned the ringlets around her face.

"You are very pretty, Mariah," he said, voice low and earnest. "Has anyone told you that before?"

"I...no, I don't believe so."

She angled her face further towards the journal to hide the color she knew had risen with this compliment. Staring at words that she barely comprehended, her heart pumped with fear and something she couldn't quite identify.

"I can hardly believe that is true. A girl as pretty as you are."

Glancing up, she found their faces were just inches apart.

He leaned in for a kiss that was chaste and somewhat embarrassed.

The journal had slid from her grasp, thumping against the porch planks.

With a muttered apology, Clive handed it back to her, disappearing inside the house with a final worried look—whether for himself or for what she might think, Mariah would rather have died than ask. It was the first and only time a man behaved so boldly to her, though Mariah had sometimes thought others wished to pay her the same kind of attention.

Arthur Widlow was harder to read. His gaze bore the same admiration as Clive's, but his manner was far less impulsive. Keeping his feelings beneath the surface, he said nothing until a crisis late one day forced them suddenly into the light. "You are angry with me," he guessed, his breath coming in gasps as he looked up from the bed in his sick chamber. "I should not have worked so long, I know, but there is only my father to bring in the harvest. The rain was not expected, and I returned as quickly as I could—"

"Shh." She daubed his forehead, alarmed by the panic in his features. The rain had done his illness no favors, a high temperature coming on shortly after. She felt relief that they had sent for her—to her mind, a man who would let his son work in this state of health, necessity or no, seemed unlikely to send for a woman physician's opinion on the cure.

She was patient with him, spooning down medicine that had previously helped. "This struggle will pass shortly," she said as he fought to get comfortable. "It is not your time."

"You cannot promise that." His faint laugh turned to coughing as if to prove it. "Only the Maker knows our final hour," he said, recovering his voice. "No earthly remedy can trump His Will, however good it may be."

"I believe there is only nature and human error to account for the time of one's death," she replied mildly, ringing out the cloth in a basin. Wiping his brow again, she let herself smile a little. "Yours, Mr. Widlow, shall not be on my conscience."

"If it was my time," he challenged, forcing a deeper breath, "and I was to be dying right now—what would you say? No false assurances; only the comfort you should wish to hear in your own distress."

She paused. It was an intimate question for people who met just recently in their lives. Seeing it might take his mind off the pain, she decided to reply, "I think...I would not want them to say anything. I would only want them to take my hand so I could feel their warmth. A touch that was gentle instead of clinging." As she spoke, she reached for where his lay on the quilt, holding it loosely, to see if he minded.

"What else?" His voice cracked this time with emotion instead of illness. "You would wish something more from a loved one," he suggested. "An admirer, even."

"This," she answered, her free hand reaching to cradle his face. His eyes closed in response. Mariah swept her fingers along his jaw to brush the mouth that was partly open. A tender touch she instantly questioned, pulling her hand away as she said, "I am sorry—"

"Don't be," he said, gently guiding her hand back to press against his lips.

Skin tingling from the brief connection, Mariah wondered how a real kiss from him might compare to that of her other suitor. His hands still held hers, gently, without the clinging she had decried moments before. Leaning down before she knew what she was doing, she felt her lips steal the kiss that was shorter, but far sweeter than her first one.

After that, it was no use pretending they were only acquaintances.

Mariah continued to nurse him, surprised to see how quickly the vigor returned to his build, his lungs sounding clearer beneath her stethoscope with each daily check. Her triumph was lessened only by the knowledge it would speed his enlistment, a plan he continued to talk of despite the connection between them.

One afternoon, standing in the parlor where first they spoke, he gripped his hat nervously between his hands. "There is to be a recruitment meeting in a nearby county next Saturday," he confided. "It may be my last chance for a while."

"Then you must go," she said, attempting to seem supportive and not disappointed as she spoke again. "You are well enough—"

"That is not why I ask." He pulled her closer, foreheads touching in a brief show of tenderness while no one else saw. "How can I leave without making you my wife?" he asked, his hand cradling the curls knotted behind her head.

She buried her face in the wool coat, heart racing at the suggestion he offered. "We have known each other so little time. Six weeks or less."

"And I have loved you most of it," he said. "I will be strong, though, if you can do the same. This war cannot last long, and we will marry as soon as I return. Until then, in my heart I will be yours as truly as if we were man and wife already."

Mariah promised the same, though tears choked her reply part way. That night, she recorded the progress of her patient in the daybook that held all her notes, pen sweeping over the page in cool, steady strokes to make the final entry for the farmer's son as if he were an ordinary patient and nothing more.

April 3rd, 1862: Mr. Widlow, having recovered fully from his infection, is now prepared to don the uniform of a private. If I believed in a loving God, I would beg His forgiveness for restoring a young man's health only to send him to face the horrors of the battlefield. My patient could not be persuaded to do otherwise, his allegiance to his home strong, as no doubt it should be. May he somehow stay safe in this madness we hear of daily.

12

November 9th 1862: Have been to the Lesley house, where the evidence of Mischief Night was still painted on the door. What a strange prank for the children to play, though most have taken it with a laugh and a shake of the head. They talk of ghosts and goblins and supernatural gifts with the same ease as they might the weekly sermon, and some believe it almost as much.

The doctor saw it before she reached the farmhouse.

Blood red and scrawled in the shape of a half moon, a broken arrow laced through it to resemble a letter 'V'. Not frightening, but strange and childish, somehow. As if small, careless fingers had painted it there.

Her hand avoided touching it as she rapped on the door. Footsteps pounded on the other side, the door opening to reveal a boy's somber face.

Blain, the couple's only child and sixteen years old—enlistment age, in some people's estimation, answered the door. "Mama's in the kitchen," he told her. His gaze shifting to the mark on the door with a sense of distaste. "Strange, ain't it, Miss Mariah? Put there by nobody knows who."

"Very odd," she agreed. "Why would they do such a thing, Blain?"

A slyness appeared in the boy's face. He turned

away, motioning for her to follow, as he said, "For a prank, 'course. Same as always this time of year. You never heard of it?"

"Of Mischief Night?" she asked. "No, not before I came here."

Nell's grandmother had spoken of a similar ritual from the Scottish Highlands. The broken buckets left by the Darrow's gate that evening had been a sort of offering to the children in search of something to steal or burn. Harmless fun, so they said.

"Never heard of it?" Blain glanced back at her, wonder in his eyes. "I thought everyone did the same as us."

Smiling at his disbelief, she followed him through the narrow hall to the kitchen. Here, the farm wife shelled peas into a bowl while her husband read the county newspaper from a rocking chair by the hearth.

Mariah glanced at the headline, heart catching as she read the words "Skirmishes Rumored Along Northern River" in bold print. She had already heard it spoken of many times, the details vague enough to leave equal room for both hope and worry.

"You have seen it then," the farm wife said, rising from her chair as they entered the room. "That ugly-looking mark on the door. More than a week now, and still he refuses to sand it off." This was said with an exasperated look to the fireplace.

Mr. Lesley continued to read, a slight narrowing of the eyes the only indication he heard his wife's complaint .

"I have never seen such a drawing before," Mariah admitted, setting her bag on the table. "What does it mean?"

"Never seen it anywhere but on graves," the

woman confided. "Not natural to find it elsewhere—a bad sign. Work of youngins, I suppose, but 'tis work of the devil all the same." With a sigh, she took her seat at the table again. The collar to her dress had been loosened, revealing skin that was badly inflamed below the neckline. "All across here, it goes," she said, running a hand over the upper part of the gown's bodice. "Itches something fierce."

"How long has it been this way?" Mariah asked.

"Since yesterday," the woman replied. "Tried buttermilk and it only grows worse."

It was likely from contact with a plant. The foliage that grew by the spring was rife with plants of a poisonous or prickly nature. One might have become tangled with the garment during washing, or else transferred through the woman's touch.

"I know of a tried and true method," Mariah began, knowing the Lesleys preferred medicine of a traditional nature. "I will need your hearth to prepare it."

Wordlessly, Mr. Lesley scooted his chair towards the wall, freeing a space for her to work by the fireplace. No doubt, he disapproved of her being summoned in the first place. But his wife was not one to suffer in silence as Mariah knew from the morning's conversation.

The boy was seated on a wooden stool by the door, watching her combine the lard and sulfur. His gaze searched her features with a quiet admiration that went unnoticed by his mother as she continued to rant about the children's mischief.

"I can hardly understand why they should go and spoil *our* door, not after we left a whole gate for the bonfire. What should make them draw such an evil thing?"

"Oh, quit your worrying, woman," came the response of her husband. "It's an old symbol with more than just the grave to give it meaning. Stands for the changes in the weather, I've heard."

"Means death," the woman insisted, "and I'll not be having it on my door. Be it by children or the devil that it came there."

Folding his paper, the man stood with the finality of one preparing to depart. "Better to have a bit of paint on the door then to find the wheels removed from the wagon. Or wake to find the cattle let out of your pasture as Martin Cray done found." Smacking the newspaper lightly against his son's head, he ordered, "Help me mend that hole in the fence, 'fore our livestock's out roaming the town."

Blain straggled sullenly after his father.

The doctor felt sorry for him, wondering if his parents always carried on this way. The Darrow household, for all its flaws, was gentler in its words of unhappiness than those she heard exchanged here.

When the visit drew to a close, the patient handed her a basket of eggs in payment. Looping it over her arm, Mariah advised, "Send for me again if there is no improvement within the week." As she left, her gaze wandered to the symbol on the door with its lurid shade of red.

Mariah saw it again when she called at the Tate's cabin further down the spring. Heavy with child, the lady of the house could barely rise to answer the door, her only companion a girl of five. Her son, Billy, was already in school.

"The pain is so bad at times," she explained, "and my fingers swell so, I cannot even write to my husband in the camp. Billy takes it down for me, but one can hardly say all they wish through another's hand."

Mariah felt herself pale with the words. She picked up a corn shuck doll the girl had dropped nearby. "Does your husband write of the camp's movements? One hears such talk of battle. It seems everyone's chief worry these days."

The lady shook her head. "Word has not come in almost two months' time, nor pay, goodness knows."

This was a hint that no fee would be met for today's visit.

The doctor collected her bag, returning the doll to its owner's small hands. The little girl's dress seemed as rumpled as the corn shuck, her pale eyes gazing at Mariah before she turned to go.

❧

November 10th , 1862: One thirty, a new patient, a female of nineteen years, arrived lately from Jefferson County to wed Mr. Lucas Kendrick. Patient complains of a cough and abdominal pains. I have started Mrs. Kendrick on castor oil and quinine, with a promise to call again tomorrow…

Geneva Kendrick's girlish figure and hazel eyes reminded the doctor of her own mother. Or rather, what she remembered her mother looking like from when she was a child of five years, sitting on her lap in the foyer outside her father's study.

She knew the delicate features were similar, the brown hair wound into a coiffure. If the too-pale complexion was also familiar, she didn't linger on the thought.

"I have been ill before," Geneva told her, hands clasped in her lap. "At finishing school last February. A fever dimmed my eyesight for more than a week."

"But you fully recovered it?" Mariah asked, looking closely at the girl's dark orbs, seeing only anxiety to mar their depths.

"Oh, yes. As clear as before, or even better, since I learned to appreciate it more."

They were sitting in the parlor to Lucas Kendrick's house, a room furnished with articles belonging to the man's former wife. Common knowledge said the first Mrs. Kendrick died several winters back from an unsuccessful childbirth. In her absence, the curtains and rugs, tables, chairs and other accessories had grown pitifully old-fashioned and faded.

"Have you been ill since the time in February?" Mariah asked, pulling a stethoscope from her bag.

The girl frowned. "Not physically. There was a…a time after my parents' accident when I was greatly indisposed. I had no appetite and took to my bed more often than I should."

"That is quite understandable." Mariah's tone was softer than she usually allowed with patients. "I lost both my parents, my father quite recently. You need not explain the cause of such weariness."

Geneva said nothing, but squeezed her hand briefly in response. She was still a child in most ways. Her marriage to the older farmer had likely been a means of surviving poverty when her parents' lives were claimed in a carriage mishap.

"I began corresponding with Mr. Kendrick two months ago," Geneva told her, chattering nervously. "My aunt saw his advertisement in a newspaper and advised me to answer it."

Mariah didn't comment on this, listening for the patient's pulse through her stethoscope. It was a trifle fast, but that was explained by nervousness as much as the illness.

"He is a very gentle man," Geneva continued, more to herself. "Kind and patient, as well. I think he must have been lonely here without a companion for so long." She sounded lonely herself, a hollow ring to the words of praise for her new spouse.

Mariah wondered that she had attempted no changes thus far to the house, big enough despite its plainness. Perhaps loneliness left her with no enthusiasm for such tasks as homemaking.

Listening to Geneva's chest and lungs, Mariah heard a rattle each time a breath was drawn. When she pressed a hand to the patient's forehead, she felt warmth that might only be from the parlor's hearth.

"Does your husband share any of your symptoms?" she wondered.

"No—that is, he says nothing to suggest it."

Mariah knew the farmer was unlikely to seek her advice, even if he suffered the same illness. Few men consulted her and only one had shown faith in her work's results. The same one who made her presence here bearable after months of rejection, his loving correspondence now the only consolation for the absence of his touch.

"Are you married, doctor?"

The question snapped her out of the memory. Laughing, she said, "How could I be? I would hardly be a doctor if I were married, you know."

Geneva echoed the laugh, though hers was raspy sounding. "I only ask," she explained, "because I know so many here have seen their husbands go to battle."

"They have," she agreed, slipping the stethoscope from around her neck. How close she had come to sharing their same fate wasn't something she cared to think about.

"I am fortunate that my husband does not have to enlist," her patient ventured, referencing the farmer's misshapen leg, the result of a haying accident in his youth. "It is nothing to be ashamed of, I tell him. Though I fear he sees it that way."

"Perhaps, it's only natural for him to do so," Mariah advised, thinking the girl must know little of men after so many years in a finishing school. "He must feel obligated to protect his home."

Geneva fell silent as if mulling this over. Hands twisted in her lap as she waited the doctor's verdict on her examination.

"I do not detect a fever," Mariah told her. "That is a good sign, at least. But you must send someone to fetch me immediately if you began to feel the symptoms of one."

"Of course."

At this point, Geneva turned away to cough, a hoarse sound the doctor had heard only twice since their consultation begin. "I am sorry," she said, words muffled by the handkerchief applied to her mouth. "It is worse in the evening. I could not sleep last night."

Quinine and castor oil were the favorite solutions for this type of case, and Mariah supplied both. Her patient seemed instantly at ease, turning the glass vials over with a kind of wonder.

"I will come back this same time tomorrow," Mariah told her, repacking her bag's contents. "If it's convenient for yourself and Mr. Kendrick, that is."

"It is fine," the girl answered. In a confidential

tone, she added, "Please do not think me impertinent, but I must tell you how glad I was to learn of *your* being the physician. It is much easier to speak of such things with another woman, you understand."

Surprised, Mariah could think of no immediate answer. "I am glad to hear it," she said at last, accepting the coins the girl fished from her skirt pocket.

Mariah saw her wave once more from the parlor window, feeling the sad gaze watch her further down the path. She would not come back the same way until dusk due to another visit to the Tate's cabin spent reassuring the restless mother-to-be.

A raven cawed somewhere in the woods, making Mariah quicken her pace. This was a shortcut back to her lodgings, its path rockier than the road that cut around the spring. She pulled her coat closer as something splashed in the water flowing below.

"Hello, Rufus." She stooped to pet the dog that bounded suddenly up the spring's embankment. Its coat was damp and muddy as were the feet of its owner, who appeared behind it moments later.

Mariah had not seen the Hinkle boy since she removed the stitches from his injured leg. The desired scar had appeared in a raised, pink line below his left knee. It was caked in grime, as was the rest of his skin.

"Evening doctor," he said, showing his toothy grin. "Been to the Tates'?"

She nodded, wondering if her movements were always known among the neighboring homesteads. It was to be expected, yet she found it distasteful for her patients' sake as much as her own, considering the personal nature of the visits.

"Thought maybe you had seen the plat-eye," he

said, voice hopeful with the suggestion. "Billy saw it down by the cavern one night. Said it came at 'em from the water."

"He said nothing about it to me," she replied. "But then, his mother may forbid him to spin such yarns beneath her roof. She is a sensible woman, I think."

"Guess she don't believe in spirits," Charley said thoughtfully. "Reckon you don't, either."

She smiled at his obvious disappointment. "It is not my way. Not in my blood, as you might say."

This explanation seemed to satisfy him. Ruffling the dog's fur, he said, "Rufus caught a fish. Caught two myself but threw 'em back." A wheezing sound punctuated this last part, the boy smothering it with his jacket sleeve.

"When did that start, Charley?" As she spoke, the doctor scrutinized his face. There were no signs of illness like those of the young Mrs. Kendrick. His eyes were bright, cheeks flushed from the exercise.

"Dunno, really," he told her. "Sort of comes and goes."

"Anything else troubling you?" Absent-mindedly, she stroked the dog's fur, her gaze focused on the boy to see his answer.

It was one of indecision before he spoke again. "Sometimes my leg hurts. Where the stitches were, I mean," he said, fingers tapping the jagged line.

She shook her head, relieved. "That will stop soon. I promise." As an afterthought, she told him, "You should stay out of the water on cold nights, Charley."

It must be the dampness causing that slight rattle in his breath. Surely, that was all.

"Yes, ma'am. I'll try." He looked at the dog, its fur rising in response to a creature stirring in the hollow nearby. A rabbit poked its head from the foliage, then streaked down the path. Rufus pursued with deep barks.

Neglecting to say good-bye, the boy chased after his pet into the gathering darkness.

13

November 11th 1862: Must use the buggy to retrieve an order of medicines from the dry goods store. Supplies from Mobile come few and far between, but anything is lucky to make it through our muddled postal routes. More welcome would be news from the regiment. How much longer shall we be forced to wait for tidings of our young men?

Mariah pulled away from the sudden brush of fingers against her arm at the dry goods counter. She turned to find a woman of middle age, fair hair tucked beneath a sun bonnet. "Mrs. Camden," she said, matching the face to one of her more recent medical cases. "How is your wrist?"

"As if it never broke," the woman replied. Hesitating a moment, she folded some bills into Mariah's palm. "I can finally repay your kindness."

Mariah had not seen so large a sum since her days in Mobile. It was not one a widow whose only son had gone off to war should be able to pay, however. "Surely this is needed in your household," she said.

"It is all right." Pride in her voice, the woman said, "Wray sends me his soldier's pay, what he gets of it, anyhow. I only wish he wrote more of himself in the letters that bring it. Too much like his father, all silence and strength." Her voice dropped slightly with this reference to her deceased husband. His violent death was still spoken of in whispers by some in the community, his grave isolated from the others in the cemetery.

"Your son sounds a fine sort of man," she said.

"Oh, he is. Blessed in character and looks, both. More than one heart was broke when he left us for the regiment." She glanced out the window. "I must be on my way now. My neighbors wait to drive me home, as you see."

She referred to the cart outside, Mr. and Mrs. Widlow visible behind the reins. The two families shared a property line and a drinking well, though it was deep friendship that bound them closer than the proximity of their homesteads.

Mariah's relationship with the Widlows had been one of begrudging acceptance that quickly vanished once their son was no longer under her care. At times, she wondered if they would have preferred his slow death to the bronchial infection rather than the danger he now faced.

Twelve o'clock: Have gone to the Kendricks to find patient is worse. Became feverish last night and complains of dysentery, in addition to the cough and stomach pains. More alarming still is a revelation that makes me certain she is not the only one from our community to suffer this affliction...

"You should have told me about this before." Mariah's tone was accusing, as she folded back the collar to the girl's calico dress. Beneath the lace, a patch of red, mottled skin traveled beyond her sight.

"Forgive me. I should have mentioned it the first time. It is just that Mrs. Lesley already told me of the lard and sulfur you gave her, so it seemed pointless—"

"It was not," Mariah interrupted. Her voice was

sharp with anger. She calculated how long it had been since Mrs. Lesley's rash appeared. By now, the other woman must have experienced the same symptoms as the girl before her but simply chose not to consult her about it.

"I am so sorry—"

"Do not apologize." Mariah rubbed her forehead, weariness replacing the flash of irritation. "But we must agree to have no more secrets about this. You must understand, Mrs. Kendrick, how vital every detail is when forming a proper treatment."

"Please," the girl began, somewhat shakily, "would you call me Geneva? I have so few friends here, no one to remind me of home. This new name is still so strange to my ears."

Her request—so unexpected and so badly timed— met with a long silence from Mariah, who scribbled something in her daybook before she formed an answer. "I...I am not accustomed to addressing patients so informally. Perhaps, for now, it is best if we continue as we are."

"Of course," the girl murmured.

She seemed to shrink a little in her chair, fingers toying with the brooch she had removed for the exam. Dampness spread beneath the hazel eyes, her gaze moving away when someone rapped against the parlor's wood trim.

A man stood awkwardly in the doorway. He was tall with clean shaven features and hair that turned gray at the temples. "All right if I come in?" he asked, pulling a straw hat from his head.

"Quite all right," Mariah told him. She noted the hitch in his step, the injured leg dragging slightly behind the other. Aside from this deformity, he seemed quite robust, with none of the illness that marred his wife's features.

"I am afraid that Mrs. Kendrick's condition is much worse," Mariah told him, "and I will need your help to see that she makes a recovery as soon as possible."

"I will do what I can." Coming behind the girl's chair, he placed a tentative hand on her shoulder.

Her fingers returned the touch, light against his stronger ones. Liquid swam in her eyes, but the tears from earlier had been wiped away.

They listened attentively as she gave instructions on medicine and bed rest. When she was reaching for her bag, the husband cleared his throat. "I remember the apothecary used to give a paregoric—"

"I have something stronger among my supplies," Mariah interrupted, handing him a bottle of laudanum. The only drug to ease her mother's cries in the final stage of consumption, it was her first choice for dealing with a powerful illness. She found the smell repugnant. It brought back memories she would sooner forget. "I shall call again in the morning," she promised, rising to see herself to the door. "Until then, I must ask that you follow my advice. Do try and rest, Mrs. Kendrick," she urged the patient whose gaze remained elsewhere.

As expected, Mrs. Lesley now complains of a cough and stomach pains. Her fever is mild, but will, no doubt, require confinement. If only she would accept this before it becomes inevitable.

"You can't expect me to leave off the cooking and chores. What with the men working all day, there is no time for laying in the bed and what not." This was spoken by a woman who looked as if she should be there already, her face flushed and hair plastered to her forehead. The rash had spread to her shoulders, neck, and torso, though she refused an examination of it.

"I only tell you what is necessary," Mariah insisted.

"Says one who knows naught about it," her patient retorted. "Your mother may have been one to have the servants run the house, but this family depends on my hands alone. Think what you are asking of me."

"The illness will demand your strength without asking. There will be no choice if the chills take hold or the dysentery—"

Mrs. Lesley silenced the doctor with a hand on her arm, her gaze flicking to the gangly youth who peeled potatoes by the fire. Though he faced away from them, the tilt of his head indicated not a word of their conversation escaped him.

Lowering her voice, Mariah said, "Anything of a contagious nature places our whole community in harm's way. You put your family at risk by refusing to hear the truth of this illness."

"My family," the other woman responded, "is my responsibility. I may trust a physician for the odd ailment, but don't be thinking I need you to run the house."

She found a more receptive audience waiting at the Hinkles' cabin, where young Charley was already put to bed with a quilt, his furry companion, previously banned from crossing the room's threshold, now present in the chamber.

"Knew you would be seeing him once I heard of the Kendricks' trouble." Mrs. Hinkle lugged a tumbler of fresh water across the sick chamber's doorway, splashing its contents into the nearby basin. "Don't want the baby near sickness of any kind. Nor the others, though it will be near impossible keeping them away from here, goodness knows."

Mariah felt the patient's skin, the cheeks once ghostly pale now a shade of pink.

His gaze followed her movements with childlike curiosity. "That a potion?" he asked of the dark liquid sloshing in the medicine vial. "Looks like one Harvey Stroud brought to school. For making the hair grow on his face."

"It is something to help you sleep," she told him. "And while you are dreaming of plat-eyes and Harvey Stroud's potions, this medicine will cool your fever."

"What about Rufus?" As he spoke, his hand moved protectively to where the dog's head rested on his knees. "Is it safe for 'em? Can he catch the sickness?"

"Rufus is safe," Mariah assured him. She measured off drops of the elixir into a teaspoon before cautioning, "Your brothers and your sister are at risk, however. They must not come any closer than the doorway."

Swallowing the medicine, he wiped the back of his hand across his mouth. "I don't ask 'em to come. They sneak in while I'm sleeping. It is only Rufus I want with me."

His mother made a tsking sound, as she dipped a cloth into the basin of water. "More trouble than the other five put together, aren't you?" She pressed the cloth to his forehead.

Mariah stroked the boy's hair, feeling the dampness from the heat within. "I will come by early tomorrow and see how you get on. Remember, sleep and good dreams."

In the hall, she instructed his mother on the dosage of the medicines. A last look at the boy's door showed the other children crowded outside, hoping for a peek at the patient before their mother shooed them away again.

The boy Charley shows the same symptoms as the two women. At present, his fever is mild, and the rash seems to give him more trouble than anything else. Because he is so young and already of a frail disposition, I feel that —

Mariah paused in her writing as footsteps sounded in the hall. A shadow hesitated just outside her door, a girl's form appearing close behind. The Darrow daughter, her expression obscured in the hall's shadow.

"You are busy," Nell apologized, turning as if to leave again.

"Wait," Mariah told her, placing aside the pen. "Has someone called for me?"

"No. It is only…I wished to look for a book I lent my brother some months ago."

Of course. She sometimes forgot that the former occupant's belongings were still scattered throughout the room, including a set of dog-eared paperbacks on the bottom shelf of the book case. Volumes of travel and history, cheaply printed from decades past, the words *Property of Henry Darrow* written in childish script inside the covers.

"Search all you want," Mariah urged. "The books have not been moved."

Smiling, the girl advanced into the lamplight. She

was considered plain by their neighbors, Mariah knew, her features as honest and simple as her manner of dress. This lack of beauty was more than compensated for by the gentle civility that so many of her elders seemed to struggle with.

"So many books," Nell said. Her gaze had wandered to the upper shelves where the doctor's collection of sturdy leather bindings filled the space. "You are fond of reading." She glanced over her shoulder.

"When I have time, yes." Detecting the girl's interest in the volumes, she added, "You may borrow one. Or several, if you like, though you may find the medical ones a little harder on the eyes."

"I should think so," Nell laughed. This friendly curve of the mouth rendered her a little less plain, her fingers brushing the book's rigid spines. Two of these bore Mariah's father's name, Barnaby Moore, M.D., his textbook writings used in several of the Alabama hospitals.

Nell continued down the row, past novels by Charles Dickens and George Eliot, pausing when she reached a volume that was larger than the rest. Pulling it free from the shelf, she turned it over to reveal a cover that was embossed with a spiritual design.

A wooden cross and a ragged robe. The bloodstained fabric entwined with gilded lettering to create a title for a Bible with copperplate illustrations. The girl's gaze held more than one question as she glanced up from the image.

"My mother's," Mariah explained.

Part of her wished to pack the volume away, someplace free from prying eyes and questions. But a lingering memory connected her to the pages, ones she hadn't touched in years. The feel of her mother's arms encircling her, helping her to balance the heavy book as they sat on the family staircase.

Her small hands flipping through the pictures of Noah's Ark and the Ten Commandments, of Christ healing the sick and calming the storm. His feet and hands nailed to the cross, blood weeping past the crown of thorns upon His brow. Images which had seemed moving and real enough to her mind as a small child, although now they seemed less so in the face of science texts and modern philosophers.

"This has been well-read," Nell observed, turning the pages with care. "I see fade marks where passages were studied often. Your mother's faith must have been very strong. "

"It was." Mariah's voice felt tight in her throat. "That was her favorite possession. Reason enough for me to keep it, I suppose."

"Yes, of course," Nell replied. Quiet sympathy shone in her eyes as she flipped the cover closed. As if sensing this was not among the copies to be borrowed, she slid it back in place. "She would wish it to be near you, I am sure."

In my hand you mean. She suppressed the sardonic response, her first reaction to anyone who challenged her spiritual apathy. Arthur had tried and failed many times, proving not even a lover's influence could break through her resolve.

The girl had finished her search, pulling a battered copy of *Robinson Crusoe* from the shelf, the bookmark still in place where its previous reader abandoned it. Pausing in the doorway, she hugged the book to her chest.

"Is the Hinkle boy very ill?" she asked. "Someone

told me he has remitting fever."

"I see no reason to fear the worst," Mariah answered, going back to her work. "Especially since it is not remitting fever, as idle talk says."

What it was, though, she couldn't yet say.

❧✥

The knock came at seven o'clock, a mad pounding that interrupted the Darrows' mealtime blessing. Exchanging looks of surprise, most of the family rose from their chairs, though it was Nell who answered the door.

On the other side, a frantic looking Mr. Kendrick sought the doctor's face. "My wife," he said.

It was all the words necessary for Mariah to fetch her bag and coat from the hall. She would have gone alone, except that Mr. Darrow insisted on driving her in the buggy. "May not be back 'til late," he reasoned, voice gruff with meaning as he took his hat from the hall table.

They took the dirt lane past the spring at a bumpy pace, the worried husband urging his stallion far ahead of them. When they reached the house, he helped Mariah from the cart, steering her anxiously towards the door.

"When did she last take medicine?" she asked.

"Right before I came for you. She…she couldn't keep it down, though."

Mariah could smell the sickness before they reached the hall, an odor familiar from years of work in her father's practice. Her patient lay in bed, propped against pillows as she clutched the quilt in silent agony. Her night dress was soaked with sweat, dark hair clinging to her thin, shaking shoulders. Seeing Mariah, she tried to sit up. A spasm of pain twisted her features as she gasped, "It hurts...please..." Words that died away as she retched violently into a nearby pan.

Mariah rummaged through her bag, unearthing some paper packets. Thrusting them into Mr. Kendrick's hands, she told him, "Boil plenty of water for tea. The ginger root will help to settle the stomach pains."

He seemed relieved to have the task, pushing past Mr. Darrow, who watched from the doorway.

Motioning the other man forward, Mariah whispered, "If he will let you, bring the tea in his place. I do not want him to see what may follow."

Glancing at the girl, he gave a reluctant nod.

Geneva's expression had a wildness about it, fingers clawing at the covers as she rocked in silent despair. Anyone might think she was close to death—and she quite possibly was.

When he had left them, Mariah arranged herself carefully on the bed.

Her patient seemed not to notice, hugging herself as she muttered something between coughs.

Forcing calmness to her voice, Mariah began, "Mrs. Kendrick, you're hurting I know—"

"Mama?" The girl was looking past her shoulder, eyes wide and searching as she propped herself up to see the door. "Where are you?"

"It is your doctor, Mrs. Kendrick," she said gently. "Do you recognize me?"

But the girl was still searching the empty doorway, panic building in her features as she called, "I'm sick, Mama. Please hurry. "

Cold fear touched the doctor's bones.

Geneva Kendrick was hallucinating, a side effect of the fever that flushed her normally pale skin.

"Do not distress yourself," Mariah soothed, attempting to draw her attention. "It is all right."

"Where are you?" the girl begged, almost screaming this time as she tried to rise from the bed.

Mariah held her shoulders, afraid she might somehow crawl to the floor in her desperation. She had kept watch at many troubled bedsides while working in Mobile, but never one so disoriented. Only once did she hear such agonized groans, such fits of sobbing. Those were the sounds from her mother's room, where the door had been cracked wide enough to show a form writhing in pain on the bed, servants rushing to hold it back.

"Stay with me," Mariah urged, clinging to the restless patient. The girl batted her hands away, sobbing as she clutched the blanket to her chest.

The laudanum and other medicines lay on the nearby table, along with the pearl brooch Mariah had seen the girl wear that morning. A pang of guilt shot through her at the sight, eyes closing in something that might have been a prayer were she someone else.

"Geneva." She touched the girl's face, a firm but gentle pressure. "Look at me, Geneva. You must hear my voice, please."

For a second, the girl's gaze rose to meet hers. Tears and confusion clouded the depths before another cough was racking her frame.

Mariah turned at the sound of footsteps, grateful to see the steaming cup in Mr. Darrow's hands. "Help me raise her," she told him.

The task proved difficult as the patient fought

their hold, striking blindly at the air.

"Hold her arms." Raising the cup with shaky hands, Mariah forced some of the liquid past her lips, only to have it spewed back again as the girl gasped and retched, eyes rolling to the back of her head. "Geneva? Wake up, Geneva!" She shook the younger woman, watching her sway like a broken doll, pulse fast, mouth slack as burbling sounds issued from her throat. "Wake up, wake up," Mariah pleaded under her breath, clutching the face that hung lifeless beneath dark strands.

There was no response, no movement from the passive features.

Mariah yanked a bottle of smelling salts from her pocket and waved it under the girl's nose. A few breaths of the eucalyptus scent were followed by a gulping sound, Geneva's eyes fluttering open. They settled hazily on the worried doctor.

"Just breathe," Mariah urged. "Calm and deep breaths."

They stayed like that for a while, the patient resting against Mr. Darrow's weight. She took a swallow from the cup of tea when it was offered, then another. Tentative draughts, with spells of coughing in between.

"A little more," Mariah told her, mixing the medicine into the cup's remaining liquid. This was taken without complaint, the patient's eyes drifting shut from exhaustion. Her breathing, though ragged, came slow and steady.

Mariah checked her pulse to find it had calmed somewhat. Placing the cup aside, she offered, "Let me sit with her while she rests. It may be some time before we know she is out of danger."

She cradled the drowsy patient like a child, tucking the quilt around her sleeping form. She rested her head against the wall, gaze focused on the glow of the oil lamp by the door. No shadows stirred, the murmur of masculine voices audible from further down the hall.

Hours passed, Mariah conscious of a clock ticking somewhere nearby. Twice she drifted off, the dreams changing the weight in her arms to resemble something else. First, it was the bag she held on her journey from Mobile; then, her mother's Bible, its heavy binding threatening to tilt away from her childlike grasp.

Fearful panting sounds told her the patient's rest was equally troubled. Geneva stirred then woke from her stupor with a groan. Blinking the sleep from her eyes, she seemed to recognize Mariah's face in the lamplight.

"You came," she said, pulling herself up, limbs shaking from the weight, as she glanced around the room. "Lucas was so worried. He thought...where is he?"

"He is in the kitchen," Mariah told her, steadying the girl's shaky form. "Your fever is starting to abate," she said, feeling her forehead and cheeks. "Are you still in pain?"

"Not as much. I feel weak, a little dizzy—"

"You should have another dose of the medicine." Shifting her carefully onto the pillows, Mariah rose from the bed. "I will fetch some more tea—and your husband."

Mr. Kendrick met her in the hall, shuffling a little from the hours of weight on his weakened leg. "Is she—how is she?" he managed, searching her expression anxiously.

"Come and see," she told him.

He crossed stiffly to the sickbed, pulling a chair alongside. His fingers reached to cradle those of his wife, lips mumbling words of comfort as he pressed their foreheads together. There was none of the usual hesitance between them, the trial seeming to bring them closer.

"Will she be all right now?" he questioned, finding Mariah in the kitchen a few minutes later. A lamp burned on the table. Mr. Darrow sat tiredly in one of the chairs.

"She must continue with the medicine," Mariah told Mr. Kendrick, "and the tea is beneficial as well. I will leave you some green and black varieties, along with the ginger that soothed her tonight."

He nodded, hands splayed across the tabletop. "It is not over then. She could get worse."

"Possibly," she admitted, stirring her cup of brew. "I will stay until she sleeps again. For tonight, at least, I think she is out of danger."

They left at first light, Mr. Darrow clutching the reins in grim silence. When they had gone almost half a mile like this, he spoke without looking at her. "Will the girl live?"

"I don't know." She adjusted the doctor's bag on her lap, the supplies clinking together inside. "Geneva has responded well to the medicine. That gives me hope, if nothing else."

She was hesitant to say more, troubled by the girl's sudden downturn. Mere hours before she had seen her resting, her fever mild and seemingly under control. There was no way to predict such lapses, of course, but part of her felt responsible for the brush with death.

Perhaps it was a turning point and meant only that the worst was behind them. Similar cases her father had dealt with were heavy on her mind, the instances of putrid fever she helped him to treat as a doctor-in-training. Her young hands had bathed brows and checked pulses between the long hours of bedside vigil.

She let her head nod in motion with the buggy, eyes drifting open and shut to study the breaking day, until something outside the Hinkles' cabin caused her to sit upright, breath coming sharp in her lungs. "Stop," she said, grabbing Mr. Darrow's arm. "Something's happened."

Crouched on the steps, clad only in their night clothes, were five of the Hinkle children. This included the baby, who was wrapped in a shawl in his sister's arms. Small cries from his mouth formed clouds in the morning air.

Mariah climbed from the buggy before the wheels could roll to a full stop. Gathering her skirts, she ran towards the steps, seeing the door was already half-open despite the morning's frost.

"What happened?" she asked the children seated there. Not waiting to hear the answer their scared faces had already told her, she swept past them to the rooms inside.

A low wailing sound filled the hall, quickening her steps and her heart, as well. She stopped numb at the bedroom door, gaze lighting on the two figures huddled inside.

One of these was Nell, her shawl and nightgown poor comfort against the cabin's chill. Her arms supported the shaky form of Mrs. Hinkle, the older woman's face buried in the shawl as her fingers twisted and pulled its fabric in distress.

The shape on the bed had been covered with a sheet, the black and white dog continuing to guard its master. Its paws were crossed protectively over the small form, head cocked to study Mariah with animal-like confusion.

Tears the doctor held back from previous hours now spilled freely down her face. More burned against her eyelids when she tried to block out the scene, her face resting briefly against the door way. She could feel herself sinking under the weight of grief and exhaustion, frame sliding softly towards the floor. Slumped there, she stared emptily at the women across from her.

November 12th 1862: Charley Hinkle died early this morning. I have listed bilious fever on the death certificate, as I was told he suffered the loss of fluids most heavily during his final hours. His fever grew worse and similar to that of Mrs. Kendrick's. There was much confusion in his thoughts.

None of his siblings appear to share these symptoms, but I dare not hope it remains that way. Already I have learned the entire Lesley household is infected, and a message has come from the Stroud family requesting medicine for a child with a fever.

I fear we may be facing an epidemic.

❦

A cellphone's jingle echoed off the walls of the historical society. Jenna silenced it, scooping up the medical journal as she moved into the hall.

"Well?" her agent's voice prompted. "This better

be good, considering all those messages you left. Something about finding the next History Channel documentary?"

When she had filled Joyce in on the details surrounding the town's legend—and the real danger that worried its citizens' lives—she sensed a startled silence on the other end. "There may be more," she teased, "since I haven't finished reading the doctor's journal yet. Plus, Mrs. Maudell is going to show me some letters the soldier wrote from the battlefield."

"Perfect," Joyce told her. "Any progress on the actual cemetery restoration?"

She frowned, thinking of her last meeting with the headstone carver. The man's abrupt good-bye still stung for reasons she couldn't explain. "I'm about to head out to the cemetery now," she said.

Reluctant to abandon the doctor's journal for another day, she wished the storm would last a little longer. Sunlight had already fractured the clouds, though, orange and gray painting an autumn sky above the town square.

One quest postponed for another. The daybook would be here when she came back, while the headstones faded a little more with each passing thunderstorm, taking with them a part of the town's past, secrets strange and wonderful to a historian's eye.

14

Con's fingers traced the stone's familiar pattern, following the V-shape where it tapered to an arrow's point. Drops of rain spattered the gray surface, smudging the dirt around the carvings. He brushed them aside to study the name inscribed below.

Strange. He supposed the families around the spring must have been too poor to afford the average stone carver's charge per letter policy. At least, that was the explanation he often heard for the lack of surnames and important dates on older headstones.

"Charley," he muttered, reading aloud the name on the headstone.

"That was a victim of the curse," a voice informed him. He recognized it even before he turned to see the history writer standing behind him.

She wore the same coat and scarf from the day before, her curls partly hidden by a red beret. Instead of her usual knapsack, she carried a backpack and a heavy duffel bag, their contents clinking as she lowered them to the ground.

"Cleaning supplies," she explained. "I got permission from the county to start restoration on the headstones. Which pretty much means scrubbing off the grime, or as much of it as I can without causing damage."

"You mean further damage," he said, with a glance to the scattered markers.

She replied with a shrug, as if uncertain what to make of his presence in the ruined cemetery. Not fully trusting him, perhaps, considering the indifference he showed in their last meetings. It occurred to him she might even see him as a trespasser of sorts. After all, she had never invited him to visit the burial ground or even told him where to find it exactly. He wiped his hands, stepping away from the tomb with the Celtic engraving.

"You probably need to get started," he said. "If you want me to leave—"

"Hey, it's public land." The glimmer of a smile told him she wasn't entirely begrudging of his presence. Unzipping the duffel bag, she tossed him a spray can. "If you stay, though, you'll have to work. Agreed?"

He nodded, holding their gaze long enough to see the expression soften a little in her eyes. The stare was broken when Jenna crouched beside her duffel bag, rooting through its contents.

"So," he began, shuffling the can awkwardly in his hands. "What's this about a victim of the curse? Not that I believe it, of course, but it sort of stirred my curiosity."

"I'm not sure I should tell you."

She didn't look at him as she spoke, making it hard to see whether she was joking or not. Golden hair fell across her face as she fished a jug of distilled water from the bag's depths, curls that seemed as lively and unpredictable as her mood this morning.

"It's kind of like spoiling the end of a novel," she continued. "You might not be able to keep it secret."

He caught something playful in her tone this time, making him bold enough to match it. "Who would I tell? All my customers are dead."

"That's not exactly true, since someone has to commission their headstones. You're part of this community, and something tells me they won't enjoy having their favorite legend debunked after all this time."

"I'm not a native, remember?" He crouched beside her, for once closing the distance he usually preferred with other people. "There's not a lot of love lost between myself and Sylvan Spring. If it weren't for the masonry shop, they probably wouldn't know I exist."

"Then you *are* a recluse."

Con's face burned, the words like a slap despite the truth behind them. He realized she must have heard the gossip by now, the usual stories surrounding his tragic loss. Shreds of truth in every rumor, making it difficult to deny.

"Sorry." She handed him a plastic scraper from the tool kit, her touch a rush of warmth against his skin. "I shouldn't have said that. It just puzzles me somehow— your living out here alone, no family or connections."

Questions flooded the gaze that quietly searched his. Not pity or ridicule, but a genuine interest that made him equally uncomfortable.

Shifting back onto the leafy ground, he told her, "It's not a big secret or anything. I like this place, these woods—" He nodded to the smoke rising above the tree line. "My farmhouse is one of the few original structures left in the county. Something worth preserving, you might say."

"That's your specialty," she pointed out. "Preserving things. It should really be you restoring the old cemetery. Or at least, leading the effort, since you're the most qualified."

He paused over the answer, not wanting to hurt her with it. The fact he was too tired, too bogged down in work to tackle such a major project. And then the real reason: he didn't like to make things personal, not when he had the luxury of shutting out even the most well-meaning of friends and strangers. "You're the historian," he said at last. "More than anything this place needs some identity, something to make people care about it. Unless that's part of the secret you have to protect."

A flicker of resignation appeared in her eyes. Lifting the gallon of water, Jenna motioned for him to follow her towards a sycamore tree in the far corner of the graveyard.

"This is the secret," she told him, pointing to three headstones planted beneath its shadow. "Or part of it, anyway. One of these people—the one with the Celtic symbol on their grave—may have known the truth behind the town's curse."

It was a flat marker, the carvings lined and cracked, compared to those of the marble headstones beside it. Mildew obscured part of the owner's first name. As he watched, Jenna began to pour water over the residue.

She worked a soft bristle brush through it, gradually revealing the letters carved beneath. A type he recognized as square cut, shaped from a flat headed chisel to spell the name *MARIAH MOORE*.

"Who was she?" he asked, kneeling to study the beveled lines, simple yet beautiful somehow.

"She was a doctor. The one who treated the sickness everyone *thought* was part of a curse. Or a punishment from God, if they believed in Him."

They sat beneath the tree's sprawling branches,

Jenna cleaning the stone as she caught him up on the knowledge gleaned from its owner's writings. Fragments of everyday life from 1800s Sylvan Spring, the doctor's narrative revealing more than the average medical records.

"Dr. Moore was an outsider, but I think she truly cared about them. I get this sense of compassion between the lines, like she's holding back emotions she can't put into words."

"Probably she didn't have much encouragement." He leaned back against the sycamore, fingers brushing its gnarled root system. "A woman doctor was hardly the norm back then, and I'm guessing Sylvan Spring wasn't too accepting of strangers, as it was."

"I got that impression." Passing a sponge over the grime, she told him, "Someone like you might argue they haven't changed much. Although you're hardly an outsider if you've lived here for fifteen years." Green eyes flicked hesitantly in his direction with this statement, as if she expected him to get angry or maybe walk away with the unwanted subject change. "You must have something else to tie you here," she urged, her voice gentle. "Friends, a church family—"

"I haven't been to church in a while," he admitted. Shame crept over his features in the form of a blush. Helpless to cover it, he let another confession slip out, saying, "My faith was sort of put on the back burner after Colleen died. Not because I'm angry or anything, just kind of…numb."

"But you still pray, I hope." Her tone was more gentle concern than judgment as she met his gaze over the headstone. "You don't have to be in church for that. He wants to hear from you no matter what."

"I try to," he said. Resisting the urge to look away,

he added, "It's more automatic than anything. But it can lighten the load when I let it."

"Good," she said. A more hesitant edge peppered the next words she spoke. "Can I ask how she died?"

Somehow, the words tumbled from his mouth unchecked, voice rough with emotion. "A brain aneurysm. She just collapsed apparently, no warning except for something about a headache—" He broke off, raking a hand through his hair. "She died before the ambulance could get there, before anyone could help. The hospital said it was bleeding in her brain, that she never had a chance."

"So you weren't there when it happened." The words were little more than a whisper. Regret lined her face, the hint of tears in her glance. "I shouldn't have asked."

"It's all right," he said. "I should be able to talk about it after two years."

She drew her legs up, letting her chin rest thoughtfully on her knees. "But you're still in pain."

"There's no expiration date on grief," he said, an expression his former instructor was fond of using. "Mine has run the same course as most people's, I guess. I visit Colleen's grave, talk to her sometimes…it helps."

"I saw you there," she said as if grasping something that puzzled her before. "My second day in town, when I visited the main cemetery. You were by this grave with an incredible ivy pattern."

"Plants were her livelihood," he explained. "She co-ran the herb shop in town, but she grew all kinds in her private garden. English Ivy was her favorite—she wouldn't let me trim the vine on our house until it started growing down the chimney."

The fact he had been the one to carve the headstone was something that went without saying. As did the ivy leaf's symbolism for love beyond the grave, a coincidence that tore ragged sobs from his throat the first time he discovered it.

A raven's cry echoed harshly through the woods, startling him from the memory. Black wings cut the air as it flew from the branches in a nearby tree.

"Look," she said, pointing where it sailed down to one of the damaged headstones. Perching there, it turned a beady, inquisitive eye on them.

"Would your Dr. Moore have seen that as an omen?" he wondered. Half-teasing, half-serious he looked at the symbol carved into the stone before them. "For someone who supposedly scorned the town's superstition, she bore its stamp in death."

Jenna frowned. "I think she hated their fear. Maybe because it meant believing in something she couldn't explain. Although, I think the idea of God's existence troubled her more than she let on."

"You've given this a lot of thought," he said. "Really immersed yourself in it."

A flush tinged her cheeks. "I tend to get emotionally involved in my research. Reading her private thoughts, it's almost like I know her. Like she's writing to me, like we're sharing this whole strange experience together." She paused, a look of discomfort replacing the burst of enthusiasm. "Too creepy?"

Laughter was hardly a reflex action for Con these days, making him all the more surprised by the sound that worked past his lips as one hand rose to block it.

Though she didn't seem to mind at all, her mouth curving in response to his warmth.

"Don't worry," he told her. "Tombstone carvers

have a higher threshold for the strange than most people."

"I guess that's true. Most people would say I'm crazy, but you..." She trailed off, a confused look appearing on her face. Pushing herself up from the ground, she moved to examine another headstone, its surface stained green.

"This moss is pretty entrenched." She scraped a fingernail along the sediment, face angled away from his as she inspected it.

On purpose, he supposed, their roles reversed as she seemed suddenly unsure of herself.

Glancing back, she offered, "Want to start on one of the others? There's over twenty more, some worse off than this stone."

He took the hint, feeling a breather was needed. Physically, they were too close at this moment for people who met just days ago. Con never trusted anyone this quickly, but he assumed this girl was used to forging impulsive connections. Part of the job even as someone who traveled in search of other people's stories and lives.

Was that her interest in him—to get his story, the same as the people whose resting place lay beneath their feet? He dropped this notion in favor of studying the yard around him.

A cursory glance revealed more than half its stones were broken in some way or other. Some were reduced to nothing but fragments buried in the earth; others had split apart with cracks as fine as a spider's webbing. Only one wrong tap was needed to leave them in a heap, he knew, gauging the damage with a knowledgeable eye.

He was cleaning the mildew from one of the

monuments engraved with the Celtic V-rod, when Jenna came beside him, camera in hand. "Does that say they were a teacher?" she asked. Her hand reached excitedly for the newly polished letters, as she bent closer.

"Anne Mitchell, School Teacher," he read from the stone. "Fifty-one years."

"Where did I read that name before?" She chewed her bottom lip, mind working to recover the information. "Not the doctor's journal, but somewhere...oh, right. A girl's letter to her brother in the Confederate Army. It said she was going to be a teacher if someone named Miss Mitchell decided to retire."

"Maybe she didn't have a choice," he said, tapping the moon engraving.

He glanced up from the stone to find her raiding the backpack she'd brought that morning. He was puzzled to see her remove a set of 8x10 mirror tiles and arrange them against some nearby tombstones.

A little tweaking angled the glass to cast the sunlight against the teacher's headstone. "Ta-da," she grinned. "Neat right? Helps the carving stand out for a clear picture of the headstone."

"Where'd you pick that up?" He raised his brows at the unconventional method he'd only seen referenced in old genealogy manuals.

"My college boyfriend, actually."

The answer surprised him, as did the flash of jealousy that followed. With no wedding band, he assumed she was single. Which didn't rule out a serious relationship, or even a fiancé, come to think of it.

"He must've been a history major, too," Con

supposed, picturing a serious type as he spoke, the kind who wore glasses and a loosened necktie. Someone who wowed their colleagues with obscure historical facts collected for their groundbreaking dissertation.

"Nope." She smiled, adjusting the camera lens for a closer shot. "Photography student. He worked summers as a cemetery caretaker and thought we should use the grounds as a backdrop for a class project. Probably where I got the idea for this book."

"Maybe you should dedicate it to him," he joked, pushing the subject further than he intended. "Since he inspired you, I mean. Unless you're not on good terms."

"Mm." A noncommittal sound, as she snapped a photo, then another. "We didn't really break up, just sort of …petered out. No chemistry, I guess."

He waited for her to reference a newer connection, maybe someone from her home city or a fellow writer she considered more than a friend.

Instead, she let out a gasp as a sudden breeze ruffled her hair and coat, lifting stray locks of gold from her shoulders. Leaves fluttered down to circle her, red and yellow hues she tipped her face back to meet with a smile. "Aren't they gorgeous?" she called, laughing as a few were caught in her scarf and hair, the camera in her hand neglected for the passing moment.

Con put the tools aside, dusting his hands against a pair of already faded jeans, a smile cracking his face as he offered, "How about a break?"

৵৽

"Sweet tea," Jenna surmised, taking a sip from the

tumbler. "Genuine Southern style, too."

She pushed aside her notepad and pencil, making room for the craftsman to fill a second glass with the rich brew. Dark liquid splashed over a bed of frozen cubes as he noted, "The syrup can be too much for some people. It took me years to get used to it, but I'm guessing you were raised on it."

"I was," she said, fingers cupping the glass fondly. "My grandmother made a raspberry version sometimes. She made sun tea, as well, but that seems kind of risky these days."

"So do a lot of old-fashioned things," he told her, pulling out the chair across from hers.

They were seated in the farmhouse's rustic kitchen, sunlight pouring through the windows to show off a pine floor and white, distressed cabinets. A stone hearth pointed to the original owner's handiwork, but all the modern conveniences were present, too.

"Do you know which family built this place?" she asked. "You said it belonged to one of the first settlers." Part of her was thinking of its close proximity to the woods, wondering if the residents were someone she would recognize from her research.

"The history is kind of sketchy," he answered. "It changed hands a lot of times, but no one had lived in it for about thirty years. Part of the roof had crashed in, a lot of the floor was rotted—a stray herb garden out back was pretty much the only sign of life."

This made her glance to the window, where bundles of rosemary and basil were strung to air dry. "You decided to rescue it," she guessed. "To repair the damage like the headstones in your mason shop."

"Actually," he said, reaching for his tumbler, "that

came later. The first time I saw it...well, I helped break the windows out."

Jenna almost choked on her tea. "Excuse me?" she asked, eyes widening as she took in the full meaning of his words.

"I kind of...fell in with the wrong crowd in high school," he explained. "Breaking curfew, a little drinking, some vandalism. We even smashed some of the old headstones in the town cemetery."

"You're kidding." She couldn't reconcile this image with the craftsman's serious demeanor. Not when he chiseled stone for a living and handled the ones from the neglected cemetery with such care and precision.

"It's true," he insisted. "It was how I became Mr. Sawyer's apprentice— reparation for my crimes, except I ended up staying of my free will later on."

She forgot her tea, arms folded on the table as she absorbed more details from his unlikely start. The years of training under Mr. Sawyer's careful eye; the arguments with his parents about a youthful mistake snowballing into a career.

"They thought I would find something else if I went to college," he said. "But mostly, I think they were surprised that I ended up staying in Sylvan Spring, while they moved back to Kansas. Ironic, since my dad's job was the only reason we came here in the first place."

"My folks thought I would teach history instead of writing about it," she recalled. "There were some doubts on their part, but they told me to follow my instincts. Faith was a big part of it, too, since it was something I felt called to do." A laugh escaped as she added, "The travel part doesn't sit too well with them, though. I spend more time in motels than the apartment I'm leasing. They've lived in the same neighborhood their whole lives, so it's hard for them to understand."

"No other ties to home?" he asked, curiosity buried in the blue stare. "I assumed there must have been someone after the photography major. You know, a more serious connection."

After their discussion in the cemetery, it seemed wrong to hold back details of her romantic experiences. Even if there wasn't much to tell, considering her last relationship had been a long distance one with a documentary writer. That had lasted mere weeks, the same forces that brought them together ultimately making it impossible to find time for each other.

"I'm not seeing anyone," she admitted at last. "Relationships are hard to build between the hours of research. Another reason for the family to question what I'm doing, though it's said with good intentions."

He smiled, a half-curve of the mouth that seemed almost boyish. "Your family sounds close," he said. "My parents appreciate what I do in their own way, but I think it's hard for them to explain it to others. It can sound kind of morbid telling people your son makes gravestones for a living."

"No one who's seen it could think so." Warmth had crept into her voice before she realized it, her admiration for the work extending to its creator. If he guessed her thoughts, the only sign was in the gaze that cut away from hers.

Con cleared his throat as he changed the subject.

"To answer your first question, the house is from the 1830s. I wasn't sure any of it could be salvaged, but the building inspector said the foundation was sound.

We ended up replacing the floor and roof, but the layout and stonework are basically the same."

Her gaze roamed the small interior, trying to picture how it might have looked back then. No sink or fridge, of course, and no stove, with the hearth used to cook their meals instead. They would have gotten their water from the spring, or maybe a water well, if one was closer.

It occurred to her that Dr. Moore might have been here, might have shared tea with someone in this same kitchen more than a hundred years ago. A shiver passed through her with the thought, picturing time as a thin veil between her and the room's former occupants. Not ghosts, but shadows of the past, the kind she could reach out and touch if only the right information could be found.

A small cough summoned her thoughts back to the present.

"You look lost." Con studied her thoughtfully from across the table, ice melting to water in his tea as he moved it aside to rest his arms in its place. "Anything I can help with?"

She could use a time machine, a portal to the past that opened to the year 1862. Neither was a reasonable request, but she could think of more practical ones. Preserving history was just as important as understanding it, and the wooded cemetery was in limbo until the county decided how to protect it.

"There is one thing you could do for me," she told him. "A sort of temporary favor."

"Anything," he said.

The overhead light flickered then came to life, bathing the interior of the masonry shop in a soft glow.

"Thank you again for doing this," Jenna said, easing a cardboard box onto the nearest counter. Inside were pieces of the broken tombs they had cleaned and photographed that morning. They had marked their original cemetery spots with corresponding tags, packed the fragments in plastic bags, and then placed them in boxes she'd had in the trunk of her car.

"I'll feel safer knowing they're here—at least until something permanent can be arranged." She gave the contents a farewell pat, turning to see Con set his container on the floor.

It was the heavier of the two boxes, the fragments in large chunks that could be reassembled for future display, an event that Jenna didn't see happening, unless it was supervised by the craftsman himself.

"Will the county apply for a grant?" He was gazing into the depths of the box, a last look before he taped its lid shut. She detected a trace of discomfort in the words, as if he shared her thoughts on the cemetery's fate.

"They might," she answered. "Of course, that sort of project takes time—and interest from people in the community."

She trailed her fingers over dusty countertops, footsteps taking her to a work bench in the far corner. A canvas cloth covered a work-in-progress, making her think of the cross-shaped stone she had seen on her first visit there. On impulse she gave the cloth a tug. It slid soundlessly to the floor, revealing a monument of polished black beneath.

Ribbon was engraved to loop a pair of hearts together, the first of these bearing the word 'FOR' in old-fashioned, block lettering. White pencil marks outlined the second part of the message, *'ALWAYS'* inside the companion heart.

"I'm sorry," she said, blushing as the craftsman came beside her. "I should have asked first."

"Like it?" He ran a hand across the surface, brushing aside specks of dust. "It's for a couple's monument, World War II era. Their first marker was a wooden one that burned in a wildfire."

"It's perfect," she said. "Very romantic design."

"The family wanted something more elaborate than the original marker. There'll be more ribbon for the border and some gold leafing to help the lettering stand out."

As he spoke, he rolled up his sleeves and reached for a chisel and a small brass-handled mallet that resembled a kind Jenna had seen in sculpting kits. Angling the chisel inside the markings for the letter 'A', he brought down the mallet with a sharp *ping!*

Quick, firm taps chipped away layers of stone. Jenna thought of a whittler shaping a piece of wood, amazed the substance could be so rough, yet delicate at the same time. Her gaze followed Con's expert rhythm, the play of muscle beneath his skin as he deepened grooves inside the pencil lines.

"It looks effortless," she said, amazed by the fluid motion. "Like the tools are a part of you."

He nodded, surprise in the blue eyes. Then, holding out the chisel, he said, "Now, it's your turn."

"Me?" Jenna's tone was incredulous, as if he were asking her to finish a master's canvas when she had never dipped a brush in the palette. "I'll mess it up," she said.

"Slate requires more precision than strength to

mold." He waited a breath's pause before adding, "If you'd like to try, I could show you."

The offer was more than a kind gesture, she knew. The artist's work was more or less an extension of himself, a glimpse to his innermost thoughts and emotions. This was a chance to experience part of his world, a taste of the forgotten craft she had learned to love these past weeks. For this reason, she found herself, asking, "Where do we start?"

They had barely touched before, mostly accidental brushes while exchanging some object. But Con was all but holding her as they began, arms pressed close to her sides as he guided her hands in place over the stone.

"You've got this," he promised, his fingers closing over hers to grip the tools carefully in place.

A tremor passed through her, whether in response to the contact or the challenge of carving, she wasn't sure. If she turned her head, she would feel the sandpaper of his jaw, his breath soft on her face when he instructed, "Ready—and now."

A steady clink of metal was the only sound as they worked the chisel over the stone. Con turned the instruments where they needed to go, his pressure firm but gentle on her fingers.

"That's good," he encouraged. "Stay with the line; it's your map."

She let his touch guide her, vaguely aware of the strength in his build, the smoky scent of aftershave filling her breath. Confusion blended with wonder as she watched the shape taking form beneath the chisel's tip.

Briefly, Con relaxed his grip, forcing her to take the lead. A sense of panic was quickly replaced by astonishment for how natural it seemed. The tools did most of the work, shaving layers of stone with almost feather-light taps.

Stroke by stroke, they filled the pencil outline, until a swirling letter 'L' took its place. Dust floated off the surface, bits of stone scattered across the hollowed portion. Their fingers slid apart, the tools falling to the work bench with a soft clink.

"Well." Jenna's laugh was shaky as they pulled away. She avoided his glance, afraid a blush might be on her face. "Thank you," she managed at last. "I never...that was different than I pictured." She stroked the newly fashioned letter, as if to check it was real, scarcely believing her hand was responsible for its appearance, despite the very real memory of Con's instruction. Her skin burned with the thought, her heart pounding despite the distance now between them.

"That was impressive," he said, with a nod to the monument. "Beginners usually put too much force in the mallet and bruise the stone. Your pacing was perfect."

Did she imagine the catch in his tone? Tension was visible in the hands that gripped the edge of the work bench in front of them. Hands that felt so confident when they held hers just moments before.

"I should go," she said, fingers closing around the car keys in her coat pocket. "It's getting late, and there's not much else we can do for the cemetery. Not that I expect you to," she added, realizing how presumptuous that sounded. "You've already helped more than enough by storing the broken headstones." As she spoke, she moved towards the door.

Con held it open for her, his expression hard to

read as he followed her down the gravel drive.

She had reached the car outside the gate.

"Wait. Miss Cade—Jenna." He let the name hang in the air, as if asking permission to use it. When she didn't object, he continued, "There's something else you might want to see. The headstones at the Lesley property and another homestead near there. I don't know if all of them have the Celtic symbol, but it could be worth checking out—for your book, that is."

"I can't ask you to spend more time on this," she protested. Secretly, she wanted to accept the offer, but not because of anything to do with the impending manuscript. Then again, maybe his reason for making it was the same—less to do with her research than the emotions stirred in their brief carving lesson.

"What are you doing Thursday?" he asked, naming the day after she would call on Josephine Maudell for the soldier's letters. "We could meet here early, around eight o'clock. It's a few miles to cover, so you'd need walking shoes. "

Breath lodged in her throat along with the answer she *ought* to give. To see the stones would be nice but hardly necessary when she already had the wooded cemetery to document and so much research left with historical manuscripts.

Yet she found herself agreeing to the plan as she slid into the driver's seat. "I'll be here," she told him, seeing the hint of a smile in return before she pulled away from the farmhouse. Her gaze sought his image in the rear view mirror until it vanished with the curve of the road.

15

The door opened to Jenna's second knock, the friendly face of Mrs. Maudell's caretaker on the other side. "Morning," the woman smiled, pulling the door open wider. "She's expecting you—wore out from it, actually." This was said with a laugh, as she motioned Jenna to follow her up the mahogany staircase.

The banister was scuffed, the carpet beneath their shoes faded here and there among the floral pattern. Glancing back at her, the nurse continued, "Mrs. Maudell doesn't get many visitors these days. Your showing up this way has been good for her—gives her a chance to talk about the past with someone who'll do more than nod and smile."

"She's the one helping me," Jenna insisted, pulling a notepad from her bag. "Does Mrs. Maudell have any family left in Sylvan Spring?" she wondered, as they drew near a door that was slightly ajar near the end of the hall.

"Just some distant connections, I think," said the nurse. "Her husband's family, mostly. Her kin is somewhere over in Georgia last I heard." She pushed the door the rest of the way open, revealing a spacious bedroom.

A fire crackled in the grate, heavy drapes pulled aside to shed light across the antique furnishings and rug.

Resting against the pillows in a four poster bed

was Josephine Maudell, her bony frame wrapped in a quilted bed jacket. "Sit down," she said, a frail hand patting the nearby chair. To the nurse she said, "Fetch the boxes from the wardrobe, Mollie. The two on the top shelf." She picked excitedly at the comforter spread over her lap, gaze shifting to Jenna as she asked, "Do you take coffee, Miss Cade? I'll have Mollie fetch some—"

"No, thank you," she said. "I had some with breakfast." Taking the offered chair, she hung her knapsack across the back. "I have so many questions to ask you," she said. "All for the book, of course. I hope you won't object to being quoted, since your ancestor was so prominent in the town's history."

"I won't mind," Josephine said, after a pause to consider. "I'm used to it, with the newspaper calling so often. If by some miracle I *should* live to be a hundred, they won't have anything left to write about." She chuckled at Jenna's expression. Reaching to pat her fingers in a kindly gesture, she said, "Don't worry. I'm not counting on more than a few months at best. The doctor thinks he's smart, but I've read my future in the words and glances. Now it's just a matter of the Lord's timing."

Jenna was saved from making a reply by the appearance of two flat storage boxes. The nurse placed them carefully in her lap and then withdrew to a wingback chair to take up her cross-stitch hoop.

"Open the top one," Josephine said, shifting impatiently among the pillows.

Jenna did as instructed, moving aside the lid to find the contents shrouded in tissue paper. The layers folded back to reveal a jacket of gray wool, badly frayed and moth-eaten. The buttons were tarnished. A stain that might be rust or something worse spread across the left shoulder.

Lifting it gingerly from the box, she found a cotton shirt and trousers folded beneath. Both were full of holes and scarcely recognizable as any kind of historic treasures. Jenna's heart beat as if they came from the Smithsonian collection, hands shaking as she held them up for closer examination.

"Sewed by his mother, I've heard," Josephine said, touching the jacket's edge. "Army regulation."

"Arthur wore this. I…it's hard to wrap my mind around." She shook her head, searching for something more intelligent to say. All she could think of was how the patient described in the doctor's notebook actually donned this uniform, wore it day to day through the camps and trails of a soldier's life. Wore it into battle, too, she supposed, with an eye for the dark stain that marred the fabric.

"He must have been tall," she noted, taking in the size of the clothes. "Muscular, too."

Beneath the uniform, she found a stack of stationary bound together with an old ribbon. "These must be his letters," she guessed, running a finger along the edges to count a dozen or so pages. Not as many as she hoped for, but posting mail had been a more difficult process for members of the Rebel army. Sliding the ribbon off, she unfolded the topmost sheet. "Dearest Mariah," she began. Her lips ceased to read the tender lines that followed as she stared in disbelief. *Mariah?*

Slowly, she looked up to face the woman in the bed. "Your great-great grandfather," she said. "He and the doctor…they were sweethearts?"

A slight chuckle escaped the older woman for her

look of shock. "I suppose they must have been, for a time at least. He would have had many girls interested in him, a man of his looks and character. Including my great-great grandmother, who was a bit younger than him, I believe."

Jenna glanced through the other letters, seeing all were addressed the same way. "It seems so strange," she said. "Why would your family still have these? I mean, obviously things didn't work out between them."

"Perhaps she gave them back to him. In a quarrel, or some such incident. He married somebody else, you know." Her hostess wore a troubled look, as if trying to recall something well out of reach.

Gently, Jenna suggested, "Someone in your family must have talked about it. Stories passed down, that sort of thing."

"Oh, no one talked about those things back then," she said, dismissing the idea with a wave of the hand. "People didn't air their troubles for everyone to see. It was private and more respectful."

Jenna wanted to ask more—to know why lovers who supposedly broke apart would later be buried beneath the same tree, especially when one of them had a spouse also buried in the same spot.

Her hostess seemed eager to change the subject, though, telling her, "There's more papers in the bottom of the box. Things to do with his regiment and a few from the town."

Digging deeper, she found a military discharge certificate that showed Arthur was sent home due to 'chronic ill health.' Yellowed newspaper clippings depicted events that took place long after the war, including the construction of the grist mill and later the county hospital.

There was an engraved county map that might prove helpful in tracing the background to the old homesteads. To her surprise, there were also photographs, sepia images of young people crowded in front of a whitewashed building.

"That was a one-room schoolhouse," Josephine explained. She tapped a knobby finger against a tall, dark-haired youth in the back row. "That's Arthur. He would've been seventeen or so."

"Handsome." Jenna smiled at the face that stared boldly into the camera. Beside him was a youth even more striking, with sharp cheekbones and a half-lidded gaze that made him seem a trifle arrogant.

They were the oldest members in a class of students ranging from teens to a boy still in short trousers. Plain, honest faces for the most part, with clothes to match. The gray-haired woman seated among the smaller children must be the teacher, the one whose headstone she helped clean the day before.

"Do you know why Arthur was buried in the old cemetery?" she asked, coming back to the question that continued to haunt her. "You said his grave's location wasn't known until I found it. You had told me he worked his father's land until he died, and I got the impression their farm was close to the town, not the spring."

Her hostess took a long sip from her water glass. "I can't say I ever heard. His parents share a plot in the town cemetery, as does one of his daughters who died young. Perhaps it was his wife that connected him to the spring."

"Maybe she lived there before they married," Jenna mused, jotting the idea on her notepad. It didn't explain everything, of course, but it was a start. If she could find more about the wife, the rest might eventually fall into place.

"Can you tell me anything about Mrs. Widlow? You said she knew Arthur before the war." Pencil poised, Jenna waited.

"Yes, a local girl. I should have told you before. There was a picture somewhere of her...and something else, as well. I don't know." A foggy look had come over the woman. She closed her eyes, pressing a hand to her forehead to rub the skin in a worried motion.

This drew the nurse's attention. Coming beside the bed, she placed a hand on Josephine's shoulder. "Time for you to rest, Mrs. Maudell," she said, voice soothing. "I'll see our guest downstairs."

"Take the letters with you," Josephine said, "and the other papers, as well. The uniform is already promised to the festival display on Friday but not the rest."

Carefully, Jenna packed the ragged clothing back in its box and placed it on the chair. "I'll bring these other things back soon," she promised, hoisting the smaller container in her arms.

The older woman seemed not to hear, face bowed against the wrinkled hand.

కిళ్ళ

Back in her room, Jenna cleared away her laptop and research papers, switching the desk lamp on to illuminate the work space. As she slid the bundle of stationary free from its ribbon, bits of paper crumbled from the edges of the long-ago letters. History turning to dust in her hands, a notion that made her shake with a sense of urgency and excitement.

Carefully, she unfolded the pages to spread across the oak surface. She sank into the chair, one leg tucked beneath her, elbows propped on the desk as she leaned closer to study the artifacts with a sense of awe. One by one, she went through them, finding emotion that seemed too private for a stranger's eyes, even those who read it a hundred and fifty years after the fact.

All were addressed to the same woman and echoed the same tone of a lover's devotion. Love that stayed steady and even grew in strength when the rest of his thoughts seemed to turn to bitterness.

April 28th 1862
A camp near Corinth, Mississippi

Dearest Mariah,

We have been at Corinth only a week now, and already we have fought and lost two skirmishes. I could bruise my fingers writing to you of all I feel, knowing that hundreds of miles stretch between us. There are not words or paper enough to describe it, though, so I will not even try. Know only that you are in my heart at all times and in my thoughts as much as this stringent new army life permits.

All day, we shoulder our muskets and practice maneuvers that are mostly forgotten when we need them. In battle, all is smoke and noise. We fire blindly into the air, never sure if our aim finds its target. Commander's shouts are lost to the boom of artillery, and every man focuses on loading and reloading his weapon, sometimes forgetting to fire in the moments between.

It is not until the smoke clears, and the cries of the wounded replace the sounds of ammunition, that we recover our ability to feel and think as we did before. Then, our senses are flooded with the notion that we are alive, still— tired, desperately thirsty, and in need of sustenance—but alive, nonetheless.

Being alive is all one can expect at times, yet I never fail to be surprised at the sound of laughter after weeks of grim silence. If I should die (and I know there is a real chance that I may), then there is little for me to regret except that I failed to make you my wife while I still had the chance. Already, I feel bound to you in my heart, as if a ring and promise had brought us together. I pray that someday it will, despite the obstacles we face.

Such obstacles seem too strong for faith even, at times, and I can't help wondering if my will and God's is ever the same. This is especially true at night when the darkness is close around me, and the silence rings loud as any battle yell. It is then I began to doubt Him ever so slightly, and often I don't believe again until the first speck of light has touched the horizon.

ॐ∙હ

Roll call was 5AM, breakfast at six. Corn cakes and salt pork washed down with coffee brewed from chicory, instead of the beans made rare by Union blockades. Then came drill session, hours of firing a musket, marching and forming ranks until the steps seemed automatic as a country dance. That was a soldier's morning, not exactly the same as a farmer's, as Arthur knew from years of rising early to break the soil in his father's fields.

How different were the fields he looked on now.

Ground that was black and barren with the scars of battle. He'd seen men burn alive in the wildfires sparked by artillery—soldiers who were already wounded, too helpless to crawl from the foliage that blazed around them. Those who tried to rescue them bore the blisters in their hands and faces, their uniforms singed beyond repair.

"Never seen fire and brimstone on earth before," panted one ragged soldier Arthur tried to bandage in the moments after such an outbreak. His breath came loud and harsh before it ceased altogether, his body turning slack in Arthur's hands before he could speak a final word of comfort.

Death stalked those in camp, as well. Cases of "the shakes," as they called it, overran the surgeon's tent and consumed the fevered patients sometimes waiting in the rain for their medicine. Those who weren't ill spent their days chopping wood and foraging food, since rations were hard to come by in the wilderness routes they often traveled.

Arthur was part of the group chosen to hunt game in the woods surrounding their summer campsite, a spot in rural Kentucky. They pitched their tents in sweltering heat, the sun bearing down on them with angry precision. Even this wasn't enough to keep the sick from freezing, as men shivered beneath their wool uniforms, struggling to perform drill maneuvers on legs that threatened to collapse.

It was a miracle that he was not among them. The bronchial attacks of old should have weakened his resistance, the doctor barely pulling him back from the reaper's grasp those weeks before he enlisted. To her gentle hands, he secretly gave the credit for this newfound immunity, though his letters to family members and the reverend back home spoke only of God's merciful healing.

I am lucky to have the strength to do this, he reminded himself, fighting past thorns and bramble in search of something to feed the hollow stomachs of a dozen tent mates back at camp.

Birds shrieked at his presence, scaring off rabbits and larger animals his company could have boiled into a hearty stew. The wild peaches he found were a poor substitute for venison, but he tucked them inside his haversack anyway for sharing with others around the fire that night.

Biting into one, he swallowed down mouthfuls of pitted fruit, worms and all. Why should they bother him, when maggots hatched daily from the biscuit supplies, and lice crawled through his hair all night long?

He ate everything but the pit, which he tossed for the birds that were still squawking in the branches above. Two of them dove for it, black birds with plumage that glistened in the sun. They scattered as the sound of boots scuffed the ground. Arthur straightened his shoulders when a familiar gray-coated figure appeared suddenly from a side path.

Wray Camden carried himself more like a commander than a private, his stalwart build adding to the sense of authority. His skin was coated in grime, a knife sheathed in his belt. There was another tucked inside his boot, a pistol buried somewhere among the contents of the haversack that dangled at his side.

"C'mon up the trail," he said, in a tone that would have seemed gruff to any but a friend's ear. "I need your help with something." Then he was gone without a glance back to see if the other man followed.

Arthur would never have considered doing otherwise, their allegiance to each other virtually unchanged since childhood games of old. Back then, it was tales of Daniel Boone and Lewis and Clark that drove them into uncharted territory, pieces of driftwood propped on their shoulders for imaginary muskets. Wray had been the leader those times as well, beating paths through the wildest parts of Crooked Wood, his steps turning wherever his instincts told them.

Now, wading after his friend through another overgrown trail, Arthur expected to find timber ready for chopping or a stream for catching fish. Instead, three bodies lay inside a dry creek bed. Their uniforms—what remained of them at least—were a deep shade of blue.

"What happened?" he asked, racking his brain for news of a skirmish before they arrived. No one had reported seeing Union troops within a hundred miles, their camps thought to be somewhere further north.

"Might have been a scouting group," Wray said, crouching to study the nearest body. "They could've run into some militia members, or even some homestead owners. If anybody lives back here."

Flies crawled over the scant remains, flesh picked apart by forest scavengers.

Wray stood and wiped his hands on a coat almost as grimy as those worn by the dead men. Disgust flickered briefly in his face, whether for the state of the bodies, or the meaning behind the uniforms was hard to tell. Wray seldom spoke of the enemy or his reasons for fighting them, even though he'd been among the first of Sylvan Spring's citizens to lend his name to the recruitment roster.

"Let's see what they left behind," he said, with a nod to where a campfire's ring had scorched the earth in past weeks.

Arthur combed the nearby weeds, finding some blankets and a knife that was broken off just above the handle. There was a haversack with tin plates and cups and a few pieces of silverware. An unfinished game of checkers was left on a cedar stump, the winning move just two spaces away.

Arthur glanced over the items, hoping to find something more useful for the men at his camp. Ignoring the previous owners proved difficult, however, his mind wandering in their direction no matter where his gaze was trained. He was used to his stench, and that of his campmates, from the limited bathing sources. A corpse was another matter. Bile rose in his throat the longer he searched the campsite. "We should bury them," he said, after a while.

"All right," said Wray, as if it made no difference to him either way, his pack dropping to the ground with a heavy thud.

They made a trench with a spade they carried for digging edible roots. Arthur covered the bodies with the blankets he found, Wray heaping shovelfuls of dirt over them. A funeral without ceremony or stone markers, like those on battle sites they'd left back in Corinth. Lonely graves for a lonely death.

He felt this way, even surrounded by rows of soldiers when the smoke billowed and artillery pierced the foliage they hid behind. Dying was a solitary nightmare, each man's experience different from the rest. This much he learned, having witnessed the final breaths of more men than he could ever count or remember.

He kicked a clod of dirt, watched it crumble at the base of the mound. Beside him, Wray stuck the spade in the ground, easing down beside it as he said, "Catch your breath a minute. There's nothing worth taking from the camp—seems they were as bad off as we are."

Arthur had heard that Union forces fared better in supplies, with plenty of coffee beans and other luxuries off limits to the South. This group had clearly not been so lucky. Their lack of any supplies made him wonder if they had gotten lost from their troop—a common enough event with men who'd never ventured past their birth place suddenly having to navigate miles of unfamiliar countryside.

Passing him a battered canteen, Wray said, "There's a spring back by the pine grove. Not big enough for bathing, but it'll do for everything else."

Arthur gulped the water down, grateful for the cool taste after their labor. He wiped a sleeve across his mouth, remarking, "It is not as fresh-tasting as the one in Crooked Wood. This wilderness does put me in mind of that place, though. It has the same towering oaks and sycamores; the rocks so big a fellow's arms can hardly span them."

"Remember stacking those stones for a barn's foundation?" Wray pushed his kepi hat back, bronze-colored hair stuck to his forehead in damp locks. "We'd help roll 'em in place then slap the mortar all around."

"The blacksmith took the flat ones for making headstones," Arthur recalled. "He would carve a few anytime the signs pointed to a wet winter."

He looked at the earth they had just mounded, guilt traveling over him like a shiver. He'd played no part in their demise, yet it brought to mind times he'd felled men on the battlefield. No smoke to veil their faces as he ran full charge, pulling a saber from his belt to plunge into their flesh.

"How scared we were to pass the old cemetery," he said, scarce believing how foolish it seemed now. "The Stroud boys would hold their breath for fear of swallowing spirits—we all did. Except you." He glanced to his friend, a puzzled smile tugging his lips. "You would have spent the night there, if any dared you to."

Wray shrugged, sampling the canteen. "Guess I knew that spirits could never bring as much trouble as the living," he said. A joke, if not for the way his jaw tightened. Did he think of the stone that bore his father's name? Planted in the northern part of the cemetery, a place often reserved for those who died in shame. In Mitchell Camden's case, being stabbed in a drunken brawl with a man he claimed had cheated him in a livestock sale.

Cold and hard in his ways—that was how Arthur remembered his friend's father, the years failing to soften that boyhood impression. At just thirteen, Wray had shouldered the weight of running a farm, his mother's sole supporter in a place still untamed compared to much of Alabama. No wonder, really, that such a youth would find little to fear in made-up stories of otherworldly spirits.

"You learned everything before I did," Arthur said. "Four months between us, yet it might have been four years."

"Think you'll ever catch up?" The cocky tone held a good-natured challenge.

One that Arthur met with a shake of the head. "How could I? You were first at everything. First to ride a horse and shoot a gun; first to venture past the borders of our birth town. The first to kiss a girl, even."

"Ada Girvin." A smile cracked the weary features. "She had sneaked a piece of hard candy from my desk. Now, every time I taste peppermint, I think of her." Glancing sideways, he noted, "You could have stolen a kiss from Nell Darrow any day."

The words surprised him, as did the need to deny them. "Nell is a good friend," he said, picturing the blacksmith's daughter as he last saw her: tanned skin and plain pinafore, carrying a handful of violets she'd picked from the woods. She had given him one of these in good-bye, lacing it through the button hole of his jacket. Later, he tucked it in his pocket, where he carried it for weeks after it had turned to dust. "She's a sister to me in every way but blood," he said, smiling fondly at the memory of warm brown eyes that met his across the rows of school desks. Unlike most of their friends, he saw no plainness in the girl's features, only the shy nature of a bird afraid to show its colors.

"You're hardly her idea of a brother," Wray said with a smirk for the notion. "Leastways, she never heaped such praise on Henry those years we were growing up."

This might be true, but he could take no pride in it. To hurt anyone so kind and caring as Nell seemed nothing short of sin. "There is much to connect us," he admitted. "A similar way of thinking, perhaps. But I can make no claim to her heart. "

"Yours already belongs elsewhere," his friend guessed.

He didn't have to answer; they both knew the letters he received from the Darrow house were not written by Nell. It was another, more elegant hand that penned the lines of heartfelt devotion he waited so eagerly to read each time the mail was delivered to camp.

Others would tease him for the rate those letters came, another arriving sometimes before he could answer the last. He would merely smile, since none of them had met the doctor before, and could never understand the reason he wrote to her and no other female of his acquaintance. To them, she was an oddity, the first of her kind in a place where healers and quack remedies were more respected than any certificate from a clinic.

"We better head back," Wray decided. "Might be those Yanks have someone looking for them. We'll need to report it along with the spring I found."

As he talked, he pulled the spade from the ground, tying it to his pack. With a glance over his shoulder, he added, "That makes one thing you beat me to—losing your heart to somebody. She must be something, this Mariah."

"She is," Arthur said. Climbing to his feet, he lost hold of the canteen. It bounced into the weeds, and he stooped to dig it out, where he found something unexpected beside it. A cluster of violets, the deep hue of purple he knew from fields back home.

It must have been the talk of old times, the memory of the neighbor girl that made him pluck one from the weeds where it grew. He turned it over, studying the petals as a sad smile formed on his lips. Then, he released it to the breeze, a movement that carried it below to the unmarked graves.

❧◦❦

Arthur carried a Bible inside his haversack, the pages worn from previous generations seeking comfort in their trials. At times, he doubted any of these could have rivaled the wretched existence of a Rebel camp. The loss of food and comfort was nothing to the loss of friends, an event made frequent between the spreading of disease and the battles they fought in the woods and fields of the rural South.

When summer came, so did the storms, lightening and hail, the rain coming down in sheets to flood the tents where soldiers slept on the ground. They marched in the rain, fought in it, too, when the circumstances called for it.

Through all of this, Arthur continued to search for answers in the faded Bible. On Sunday mornings, he gathered with others from his company to hear the chaplain speak of a love powerful enough to heal the nation's deepest wounds. Some would nod their heads; others murmured "amen." Arthur waited quietly for a sign that such a feat was still possible in the land that grew more bloodied and broken every day.

Last night, we came through a town where a deserter had just been caught from the regiment camped near Bowling Green. He was flogged nearly fifty times, crying as he said that his children were starving back home. Afterward, they locked him up to face more penance when the news should reach his company's commander.

They could have done worse by him, I know, for such a crime. Still, my heart did fill with sympathy to see one so clearly in distress for his loved ones' well-being. The many times I have thought about the risk that would be worth it to see you again, dear love, cannot be named in the space I have left to write.

He didn't dare express such feelings to any but

Mariah. His parents would say it was foolhardy, a dangerous emotion in need of dampening. Only the girl who shared his intense yearning could understand, and to her was sent the bulk of the stationary he could rarely buy.

The letters mailed in return bore details that sometimes mirrored his experiences. Mariah spent her days trekking through rough terrain along the town's outlying homesteads, a heavy satchel strung across her shoulder. She bandaged the hurt and doctored the aged, her services meeting with little or nothing in return.

She too had witnessed death in its many cruel forms, starting with that of her mother. It was this which had turned her from God while just a girl of six. Age and experience had not changed her mind on the subject, and it seemed love would not, either.

"How can you share my heart but not my faith?" Arthur pleaded on one occasion, overcome at the thought of losing her to their differences.

"Would you change for me?" had been her reply.

The look on his face had been answer enough, the doctor turning coolly away. Were she to ask him again, would he give the same reply? It bothered him that he didn't know, his heart refusing to answer either way.

"Give us, Lord, the strength to face adversity," the chaplain prayed, head bowed along with those of men who came to worship. Arthur glanced around, seeing eyes that were closed and hands clasped in earnest plea. Some were missing their fingers; others were plagued by the yellowed skin and rotting teeth of the dreaded scurvy.

Strapping boys wasting into scarecrows, their clothes just as badly torn. His friend Wray still had the robust frame of youth but with feet that were constantly bruised from marching sixteen miles a day without boots. Still, no supplies came, their rations down to cornmeal and canned peas as October brought the first frost to those who lost their tents in the summer storms.

Arthur covered his face, begging silently, *Take from us these burdens we carry. Reach out Your hand and pull us up from the depths of hopelessness before it swallows us whole.*

16

November 6th 1862

A camp near Bridgeport

Dearest Mariah,

Your eyes are not mistaken: the address I write from tonight is, indeed, within a hundred miles of where you are.

Marching orders have taken us back to home territory, our regiment sent in pursuit of Union raiders who plague the local farmers. It is a simple mission, as far as they go, and I expect surrender will be swift, since we greatly outnumber them and come unexpected. Already, some have begun to celebrate as if we stormed the camp, with prisoners taken and not a single shot.

The sun burned low as Arthur tucked the letter inside his haversack, envelope unsealed for finishing later. He would fill the paper's remaining space with details of tomorrow's raid, where they planned to surprise the enemy still at breakfast, or asleep even, if they could ferret out their hiding place in time.

This, combined with the fact they were back in home territory at long last, had brightened the mood of more than a few in the camp. Songs were raised from a smattering of instruments, shouts, and cheers accompanying the anthem "Dixie" and bittersweet chorus of "Home! Sweet Home!"

Arthur joined in now and then, his baritone fading when the hymns of praise began, lips stumbling over words he'd known since boyhood, a twinge of conscience rising inside him for the lack of enthusiasm. Given the circumstances, he should feel closer to God and not as if he were obliged to One whose debt he didn't care to pay.

Across from him, Wray dozed on a blanket stuffed with straw. In his frocked coat and bare feet, a cap tilted over his face, he looked every bit the Johnny Reb from the newspaper drawings. He stirred as the song broke, the words to *Amazing Grace* fading with the last of the twilight. "Wish I hadn't woke up," he said, propping himself on one elbow, eyes heavy from sleep. "I dreamed Hattie Cray met me by the spring for Saturday night courting. She used to put her feet in the water, just to feel the cold—said it made her feel twice as alive."

Arthur caught the wistful edge in his voice and wondered if it was for the girl or the simple memory of a time and place better than this. He was about to ask when another soldier joined them at the fire, younger in appearance, with tawny hair and freckled features that brought another face to mind.

"What will it be, then?" Henry Darrow questioned, fingers poised on the tin whistle as he glanced cheerfully around. "A love song for the girl back home?" He sent a wink in Arthur's direction.

Arthur shook his head while others nearby laughed. "Something other than music," he suggested, sending Henry digging in his pocket for an envelope that bore a woman's handwriting.

"A letter from home," Henry said, holding it up to

the cheers of the other men, some of whom had never even been to Sylvan Spring. So deep ran the hunger for news of any kind, that it mattered little who or where it came from.

"My sister, Nell," he continued, unfolding the stationary. "With a detailed account of the doings on Mischief Night."

"Knobbly Nell?" cried a boy from the next campfire. One of the Stroud brothers, his recollection of the girl's long ago nickname drawing snorts from their classmates who were close enough to hear.

Feeling protective of his childhood friend, Arthur interrupted. "Henry, your sister had a clever way of writing, I remember, from our days at school. Go ahead and read us her news."

His compliment proved true, the letter's narrative painting scenes from a world he'd almost forgotten, so altered was his notion of what it meant to celebrate. He saw again the lanterns carved from gourds, their fiendish grins alight with a candle's flame. A bonfire made from broken furnishings; four scared faces as young Wray struck the match to light a trail of snuff before a woodland shack.

Afterward, he found his face was damp, an emotion that escaped the others' notice in the firelight. He was not the only one who was in this state, but Henry and his friends were already drifting to another spot nearer the fire, where a soldier in a tattered coat sawed the chorus to a homesick tune on a violin.

Only Wray had remained, stretched over his blanket with his hands clasped behind his head. In a voice somewhat hoarse, he wondered, "Think we'll winter over here?"

"Hope so," Arthur replied. Inside, he was thinking

of how Wray's face had changed with the letter's mention of his father. Mitchell Camden was furious that night they stole his snuff for the childhood prank. His anger had left a mark on Wray's jaw, still visible in the form of a small white scar. He could see it when his friend turned towards the fire, eyes clear of the tears that must haunt his own.

"They might give us leave of absence for Christmas," Arthur said, speaking aloud the hope he nurtured in spite of himself. "We could see our families again—"

"And you could see Mariah," the other man finished, a half-smile forming on the usually stoic face. When Arthur didn't reply, he propped himself on one arm, seeking his face in the firelight. "She didn't break it off," he said. "Did she?"

"There is nothing to break," he admitted. "No promise except to write each other. There is an obstacle…a disagreement I refused to compromise the last time we talked. She refused as well," he added, to make it fair. "We couldn't see a way to make such opposite ideas live equally between us." He swallowed, frustrated at the tug from his conscience. A stand-in for his waning faith, he envisioned bitterly. "I have wondered lately if it matters as much as I thought. If it is worth driving a wedge between us," he said.

The violin was wrapping up its tune, the last sad note trailing off in a hum of strings. Wray said nothing for so long Arthur wondered if had drifted off. Finally he did speak. "Seems to me you owe her something more. For saving your life—if that is what she did."

"It was." He shoved another log on the fire, orange flames licking the bark. "She still does, in some ways.

To read her sweet words is all that keeps me sane at times. That and the picture I carry in my mind of amber hair and shining eyes." He lost himself in the image once more, her face easier to picture in the dark when nothing else could block it out. "You should write to Hattie," he said, remembering the dream his friend had mentioned earlier. "For your sake, if nothing else. To hear from one who feels for you the way I do for Mariah."

This time, no response came. The crackle of wood and coals was all he heard before sleep stole his thoughts.

17

Campfire smoke had been spotted drifting from a stretch of woods known as Crow's Hollow. The farmers who kept crops within its eight mile border were certain that blue coats were the ones foraging their winter fruits and kale. Arthur's detachment believed it too, tracking the enemy's location through a series of fields and foot paths in the hours before dawn.

"Think we'll take them without a fight?" Henry wondered, voice hopeful despite the lag in his step. Last night's revelry had worn off, the face beneath his cap pale-looking in the first traces of dawn.

"If we don't," Arthur said, "then it is nothing we haven't done before."

The boy nodded, a frown creasing his brow.

Sometimes Arthur forgot how much younger Henry was than most of the soldiers in their group, and that he would still have been studying at a school desk if the war hadn't broken out. He stood his ground with the oldest and bravest among them, his uniform battered with the same experience and regret as the rest.

"Your sister's letter was heartening," Arthur told him, thinking a subject change would distract them both from the morning's impending danger. "She will make a fine teacher if that is how she chooses to use her talent."

Henry shrugged. "She has no choice, I reckon. Unless one of our neighbors takes a shine to her," he added, somewhat doubtfully.

Blunt words that Arthur supposed were true in their own way. He imagined the girl had little choice in her future while his destiny lay between equally rocky paths. One of these found him devoted to God and his earthly parents; the other to a woman who defied both of them in her core beliefs and actions. "I envy Nell her strong faith," he said, realizing afterward how strange that must sound. "She always had a devout heart, I remember. One that kept her anchored through life's uncertainties."

His friend gave a short laugh. "You can't be expecting too many of those, with a good plot of land and a faithful woman waiting for you after the fighting."

Arthur could only manage a weary smile for the simplicity of the statement. His fondest hope reduced to one sentence without the complications of his conscience to throw obstacles in the way.

She had promised to wait for him, as Henry said. Years even, if this nightmare continued as long as he now suspected it would. There was only the question of whether her love could truly endure that long—or if he could accept it, even when no war remained to come between them. *How is it I feel Your presence in this, but nothing else?* He spoke silently to the God he still saw as real, if not entirely on his side.

The army broke ranks where the river raised, a blanket of green beside a farmer's cornfield. The crop had been harvested months before, leaving tall, hollowed stalks to rustle in the wind. Arthur thought of hoeing crops back home, of chopping and scraping weeds to stir the soil at the base of the plants.

His fellow soldiers scattered quickly across the banks, eager to fill their canteens and wash the grime from their faces. A few had waded in, among them Wray.

Even from this distance, Arthur could see the way his jaw was tightened, muscles fighting against the pain it caused his blistered feet. He'd worn the same look that morning when Arthur woke to find him huddled over the remains of the campfire.

In his hand had been a lover's memento: a piece of ribbon, a gold lock of hair twined around it. "From Hattie," he'd explained. "She gave it to me right after I enlisted. Said it would keep her in my mind, with all the distance between us. "

Beginning to understand the reason for last night's conversation, Arthur sat up, his voice full of sympathy. "She didn't keep you in hers, though."

"She married an attorney in Woolwich. Her cousin told me the other day."

Without glancing up, he'd tossed the keepsake into the embers. "Guess she knew there would never be anything but letters between us." The meaning was hard to mistake, the slight nod of the head in Arthur's direction before he rose, dusting his hands with a look of grim resolve.

Would Arthur find himself equally regretful one day? Stoking the flames with the letters he treasured as another man would a piece of gold. The thought made him reach for his bag, hand dipping inside to find the last letter she had sent to him. Weeks old and creased from multiple readings, he could have recited the lines from memory. It was the handwriting he wanted to see most, however, the strokes as sure and steady as the heart of the girl who penned them. Grasping it between his fingers, he let his eyes close briefly in prayer. *If You hear me, then guide the way of my heart. Show me how to be with Mariah, yet still abide with You. Whatever the cost, I will gladly pay it.*

A way must exist to forge the two paths of his heart together. Why else should he meet her, only to lose her to the pain of indecision? She could not have spared his life only to leave his heart in ruins. So he told himself, unfolding the sheet to study its contents with a hopeful eye.

Halfway through the first page, it happened. Crows, dozens of them, began to shriek in the woods across the river. In clouds of black, they rose from the rows of trees, startled by some unseen predator below.

A nervous murmur traveled through the field of soldiers.

Arthur stood, shielding his eyes against the glow of sunrise. One moment, he saw only foliage, and the water rippling with the tide. The next, a flash of light, the puff of smoke as musket fire exploded across the river.

He dove for his rifle and then for cover. Those around him did the same, the air thick with cursing as men scattered in every direction.

Some made it to the woods, others fell when they crossed into the open.

Arthur ducked inside a row of corn husks, his friend nowhere in sight.

The shaky youth in the next row was already reloading his weapon, powder spilling as he filled the barrel.

Arthur shot repeatedly across the water, chest tightening as he wondered how many lay in wait for them.

News of their coming must have leaked, perhaps days ago, giving time for the Union camp to bring reinforcements if they chose. Would a pack of troops sneak up behind?

The skin prickled on his neck, a sense of being hunted overtook him as he glanced wildly over his shoulder. Trees and bushes grew thick at roughly the perfect distance for another ambush. Possibilities crowded his mind, competing with the sounds of fighting that echoed around him. They could be surrounded in less than an hour, forced to run like animal prey or else be taken prisoner. Prisoners on their native soil. The idea scorched his blood, prompting him to hoist the musket for another shot. Only there wasn't time to pull the trigger. A blow from some invisible force hurled his body backwards into the dried grass. Harder than any punch a man could wield, it made his bones throb.

He saw blood pool on the ground beside him, realized it was his when the sting in his shoulder told him where the bullet had lodged. Shot. He'd never imagined the kind of pain it might bring even though he'd witnessed the screams of those whose flesh was torn apart by heated lead. Those men had moaned and writhed in agony on makeshift stretchers as they waited to meet the surgeon's awful tools.

Nausea overwhelmed him. Dropping his gun, he lay on his back, breaths coming short and shallow. Anything deeper tore cries of pain from his lungs, tears welling up in his eyes. He could feel his pulse thudding out of control, see the rays of sun blurring in and out of focus in the sky overhead.

"Stay calm," Mariah urged, pressing a cloth to the

bloody wound. "I will get you through this, just like the other times. I promise."

"It is not up to you," he babbled, too jarred by the pain to wonder how she came to be there, skirts arranged among a pile of dried corn husks. A trick of the mind, meant to distract him from the way his body contorted with pain every few seconds.

The imaginary Mariah was cradling his head now, stroking the hair in a soothing manner as she said, "You still believe that God controls your fate—that He sees you now, and makes a plan from what has taken place?"

"I don't know," he admitted. "It is too hard to think, to breathe. I can't—Mariah, I can't—"

"Sleep, then," she said.

And so he did.

છેબ

When he woke, the sun had changed position in the sky. Blood plastered his coat to his chest, the fabric stiff where his wound had staunched itself while he slept.

In the distance, gunfire echoed; the battle had moved further into the woods.

Whether his group had been the ones to pursue or retreat seemed unimportant at this moment, though he supposed all the advantage had been on the side of the Union forces this time.

Teeth gritted, he pulled himself to a sitting position. Clutching his wounded shoulder, he scanned the horizon for signs of life.

Bodies littered the field before him. Motionless, their mouths slack and eyes wide as flies buzzed over their sticky wounds. All wore the uniform of a private, no stars or bars to decorate the frayed collars on their coats.

A tawny-haired youth was face down in a patch of dried corn stalks. The familiar height and coloring made Arthur's hand shake as he gripped the lifeless head. He raised it to find the man was a soldier he'd spoken to all of twice since joining the army, a man whose discharge papers were being drawn up the last time he saw him.

Pulpy matter coated Arthur's hand where it touched them—the brains expelled from the stranger's head when a bullet passed through it. He stared dazedly at the mess and then wiped it on a clump of grass before dragging himself forward to the next figure sprawled in the grass.

All were men he'd seen around the campfire or among the lines they'd formed in battle. He left them where they lay, none breathing when he pressed an ear to their mouths.

No prayer or plea crossed his mind. His thoughts were numb compared to the ache in his bones, a strange dreamlike quality to his surroundings. The fact he was alone—and probably on the verge of death— seemed less important than his need for a drink to quench the parched feeling in his mouth.

The banks of the river loomed ahead, a series of objects scattered across the grass. Canteens and tin cups abandoned by their owners after the gunfire erupted. Rifles were propped on the shore, a homespun kepi hat tangled in a patch of weeds along the edge of the banks.

Desperately, Arthur lowered his mouth to the water only to jerk back again, gasping in terror.

Beneath his reflection, a group of faces looked back at him: bulging eyes and bloodied features, crimson seeping from the holes in their shabby uniforms. Men who waded into the river only to make it their grave.

He stared, shrinking from the soulless gaze of their eyes. Until he saw a pair of familiar green eyes, bronze-colored strands of hair scattered around them. A tattered frock coat and bare feet, a jaw marked with a light scar. Blindly, he reached for him, for Wray, beneath the water.

Water touched his face, flooding his nose and mouth as he quickly pulled back up. Still gagging, he fell on his side, pain jolting through his body as he rolled away from the shore, his wounded side pressed into the earth, he could move no further.

They found him in that same position later that day. The victors returning to care for their wounded and dead mistook Arthur for one of the latter. A murmur from his throat alerted the men who carried him that life yet remained. Barely, and for how long, was anyone's guess.

⤫⤬⤫

There is no room left in my heart for grief. It doesn't seem possible to feel such pain and still be alive, yet for three days in a row I have woken to this same corridor with breath in my lungs. What should happen to me if it finally ceases no longer seems as clear as it once did, and I feel much regret for those times we quarreled on this very subject.

I had no reason to doubt back then, no loss to grieve me the way you already did. How foolish I must have seemed to you, arguing from a boy's vast inexperience in the matters of death. Now, it is your forgiveness I must ask instead of the

God whose counsel I sought in vain."

Arthur wrote with a shaky hand, propped on his side in a bed at the hospital outside of Bridgeport. The candle flame wavered uncertainly on the table beside him, casting his writing into shadow every few seconds. It didn't break his concentration. His hand filled the page with a string of thoughts and feelings unchecked by any force.

He looked at the words, raw and bleeding on the page as any physical wound could be. Words too harsh for a lover's eyes, some might say, but there was little other choice for one in his position. It was either share his pain with someone who cared or else go mad waiting for death to come for him in this dank, smelly corridor.

They had given up on him, the doctors who practiced here. He was given supplies to treat his wound, a breakfast and supper tray left by his bedside as he slept. Too many others needed their attention, men who coughed in their sleep all night and bawled with pain as infected limbs were cut away by the surgeon's steel tools.

His haversack, along with all its contents, had been lost to the chaos of the battle. For stationary, he was forced to borrow off the patient in the next bed, a soldier whose jaw was partly removed when a Minié ball ricocheted off the tree beside him.

Believe me when I write that the hope of seeing you again is all that remains to comfort me. The doctors here have drawn up a furlough slip on my behalf, fearing this injury will leave me vulnerable to infection from others in this ward. It may be weeks before my commander receives it, but I intend to live however long it takes to make it back to you. We will meet again, Mariah, if only long enough to say good-bye.

18

Con unwrapped the bandage to find jagged scarring where the chisel had cut his hand. Flexing the fingers experimentally, he caught sight of the outline where his wedding band used to rest. The lines had grown faint, the ring itself stashed in a bedside drawer with a few other mementoes from the woman who gave it to him.

Three months. That was how long since he'd removed it, the biggest stride in a two-year grieving process. At times, he thought it would never end; other days—the last few even—he felt a glimmer of hope for something beyond the endless cycle of pain and regret.

A car's motor hummed in the distance. Miss Cade was late for their expedition, yet he wouldn't have minded a little more time before they were face to face. Tossing the bandage in the trash, he reached for his jacket.

What made him suggest this, anyway? The answer came as a flash of memory from their carving lesson. *That* had been a mistake, one inspired by the notion of Jenna looking him over, admiring his work with the stone.

Today, he would need to be more careful. No reason to take a moment of attraction and blow it out of proportion. Especially when she'd be leaving in a few days, and he'd be back in his workshop, fashioning memorials for people he'd never laid eyes on.

He grabbed a backpack and strode to the door.

Jenna had parked beside the gate and was already climbing from the car.

"I had a late night," she apologized, untangling a familiar knapsack from the passenger seat. She had stuffed her curls into a clip, small wisps escaping to brush her face. The flyaway look suited her, as did the frayed jeans and green jacket that set off her eyes.

"We've got plenty of time," he assured her. "Though I'm sort of wondering what you found to keep you up so late in Sylvan Spring."

"Love letters," she replied, pulling a coffee thermos from her knapsack. Seeing his raised brows, she added, "Someone else's. Apparently, the soldier was writing to the doctor during the war."

"But he married someone else," Con said, puzzling over the newest revelation.

"I'm hoping the rest of Dr. Moore's notes will shed some light on that." Unscrewing the thermos lid, she asked, "Want some? It's hazelnut, a little strong—"

He shook his head, but in truth, he liked the friendly gesture. Maybe that's what bothered him about it, since shying away from strangers was second nature these days. Which meant something about this one must be different, the connection strong enough to threaten firm habits.

Frost crunched beneath their shoes. The path to the Lesley homestead was overrun with weeds and brush, more so than he remembered from the last time he'd been there. He pulled back low hanging branches, the rocky terrain forcing him to take her arm at one point as they navigated a slope.

"Thanks," she said, brushing some twigs from her

jacket. "It's beautiful back here. Even untamed like this—or maybe that's what makes it so pretty."

"Not many people roam off the main path," he told her. "A few tourists interested in the spring or kids looking to get away from the town."

That was why he'd come there in his youth. Later years had been about the stone work or nature walks with Colleen. She would take cuttings from some of the wild plants, and then coax them to take root in her garden at home.

Right now, hardly anything bloomed among the fall landscape. He did notice the purple hue of violets sprouting beside a hollowed tree trunk.

Jenna saw them too, plucking one to inhale its scent. "I saw this shape carved into one of the old cemetery's headstones—the one belonging to the soldier's wife, I think. Do you know if it has a special meaning or anything?"

"Roughly a hundred." He smiled at the incredulous look this earned him. "Faithfulness, modesty, innocence—those are some of the common ones. There's always the possibility it was just her favorite flower," he added.

Twirling the stem between her fingers, she studied its delicate build. "You know," she began, "looking at so many headstones, learning the symbolism behind the designs...it makes me wonder what I would choose." She looked up, green eyes thoughtful. "It's weird, I know, but important, too. A last message to leave behind, kind of like the Celtic symbol was for these people. Only I'd want it to be something more hopeful than what they chose."

The topic shouldn't take him by surprise, considering the nature of his work. For some reason, though, he found himself uncertain how to reply as they continued down the path.

"You must have thought about it," she persisted. "Or at least have some idea what you want."

He shrugged. "I guess it crossed my mind a few times. My instructor carved his own headstone. He didn't want anyone saying the quality was inferior to ones he made for other people."

This gave her pause, eyes widening with the image.

"Don't worry," he said, a soft chuckle escaping. "I'm not thinking of adopting the same plan. Sawyer was more of an artist than I am with a whole legacy of stone carvers to defend. I have an easier time separating myself from the work."

Her lips formed a relived smile as she glanced his way. "You know, a few of the markers I found at previous sites were actually signed by the craftsmen who made them. When I traced them, it turned out their descendants had passed the trade down through the generations."

Con nudged a broken tree limb from the path, its wood grown spongy with decay. "Sawyer didn't have any children," he said. "Which is how I ended up inheriting his stonecutting tools." An irony, since the mason never quite trusted him with them in life. He had done his best to preserve them since, and to render the kind of work his mentor would have approved of in his begrudging way.

"It must have meant a lot to him," Jenna observed. "Having someone to carry on the skills he learned from his family. To keep his memory alive, so to speak." There was something wistful in her tone, and the gaze that quietly sought his.

"I think so. He wasn't the emotional type, but there was a sort of unspoken pride, at times. Hopefully, I can live up to his standards," he added, thinking the possibility was still years away in terms of his talent and experience.

By now, they could hear the flow of spring water somewhere nearby. Pointing up a steep incline, Con told her, "We're here. The Lesley homestead—or what remains of it, anyway."

A stone foundation and skeletal frame to a house that burned long ago. Big, forked trees and wild berry bushes; a pile of firewood some visitor must have left, since people often camped there without permission.

Before he could offer assistance, Jenna had scrambled ahead of him up the rocky path.

When he caught up to her, she was attaching a lens to a film camera.

The violet blossom was tucked in her hair, the rich purple like a jeweled clip. "My agent prefers digital pictures, but I try to include the old-fashioned kind, too," she explained, waving a battered-looking 35 millimeter. "It seems more appropriate, somehow, photographing history with vintage gear."

He couldn't help smiling a little at this idea, thinking it was typical of someone who stayed up half the night reading one hundred year old love letters, or spent the following day trudging through acres of wilderness in search of a few weathered monuments.

"The graves are towards the back of the property," he told her. Waiting for her to loop the camera strap over her neck, he led her to the small grove where three fieldstones were nestled among the leaves.

Time had been hard on the poorly carved tombs. Jenna crouched beside them, snapping pictures of one that was marked simply as *BLAIN, 16 YRS.* Photographing the other two, she asked, "When did the house burn?"

"Years ago, I think. No one was living in it, and a drought was causing some wildfires."

She nodded, carefully tracing the shape that was cut into one of the stones. "Dr. Moore mentioned the Lesley family among her patients. I suppose they were part of the epidemic."

"So that's what it means," he said, with a nod to the design. "All the stones with Celtic V-rods belong to fever victims?"

"Some of them do," she said. "But if the symbol was legendary enough, I suppose other people may have chosen it based on the stories they heard. With no dates on the graves, it's hard to know for sure."

They drifted towards the remains of the house, peering over the stone wall to see where a crawl space used to be. Bits of glass and pottery layered in the dirt gave off flashes of color in the morning light.

"I can't believe places like this are still abandoned," Jenna said. "There's so much potential, with the woods and the spring around it. Doesn't anyone else see that?"

He rested against the foundation, hands stuffed inside his coat pockets. "The county owns most of the land. Maybe they'll arrange for a campground or hiking trails at some point. Or a grave walk," he added, with a nod to the woods below.

"If the monuments are ever restored," she reminded him.

The words made him stiffen instinctively, waiting for her to push him to make it a special project. With anyone else, it would have been unbearable, but she had a way of making him question his deepest motivations. Including the ones he considered his only choice in his current state of mind. "The graveyard won't be forgotten anymore," he pointed out. "You've given it a better chance for preservation than most places here. Right now, the Lesley homestead is pretty much the only site from these woods people still recognize."

"Speaking of that," she said, digging through her bag, "I have something to show you."

She unfurled what seemed to be a scanned image from a map. The date 1876 was penciled in the corner, the layout showing the Sylvan Spring schoolhouse, church, post office, and other period buildings. It showed where the homesteads had been, the property owner's names inscribed by some of them. The Lesleys—which belonged to a new owner even then— was among those located by the spring, a gray squiggle representing the body of water.

"Here's the graveyard," Jenna said, indicating a piece of acreage called Crooked Wood Cemetery. "And over here," she said, running a finger to the south, "must be your property—the Darrow residence. Ever heard of them?"

He shook his head, dumbfounded by the map's detail. A brief glance revealed names that were still familiar to the region. The Strouds, whose descendant worked at the funeral home; a family called Girvin, whose distant relation ran the herb shop where Colleen had worked. There was also the Maudell house, proudly situated off the town square, its architecture still a testament to the early Victorian era.

"This says the soldier lived near town." He spotted the Widlow homestead beside that of the

Camdens. "I wonder why he's buried out here then."

"More answers I don't have," she said. "Yet."

Placing the map aside, he hoisted his backpack onto the wall. "I thought we could use some refreshments," he explained, taking out some fruits and crackers he'd packed that morning.

Jenna's face held surprise as he handed her a bottle of water. "You're better at this than I am," she said, uncapping the bottle. "Coffee was the first thing I thought of on my way here. Guess my city upbringing shows, huh?"

"Here and there, yes." He rolled an apple in his palm, conscious of the urge to flirt. To provoke the girl before him with some remark in hopes of earning a smile or touch, however brief. The realization brought warmth to his face, a warning he chose to ignore with his next comment. "You should consider bringing a guide for all your outdoor research. Someone who knows caffeine is just a way to zap your energy partway through the hike."

"I got through trails in three other states just fine, thanks." She grinned, peeling an orange to savor its tangy flavor. Gazing into the forest below, she asked, "Do you ever miss a different kind of atmosphere? I'm guessing this place was sort of a culture shock after your life in Kansas City."

"It was a hard adjustment. I didn't miss any particular place so much as the sense of belonging somewhere. In some ways, these woods are the closest I've come to that feeling anywhere I've been."

"But you don't feel the same about the town." Her fingers pulled apart slices of fruit, her expression thoughtful. "I can understand why, but it's a shame. They could learn something from your work and you…" Her voice faltered, the usual boldness disappearing. "I know it's none of my business, really. But you can't always plan to be disconnected from them. Every place has its faults. From what I've seen, Sylvan Spring is just a little random in its search for identity."

"See if you still feel the same after the festival," he joked, chewing a bite of apple before he added, "Unless, of course, you're leaving before then." The answer shouldn't matter. He wouldn't be there regardless of her plans, but for some reason his breath grew still waiting for her to speak.

"I have to attend," she said after a brief pause. "Publisher's orders and I confess a curiosity to see what it's all about." Chucking the orange peel into the weeds, she gave him an expectant look. "What next?"

He studied the map a moment. "Over here," he said, indicating a place that once belonged to someone called Roan. It was a name that must have gone the same way as the Darrows in the town's later years. "More fieldstones," he recalled. "It seems one of them had an epitaph."

"Let's go, then." She slid off the wall, stealing the map from his hands as she passed. "In case I decide to ditch my guide," she called, waving it playfully over her shoulder as she disappeared in a grove of fall colors.

❧

The shutter gave a faint click as Jenna took the picture. A twisted, barren oak was the focus, the middle part hollowed to resemble a gaping mouth.

"Watch where you step," Con advised. "There's a

few bigger roots under the leaves."

He had watched, amused perhaps, as she photographed some of the oddities tangled in the thorns and brush. Rusty old farm equipment and signposts; a crumbling chimney sunk into the ground where someone's residence used to stand.

"I think it's wilder in this part of the forest," she noted. Hugging herself, she glanced at the tree's branches overhead. Unlike the ones around it, the foliage was brown and shriveled, limbs like angry claws reaching for the sky. Standing in the shadows it cast, she could understand how people thought the woods were haunted so long ago.

"We should be getting close to the homestead site," Con promised, taking her arm as they passed through a narrow thicket.

This protective gesture made her skin tingle beneath the fabric that separated their touch. She hadn't expected him to be in such a helpful mood or to volunteer for this in the first place. Was it his love for the stonework that made him offer? The other possibility was that he wished to see her again. She shivered with the thought, unconsciously drawing closer to his arm.

"Are you cold?" he asked.

"I'm fine," she said, quickly relaxing her grip. She needed to be more careful, it seemed. Blood rushed to her face, making her suddenly thankful for the foliage that surrounded them.

Pushing past limber branches, they emerged to find a denser part of the forest. Spanish moss hung in long chains, its scaly leaves brushing their faces when they passed beneath its vines. Scattered beyond a fallen pine were a handful of grave markers fashioned from rocks of various shape and size.

She glimpsed primitive carvings that read *'BABY BOY'* and *'DEAR SIS'* on the smaller stones. Initials were all there was to commemorate the bones beneath two large ones, along with dates from the 1850s.

"Jenna, over here." He nodded to where a flat marker was encased in the earth. Rain water pooled around its edges.

Scratched into the surface was an epitaph, along with the moon and arrow symbol she'd come to know by heart. "Is there a death date?" she asked, coming to kneel beside him.

He frowned, running a hand over the faded carvings. "It's had more sun exposure than the others. I can only make out a few letters."

The marker seemed sturdy enough, its flat shape giving it a more grave-like appearance than the other fieldstones. Excited, she pulled out a blank sheet of paper and stretched it carefully across the surface. "Help me hold it," she told him, fingers brushing his when they moved to take her place. Her heart raced at the possibility of what lay beneath those fade marks, soon to be revealed before their gaze.

Working the crayon in a gentle sideways motion, she brought the meaning to the surface word by word. She could feel Con watching, her gaze meeting his briefly to find the same excitement mirrored there. The crudely cut letters took shape for a message of three lines: *Here lies Old Roan/Who lived alone/And died alone.*

"That's it?" She dropped the crayon with a frustrated sigh. No clue to when or how the man died, only that he wasn't very popular in life. Disappointed, she sat back as Con studied the epitaph with a faint smile.

"I was just thinking," he said. "What you asked earlier, about what I would put on my headstone. Something like this—" as he tapped the hermit's grave—"seems appropriate, don't you think?"

Her heart sank with the joke, thinking he had completely missed the point of their conversation. Stowing the gravestone rubbing among her other papers, she told him, "It was a serious question. One I thought a stonecutter might understand, but apparently not."

"Okay, then," he said. "What would you choose? You've clearly given it some thought."

Fair enough. Except that she hadn't found an answer those times she debated it while preserving someone else's words of remembrance. "I don't know," she admitted. She plucked the violet from her hair, absently fiddling with the petals as she talked. "So much of my time is spent researching about other people's lives. Who they loved, what they did…" She shrugged, glancing up at him. "It can make my life seem plain, sometimes. Empty, even." That was just a feeling, she knew; her faith should be strong enough to fill any void created by the lack of a human connection. At her loneliest, the pain couldn't be worse than Con's grief, something she realized with a rush of sympathy. "I'm not ungrateful," she began. "I have the job I want and a chance to do something that matters. When it comes to other stuff, people say it's impossible to miss something you never had —"

"People who already have it, usually." A wry smile broke across his features. Reaching over, he covered her hand with his, hesitant at first.

"I don't think you have to question whether you're doing something that matters," he told her. "Not when

Laura Briggs

you're giving a heritage back to places like this and the people who settled it."

"You really think that?" She couldn't help the skepticism that laced her tone, despite the way her heart fluttered from their contact.

"We're not so different," he said. "I can understand your reasons for tracing the cemetery. It makes me envy you a little, that sense of purpose."

Warmth traveled through her, from his words and the touch of his hand. Returning the gesture, she twined her fingers with his, seeing his eyes widen across from her. She was disappointed when he finally drew away, leaving her with only the flower she'd been holding before.

"Maybe I'm not the best person to be giving advice," Con said after a moment. "Still, that's how I see it." He climbed to his feet. "There's no graves at the other homestead sites, at least none I've heard about."

She could hear the catch in his voice, mimicking her heartbeat a moment before. "So this is it," she said, getting to her feet before he could offer a hand. If they touched again, she felt something might happen beyond the closeness they already shared. "You probably have work to do," she continued in a breathless tone, although she had been sitting. "I should drop by the historical society and finish reading the doctor's journal."

Understanding shone briefly in his face. With a nod to the other side of the woods, he said, "We can take a shortcut back, if you don't mind crossing the spring. The water's shallow this time of year, with plenty of rocks to make a path across."

"Sounds good," she said.

Leaving the violet on the hermit's grave, she

226

trailed after him down the path. Neither spoke. Jenna took up her camera to frame shots of an old smoke house that was partly collapsed. Its roof was gone, vines growing in the cracks between the bricks.

She peered into the depths of an old root cellar. Stone steps descended into murky darkness, the picture she took likely to be too dim when she developed the film later. Up ahead, her guide waited to see she was safe before moving into the clearing visible past a cluster of pines.

It was here the ground sloped to meet the clear flow of the spring. It wasn't as big as she imagined, the water receding with the change of the season. Jenna stood on the banks, camera scanning the horizon until it focused on Con.

He faced her, crouching to examine something among the bedrock in the shallow part of the water, hair tousled, eyes a rare shade of blue as they glanced up.

She pressed the shutter release, capturing the image. Then, without glancing away, she lowered the camera and moved towards him. Water splashed her shoes, mud coating where they touched the bottom of the spring. She was almost to him when a stone shifted beneath her feet. A sense of panic was followed by relief as he caught her, pulling her towards him before she could fall.

"Careful," he said, still holding onto her arm as they stood close together.

She looked up at him, seeing a question in the blue depths.

Con tilted his face to press their mouths together in a soft, searching kiss.

Leaning into it, Jenna threaded fingers through his

hair. Touch and taste collided with the memory of his hands guiding her to form a letter in smooth stone; arms that cradled her with the same warmth as now. Familiar senses blended with new ones in a way that made her head spin. "Wait." She pulled back to find her hands clutching his jacket, a few breaths all that passed before she closed the gap again to kiss him even deeper.

It was Con who broke the connection this time. He kept his hands on her shoulders, gaze filled with something between confusion and an apology.

Suddenly, Jenna was aware of the cold spring water seeping into her shoes and jeans. The fact her knapsack had escaped when she stumbled, and now floated against a big rock nearby.

"My bag," she said, finding her voice as she realized the danger to the papers and voice recorder inside. Her legs seemed frozen in place, feet numb as she watched it bob helplessly against the tide.

Con pulled it from the water, canvas muddy and dripping. Extending his other hand, he nodded to the embankment across from them. "Come on," he said.

They broke apart as soon as they reached dry ground.

Sitting on the leafy slope, Jenna removed damp papers from the bag and then checked her recorder with its hours of material.

"Everything OK?" Con hovered nearby, seeming uncertain whether he was welcome or not.

"I think so," she said, hearing a tremor in the words. "The recorder still works, which is the important part. The papers are a little damp, but seem all right otherwise."

"What about you?" he asked. An awkward cough

followed, as he admitted, "I've never kissed someone after knowing them less than a week."

"Neither have I," she said, looking at her shoes, which still bore the traces of spring water. "Gives a whole new meaning to getting your feet wet."

His laugh broke some of the tension. Sitting on the bank, he kept a noticeable distance between them. "That wasn't something I planned. It's not why I invited you here. It was an—an accident, sort of."

"I know," she said, aware that what happened was a culmination of events. The odd glance or touch; the fact she had been drawn to him from that first glimpse among the town's monuments and crypts. "I don't mind," she added. "What happened—it seemed like it was coming on for a while."

Instead of answering, he stared at his hands. She thought he was considering her words until she noticed the faint markings where a ring used to sit. A wedding band.

When he spoke, his voice was hoarse. "It's hard to explain. This feeling…being with you…" He glanced up, uncertainty in the look. "I haven't thought about something like that for a long time."

Jenna, having never felt that way before, had nothing to compare it with. She struggled for anything to reassure him when her thoughts were just as muddled. Finally, she pulled the knapsack across her shoulder. "We should probably head back now. If you're ready."

The walk back to the farmhouse seemed longer, neither of them saying much until they had reached the car.

Con leaned down to speak through the window. "Let me know how it turns out. If you find anything in the doctor's ledger."

"It's a long shot," she admitted, "but it's the only trail I have right now."

When he started to move away, she caught his sleeve. He stiffened slightly with the touch. "Thanks, by the way. For showing me the gravesites. I couldn't have found them, even with the map. "

He nodded, slowly easing away from the hand on his arm. "I just wish it had been more helpful," he said.

Had he meant it to sound like good-bye or had it been only a friendly gesture? His interest in the gravestones might depend solely on the way he felt about the woman researching them. For her, Con was never far from any thought she had about the wooded cemetery. Both were lost to the town's sight, hidden away in the acres of foliage and neglect.

19

The manager at the historical society saw her coming this time.

"Our Civil War fan returns," he said, fishing a set of keys from a basket on the desk. "I have your reading material right here, my dear. Though I can't imagine what's so interesting in a lot of remedies I recall from my granny's old cupboard. "

"You would be surprised," Jenna said, smiling as she thought of how such a pivotal part of the town's history could go unnoticed for so long. Especially when a whole festival was devoted to a legend no one could quite remember anymore. She took the ledger, aware she should feel excitement for whatever entries remained to be read. At the moment, though, she was having a difficult time concentrating on someone else's troubles.

Why had she kissed Con? A week ago, if someone told her she would do such an impulsive thing, she would say they were crazy. *What does it mean, Lord? I'm not sure it's possible to accidentally kiss someone, so there must a reason for it. I don't believe in fate, but Your Will is another matter.*

The idea that God had a hand in these feelings was one she hadn't considered yet. As much as she hoped there was a heart somewhere intended to be with hers, there was never any promise of it. This might be nothing more than an admiration for the work he did, the craft so closely tied to her ambitions.

And if she didn't see him again, it might not matter at all. A possibility she knew was likely, since her agent was eager to move her on to the next site. All the more reason to be concentrating on her research, a task she began by sliding the fragile text from its protective bag.

⩺⩹

November 14ᵗʰ 1862: They buried Charley Hinkle this morning in a plot of ground at the back of the cemetery. There was no coffin for the poor body and only a cloth to cover his small features. His mother wore no veil, and there were bits of foliage scattered inside the grave by his brothers and sisters.

I cannot help feeling responsible for this boy's death. No one cast an accusing eye in my direction, however. Instead, there was much agreement that God had called him home for some hidden purpose that will not be revealed until the final resurrection. I cannot rest so easy with such an explanation, and lose sleep to studying my father's textbooks for a deeper understanding of the illness that took him.

Still, no word comes from Bridgeport. How much longer must I wait to hear from A.?

The smell of grief hung thick in the air: walnut oil, boiled over an open flame for dyeing garments the color of mourning. Mariah knew Mrs. Hinkle had done this for Charley's funeral, soaking her Sunday best in the steaming brew. Its pungent odor carried for miles on the wind to mingle with that of dye pots in other communities—places where women had already learned of loved ones lost to the fighting in Bridgeport.

Sylvan Spring had yet to receive any real news of that event, either by letter or word of mouth.

Mariah was among those who waited in painful suspense each day for the post to arrive, only to glance through its contents with a sinking heart. She saw her anxious feelings mirrored quietly in faces on the street and in those of the blacksmith's family, whose son Henry had not written since the battle took place.

"Give us patience, Lord," the blacksmith prayed at mealtime, his weary tone implying he had little of it left. His tablemates would spoon dutifully at their stew or crumble bits of cornbread on a plate, eyes turned away from each other's worried expressions. Talk was of the weather, the crops—anything but what really occupied their minds it seemed.

Her next visit to Mrs. Tate found the patient poring over a newspaper. "Says here there were dozens killed and more than that injured," she said, holding it out for the doctor to see with panicked eyes. "The hospital outside Bridgeport's overflowed with the hurt, and private homes is taking the ones with no place to go."

Such rumors made focusing on her work nearly impossible, though she had more of it than ever to keep her busy. Mrs. Tate gave birth to a healthy son, and the Stroud household requested medicines for fever and stomach troubles.

The Lesleys were sick. Dying, if she were to be honest. The wife could no longer rise from her bed, the son and husband carrying on the chores, despite their own difficulties.

"Is there no one to help you—no girl from the town to see to the meals or laundry, even?" Mariah wondered, dabbing the woman's forehead with a damp cloth.

"We help ourselves," came the stubborn, but honest response. Her presence was necessary only for delivering medicine; she found, the door remained shut tight against her knocking at any other time.

November 16th ,1862: Rumor has surfaced of a foul smell in parts of Crooked Wood, and there is much fear of contaminated air. It is certainly a possibility, though I believe a contagion is proving more and more likely. It is bad news either way, and soon there will be no denying the state of the outbreak upon us. I can only prepare my medicine cabinet for all who may need it and hope that others will take their duties as seriously where action is demanded.

Two days after Charley Hinkle's burial, the schoolhouse was closed.

Mariah had known this might happen from the moment she signed the boy's death certificate. She didn't anticipate it happening so soon, since most towns denied an epidemic as long as possible for the sake of their businesses. In the case of Sylvan Spring, there was no other choice: the teacher herself had caught the illness.

The children found her half-curled beside her desk, retching into a bucket used for cleaning the stove ashes. That was the chore she had been performing when the attack came upon her, hands and face streaked from where she'd touched her cheeks in an attempt to push the stray hairs from around her face.

Coming beside her with the satchel of medical supplies, Mariah ordered the frightened students outside. "Someone bring me a little water before you leave and something to dip it with."

This task was met by a tall girl with a crown of braids, who accidentally sloshed liquid out of the bowl as she handed it to Mariah. Her eyes, wide with fear, were fixed on the teacher, who clutched her abdomen in pain. Without a word, the girl turned and joined the other students, who filed quickly out the door.

"You should not have done that," the teacher scolded, half-sitting with a grimace. "The rowdy ones will feel the liberty to go home now. No duty for their lessons, these farm boys."

Mariah shook her head, observing the red rash that crept above the woman's dress collar. "There will be no more lessons today, I am afraid," she told her, easing water past the chapped lips. The woman drank it down, sputtered a little as she covered her mouth. Her hand was lined with veins, the skin pale and thin.

She offered Mariah a frown that might have frightened a pupil. In a tone equally stern, she told her, "I shall rest a spell, perhaps. There is no reason I cannot sit down while I teach, however."

"You have the look of a fever about you," Mariah replied, "and such an illness requires rest and quiet for the body to mend itself. The children will be safer at home," she added, thinking of the contagious diseases she'd read of in her father's medical journals. She couldn't be sure this one would pass from human contact, but risking it seemed unwise.

"The Hinkle boy," the woman realized. "I heard there was fever upon him that night. Others, too. The Kendrick woman and Mrs. Lesley. Her son's been kept home all week to do the chores—" She broke off in a coughing fit, the frail body threatening to collapse against the pine boards.

Mariah took hold of her arm, carefully wrapped it

around her shoulders before staggering to an upright position. They stood that way a moment, both recovering their breath before the doctor half-carried the older woman to a curtained-off portion beyond the rows of desks.

There, a small cot stood against the wall, books piled on a knee-high table beside it. A plain dresser and wash basin were the only other furnishings Mariah noticed as she lowered the woman onto the makeshift bed.

"Do you have more blankets?" she wondered, moving towards the battered dresser with its years of use.

There was a Bible laid on top and a handkerchief with flowers embroidered around the edges. The initials A.M. stitched in the corner suggested it came from the teacher's handiwork, perhaps in her younger years.

"Leave it be," the woman replied. Propping herself on one elbow, she fixed Mariah with a determined stare. "I will not be needing your help now. It was the children who fetched you, not me. I won't pay you, so you best be on your way."

"I have many who cannot pay for their medicines," Mariah assured her, tugging on a set of brass handles to reveal a drawer full of winter clothes and fabric. "If I helped only those who could afford it, there would be no point in my being here."

She pulled a shawl free from the pile of fabric, moth-eaten wool that smelled of musty storage.

The teacher gave a laugh that might have been a shudder passing between her lips. "It is not a matter of payment—if I could afford your care I still wouldn't call on it. No God-fearing woman relies on the work of a heathen to keep her from the grave. "

Mariah froze, arms hugging the shawl before the dresser. Turning slowly around, she forced her voice to come out steady despite the anger shaking through her. "My work can pose no harm to your religion," she said. "No more than the apothecary who practiced here before me. It is an act of charity to care for one's neighbor—does your Bible not say the same?"

The woman sighed, gaze roaming the plain walls. "Perhaps you mean well," she admitted, "but your medicine could not save the boy. Perhaps nothing could have—it might be the sickness is a punishment for some wrongdoing. Many a reverend's preached it that way, and I have seen it myself when those who knew better strayed from His Will."

The words—strange enough in themselves—had a rambling quality that made her worry the fever had taken over the woman's reason. Bringing the shawl, she started to drape it across the thin shoulders, only to feel a hand clamp around her arm.

"We may have called down His judgment," the teacher confided, gaze latching onto Mariah's with unnerving force. "Called down a punishment for sending the men to hunt their fellow Christians like wild game. There must be payment for such a mistake." Fretful, agitated—the woman was mixed up in her thoughts beneath the grip of illness.

Mariah realized this, even as she wavered beneath the sound of bitter regret. As the town schoolteacher, Miss Mitchell would have seen the local soldiers grow from boyhood, their hearts and minds bearing some part of her instruction. Talk of the skirmish had probably left her rattled, the same as everyone else.

"Surely no punishment is greater than this war,"

Mariah suggested, easing free of the woman's grasp. Arranging the shawl around Miss Mitchell's frail form, she added, "We have all suffered terrible loss in its wake. Further sacrifice could hardly be demanded from any fair Creator."

The eyes watching her narrowed in response. "What does an unbeliever know of sacrifice? Those who never enter a church or seek any power outside their own." As she spoke, pain contorted her features. Her hands clenched at the bedspread, her face turning quickly towards the wall. "I can look after myself now," she said. "Tell the children what has happened, and send them home."

Mariah hesitated, reluctant to leave one so clearly in need of help, despite the harsh words between them. If she left some medicine, perhaps the woman would take it once the pain became unbearable. She started to fumble with the latch on her bag and then reconsidered as the woman's gaze drifted back in her direction. Pride and pleading were buried beneath its surface, telling her the gesture would be taken as an insult. She ducked past the curtain, fabric swinging back in place to hide the sight of the figure huddled on the cot.

Outside, the number of students had dwindled as the teacher predicted, with only a handful of curious girls gathered on the playground to hear the outcome of the morning's excitement.

"Miss Mitchell is ill," Mariah said, stepping onto the path in front of them. "She will not be able to teach you for some days. You must tell your parents about this, and tell them as well if you began to feel any sickness yourself." When no one spoke, she continued. "You may go home now. It will be your parents' decision to decide what to do about your lessons next."

The classmates looked at each other, one girl elbowing her companion with a secretive glance. They began to giggle in a nervous way, others close to them picking up on the joke with barely concealed smiles.

"What is it?" Mariah spoke sharply, annoyed by this reaction to the teacher's misfortune.

After their classmate's death, she had supposed the subject would hold a new kind of terror for them. Instead, the faces below her were almost gleeful somehow.

"What makes you laugh?" she demanded, this time with obvious anger for the quiet mirth.

The girl with the crown braid who had fetched the water earlier, now avoided eye contact with Mariah and stretched a hand to point silently to Mariah's feet.

There, in the dust of the schoolyard, someone had traced an inverted half-moon, its shape stabbed through with a broken arrow. The same as the one painted on the building's front door. Attempts to scrub the symbol from the wood planks had made the dye streak, a bleeding effect against the whitewash.

Mariah's gaze moved slowly from one image to the other. Heat rose to her face, mouth forming a thin line as she stood there. After a moment, she lifted her boot and erased the pattern from the dirt with a swift motion. "Go home," she told the children who gawked in silence now.

They obeyed without a word, some of them linking arms as they moved past the closed-up building.

With a last glance to the symbol on the door, Mariah hitched her bag higher on her shoulder and walked the opposite direction down the path through the woods.

20

November 18th 1862: Mrs. Lesley and her son died two days apart and were buried in the grove behind their cabin. The poor husband continues to lie in a stupor, and I suspect it will not be long before he joins his family in that final rest. There is no fight in him, and any chance of improvement seems to have vanished with the loss of his wife and child.

Six new cases of fever since closing the school, two of which are children. Talk runs as wild as the fear among our neighbors, and I can say nothing to turn its course. Perhaps some speck of light will shine from the darkness, a gleam of hope to dispel this talk of divine punishment and superstition.

Ending the drought of battlefield communication was a letter from the Darrow's son. Written on a torn sheet of stationary, it contained but five lines explaining he was unharmed and on the move again, his plan being to write a more detailed account of what had passed once the company settled into its winter quarters.

This was enough to send tears of joy streaming from Mrs. Darrow's eyes, the family's members embracing each other as Mariah smiled faintly from the stairs. On her way to another house call, she had paused to hear the long-awaited contents of the envelope from Bridgeport.

Unlike the Darrows, the tears in her eyes had

nothing to do with the letter's author—she knew him only as the blacksmith's son and the true owner of the room she occupied upstairs. It was Arthur she had hoped to hear of. The thought of learning his fate explained her held breath while Nell read the scant details of the fighting along the river.

Rain pelted the windows, the gloom outside less noticeable to the family with their newfound cheer. Only young Nell showed a hint of wistfulness in re-reading her brother's message, as if expecting to see something more scrawled inside the paper's margins.

Mariah couldn't miss the desperate way the girl eyed the mail over the next few days. Stealing a quick glance at the postmark on every envelope, never touching them as she did so. But all that came were more messages from town requesting medicine for stomach cramps or fever, a paregoric to soothe a baby's cough.

The doctor delivered these medicines on foot, rain dripping off the brim of a man's hat pulled close around her curls. Her boots let the water in, feet chaffing in a way that had her limping by every afternoon. She took a rest by the fireplace whenever one was offered, a cup of tea or drink of water from those who shook free of their worry long enough to summon basic hospitality.

Nell watched her come and go, at one point saddling her father's horse and leading it out to her in the muddy yard. "Take Fergus for your other deliveries, or even let me go for you instead," she urged. "You can't help others if you run yourself ragged."

This was true—more so than Mariah wished to let on. She couldn't accept the offer for practical reasons.

The horse was likely to have trouble navigating the steep paths she traveled through Crooked Wood. "I cannot take him where I'm going," she explained, handing the reins back to the disappointed girl. "Although," she said, sliding her hand inside her satchel, "if you like—it would help me greatly if you could deliver this parcel."

As she spoke, she removed a small box from her satchel, the name of Widlow written across its brown paper. Inside was a jar of liniment for the woman's rheumatism, the kind supplied to her in years before by the town apothecary.

Understanding passed over the girl's face when she saw the name scrawled on the package. "I'll take it right away," she said, mounting the horse she'd already saddled, a light kick sending the stallion trotting in the direction of town. When she returned later that evening, she handed the doctor a few coins from the patient, lingering in the doorway to tell her, "There was no news. I asked the Widlows if they heard anything, but they get no letters, they say."

Surprised, Mariah had dropped the coins in the jar on her desk before she answered, "Thank you. For taking the package, I mean." She leaned back over her work, aware that Nell watched her a moment longer before retreating to the hall.

Part of her felt guilty for ignoring this small gesture of trust. If she confided in anyone about her worries for Arthur, it should be the one who shared her devotion for him. She knew of the girl's feelings for Arthur—not those of a friend, but those of love, shared for a heart that could belong to only one of them. There was no resentment in her glance, only a quiet need to shoulder some of the pain that threatened to take him from both their lives forever.

After a while, they fell into a pattern, with Nell dispensing medicines to homes within riding distance, and to those who complained of something other than a fever. Nell took her duty to heart, riding through storms, and sometimes staying to boil medicinal teas for the ailing from her grandmother's supply of herbs. Often, she finished her work as late as the doctor herself, their suppers taken in the kitchen hours after the rest of the household had gone to bed.

"I took Mrs. Tate the calamus for her baby's colic today. She read me part of a letter her husband sent from the battlefield." Nell spoke these words softly over a plate of cold beans and bread. An oil lamp burned low in the middle of the table, casting her expression into shadow. Her voice was enough to betray what she felt, threatening to break as she said, "He wrote that Mrs. Camden's son was killed in the skirmish. That he helped to bury him, and that he heard that others from Sylvan Spring were badly hurt."

There was no other news.

Nell's hands trembled as she took a long sip of the tea Granny Clare had brewed for them in her daily quest to be of help to the younger women.

Mariah left her own cup untouched, silverware set aside with the clink of metal against ceramic.

November 19th 1862: Mrs. Tate and her baby continue to do well, and concern continues on my part for the schoolteacher, Miss Mitchell. I hear she does no better, and all aid on my part is adamantly declined.

Black smoke billows from the farms and fields, like storm clouds on the horizon. It comes from the bonfires lit every morning in hopes of purging the air of whatever disease stalks us. There is little I can say for this plan, except that it shows no effect on the illness and poses a threat to those who are careless in their movements.

The girl with the crown of braids was how Mariah recognized the patient who was ushered hurriedly into the Darrow's parlor. Tall for her eleven years of age, Annie Cray was one of five daughters born to a farming family who lived a mile north of the schoolhouse. Her skirt was singed, her hands red with blisters where they tried to smother the flames from one of the bonfires.

"We soaked them in the spring," her mother fretted, turning her small hands over for the doctor's inspection. "Look how they weep, though, how red they've grown. I've got no wrapping at the house, nothing to bind them with—"

"Let me tend them with some lard," Mariah said. She led the girl to a chair by the desk, where she had to push against reluctant shoulders to make her sit down. Fright and distrust covered the girl's features, with no sign of that curious smile she wore that day at the schoolyard.

Mrs. Cray sat in a chair by the hearth, where the blacksmith's wife and mother tried their best to calm her nerves with a cup of tea.

Nell was not with them, having gone to the dry goods store to barter for a jug of molasses for the upcoming holidays. She had met the Crays on the road, though, and seeing the mother was almost frantic with worry, had given them her horse to ride back to the house.

"Such a scare it was," their guest sighed, stroking her porcelain cup with worried fingers. "To hear her scream that way, as if she were dying—she could have, you know. My sister's youngest burned to death when his coat sparked from the hearth—"

"Do not think of it," Granny Clare soothed, hand reaching to pat her arm from the chair beside her. "She's safe now and won't be likely to venture so close again. There's only the blisters to show for it, and those will fade in time."

Mariah doubted this last part, but said nothing as she smeared lard into the badly-damaged skin. The motion brought to mind a flash of imagery from the letters she read at night: Arthur dressing the wounds of a soldier caught in a wildfire, feeling the breath leave their body as he cradled it on the hard ground.

She wiped her hands on her apron and then reached inside her satchel for a roll of cotton dressing. Beginning to unwind it, she said, "You will need to apply the lard twice a day until the skin is healed. The bandages will keep an infection from getting in, so you must see that they're tightly wound, and try to keep them dry."

Her patient gave no answer and seemed not to realize she'd even spoke.

"Annie?" She frowned, searching the pale features across from her. "Do you hear what I say? Your hands will need—"

"Listen." The child spoke in a whisper, head inclined to the figures seated by the hearth. "They're talking of the sickness and whether it's a curse for some kind of wrong doing."

Confused, Mariah tilted her head in the same direction. She caught their murmurs, soft and serious, the sound of the girl's mother saying, "…and she told me how she'd only seen the symbol on graves before, and that it wasn't natural to paint it on a door that way. She said no child would do such a thing of its own mind. She knew a great deal of children, Miss Mitchell, though she had none of her own, bless her."

The schoolgirl drew a sharp breath at the mention of her teacher, who was now interred beneath the cemetery's cold ground as the latest victim of the unknown sickness.

Gently, the doctor began to wrap the bandage around one of Annie's hands. She was about to repeat her instructions for the lard as a means of distracting her from the other's talk, when Granny Clare's voice joined the conversation across the room.

"My papa used to say, 'Dunna look for evil, less you look for death.' Not often a churchgoing man," she said with a soft chuckle, "but one with an eye for the signs of trouble." The woman's Scottish brogue seemed thicker than usual, perhaps strengthened by the nature of her memories. With a sigh, she told them, "He could find trouble in the cry of the owl, my papa could. He knew when a storm was coming by the color of the sky, and what the crops would yield by the changes in the moon."

"What of the plat-eye, then?" Mrs. Darrow wondered, sewing forgotten on her lap in the course of their speculation. "There was more than one saw it on the road before all this come about. Might be it was a harbinger for our troubles, if the old folks' ways are to be believed."

"My husband seen it," Annie's mother agreed, setting her teacup down on the worn table. "A great one for seeing things, he is. Likes to tell of his boyhood in Bowmore where he came upon the *bean nighe* washing a coat in the stream. He saw the coat was the same as his granddad's and knew it meant the man would die soon—and so he did, not a week later. "

"The washerwoman." A soft clucking sound escaped Granny Clare's tongue. "That's what they called her in my village, and what a fear I had of seeing her. A hag's face, all spotted and gray, her long hair all tangled in knots." She leaned forward as she talked, eyes straining as if searching for the same picture that formed inside her head. "The washer woman was only to be found beside a deserted stream, they said, and wailing her sad song as she scrubbed the burial clothes of some poor soul. It was said the garments she washed belonged to soldiers who would die in battle, and that's why they were stained with blood."

Mariah heard a slight gasp and felt the half-bandaged hand twist in her grasp. It was only then she realized how tight she'd been holding it. Muttering an apology, she began to wrap it again, face turned away from the hearth, though her ears continued to strain for the sound of the women's conversation.

"I suppose…yes, I'm sure I've heard that tale before." Mrs. Darrow spoke in a halting manner, no doubt thinking of her son. His recent escape in battle made no promise of future safety, and the image of uniforms soaked in blood must seem a harbinger of doom in its own right. She gave a faint laugh. "I learned the story myself from a man who worked alongside my father at the docks. He smoked a ceramic pipe, great puffs clouding the air when he talked of the old ways. The faerie, and the *bean nighe*, which he said was the spirit of a woman that died giving birth. All old Scottish tales, they were."

Her audience waited as she took up her mending again, a needle passing through the cloak she held with quiet precision. Her gaze was fixed on it when she spoke again, perhaps seeing the bloodstained shroud of the washerwoman in the threads she stitched slowly back together. "The way he told it," she recalled, "to see the washer woman meant only two things: that the garment she washed belonged to one who would soon die, and that if you saw her washing it, the garment belonged to *you*."

☍

Mariah plunged her hands into the washbasin, dark clouds rising to meet the surface. Frozen, she watched her reflection in the grimy water. Hair escaping its pins, eyes made puffy by sleeplessness. A mouth that seemed pinched and drawn as a woman twice her age. The image wavered and then broke apart as she pulled strips of fabric to the surface and wrung them out.

Salvaged from an old work dress of Nell's, they would serve as cold cloths and makeshift bandages in the doctor's scant supplies.

She draped them over the backs of kitchen chairs, water dripping from hands that were chapped from bathing so many fevered brows the past week. Ten women, six men, eight children. That was how many people she knew for certain were infected by the disease.

There were others, of course. Those who requested medicine but not the presence of the physician, and those who never called on her at all, who chose instead to rely on remedies from their own cupboard. If their suffering took a turn for the worse, she would know it by the sight of fresh dirt mounded in the wooded cemetery when she stood with other mourners around an open grave or saw the long hills and rough gravestones in the yards of a neighboring homestead as she passed by.

Poring over her father's text books yielded nothing but sleepless nights. She found herself drafting letters to every apothecary within fifty miles, asking for news of a fever outbreak among their communities. It would be weeks before she got a response, if any ever did come, and by then it might be too late.

Whole towns had been wiped out from epidemics. She knew this from newspaper clippings in her father's old study, the stories sent to him by colleagues who witnessed such events. One place in Georgia had boasted more than a hundred in its population before a wave of cholera left just four families to rebuild the ruins.

Sylvan Spring had fifty households at best. How quickly disease might spread in such a place and what disaster it might leave in its wake, left her breathless with worry. Her medical supplies were limited, the shipment from Mobile perhaps a month from arriving. Alternative means would have to be found, the reason she took to the garden one morning, Granny Clare close to her side.

"For aiding the stomach," the woman told her, piling sprigs of yarrow beside her on the ground. "Used by my mama in the old village for the babies' colic. More times than naught, it soothed their cries."

"I will try it," Mariah promised, binding the stems together with a piece of thread.

The gnarled hands searched the dirt for the right plants. The woman identified most through smell, occasionally touching a leaf to her tongue when doubtful. Her eyes bore a calm Mariah could only wonder at, the mind behind them as sharp as her own.

There were herbs for digestion and dysentery, for coughs and fevers.

Mariah gathered them all, pounding each beneath a mortar and pestle with a frantic rhythm that matched the pace of her thoughts. Funneled into paper packets, they served as teas for patients who could keep nothing else down. A few went into her pocket, slipped into her evening brew while the food on her plate went mostly untouched.

November 21st 1862: Where a cure cannot be found, the means to comfort becomes key. That is what I tell myself as more cases began to slip beyond my influence. Some improve for reasons I cannot explain, while others given the same course of treatment take a violent turn for the worse. It is terrible to watch the suffering of those who are ill and know their fate depends on chance more than anything. I will not abandon my search for the cause of this outbreak and must hope there is strength enough left in me to find it.

"Are you all right, Miss Moore?"

Geneva Kendrick studied the doctor with concern from her seat on the parlor's worn settee. She had answered the door herself, well enough now to receive visitors in the parlor instead of her bed chamber. The fever had left her, and only a slight weariness haunted the youthful features to recall what had happened.

The patient did not see the same promise in Mariah's appearance, however. "You look so pale," she told her. "Let me pour you another cup of tea. It has done me such good, especially the one made from ginger root."

"I am fine," Mariah assured her. Her voice wasn't very convincing, she knew, strained from the coughing that kept her awake at night. She was able to control it during the day, but the cold air in her bedroom made it impossible to fight the weakness dragging her down.

"You must take care of yourself," the younger girl urged. "It does no good to tax your strength this way. Your friend spoke of it yesterday—how you rest but a few hours each day and seldom eat anything."

"My friend." Mariah's brow wrinkled, struggling to imagine who she meant. The only one she could think of was miles away on a battlefield, where letters came few and far between to those who waited at home.

"The blacksmith's daughter," Geneva explained. "She came here yesterday to see how I did and to bring some of the tea from her grandmother's garden."

"Miss Darrow has been a great help to me," the doctor answered, realizing how true it was as she spoke. Nell's heart lent itself naturally to the task of healing, with patients trusting her more than they would an outsider, something Mariah was still considered to be, despite living among them for so long now.

"She spoke so hopefully of our predicament," Geneva continued, "that I began to be hopeful myself. It was different from what everyone else says. About the curse, I mean."

"What is it they say?" The words came out funny, slurred almost. She raised the cup to her mouth, attempting to disguise the sudden lapse.

Fortunately, the farmer's wife was more concerned with how to answer, her fingers playing nervously with one of the threads on her shawl. "It is idle talk," she said, winding and unwinding the same thread as she continued, "They are saying—and I do not believe it—that the houses with the Celtic mark are ones belonging to people who will die of the fever. That the symbol is a—a kind of prophecy, placed there by a spirit...or devil...that brings the sickness." She glanced down, cheeks coloring as she added, "That is why I have gotten better, they say. Because there was no mark put on our door that night."

Mariah could not speak, mouth open from disbelief. The stories of washerwomen and plat-eyes seemed nothing compared to such cruel speculation. Those who believed in it might simply lose heart to fight the illness, sealing their own fate through superstition.

Geneva assured her, "I pay no mind to what they say. If anyone mentions it before me, I am quick to tell them that Miss Moore's skill is responsible for my being well again."

"Thank you." She set her tea cup back on the table, sloshing a little into the saucer. "I have been thinking," she began, "that considering the circumstances—and how often we have spoken these past weeks—you might...well, you might call me Mariah. If you still wish it."

The girl's eyes brightened with the suggestion. "Yes, of course." With a surprised laugh, she added, "Mariah. It is a pretty name."

"From my mother's aunt," she remembered. "A midwife in their small community. So it was a fitting choice, in a way."

"Doctoring seems to run in your blood." Her young patient smiled. "My father was a clergyman, as was my grandfather. I should wish very much to have guidance from either of them now." Her face grew wistful with the thought.

Mariah hesitated before she spoke. "My father—he left his wisdom to me in the form of text books and writings from his medical career. Your father, I am sure, would advise you to look to the same book he trained from as a clergyman." *How can you say such a thing?* She scolded inwardly for recommending a path she had never followed herself.

It seemed to comfort the girl, though, her mood improving as she talked again of her family's livelihood, the church in Jefferson County she regarded as a second home.

When Mariah's tea had grown cold, she took up her bag for making another house call.

The Stroud residence had three members battling the disease inside its walls, one of them suffering from a high fever.

No tea was offered at this place, the mistress of the house far too frazzled. She did press a jar of preserves into her hand, saying, "For the herbs, and the liniment you gave me father last month. I've not forgotten it. You see, I had nothing to give in return at the time."

Walking home, the sight of smoke climbing above the treetops told her that others continued to stoke the bonfires for purging the air. Bits of ash floated down, coating her hair and clothes as she tried to brush them away. Absorbed in this, she failed to notice the shape that loomed before her in the path.

Charley Hinkle's dog, its coat matted with burrs. She half-feared the animal sensed some predator lurking in the foliage around her, given the speed of its approach. But he passed her without a glance, bounding over the low wall that ran alongside the wooded burial ground.

Without slowing, the dog made its way to the north side of the yard, where mounded dirt showed the most recent burials from the plague. Lying beside one of only two headstones planted in the section, he crossed his paws and took up guard.

Mariah came beside him, knowing already what name would be inscribed on the tomb. Directly above, chiseled where none could miss seeing it, was a shape that made her throat tighten: the half-moon and broken arrow of the ancient Celts.

An omen of death for this community's ancestors, eerily precise in its predictions.

"This is not right," she said, voice emerging shakily from her lips. "You deserve a better remembrance than this, Charley."

The dog's ears pricked up at the sound of its former owner's name. Releasing a low whine, it nudged Mariah's hand in a plea for sympathy.

She stroked the fur, rough and tangled with no one to care if its burrs were removed anymore. "Poor Charley," she murmured, still looking at the grave marker. "I am sorry—so sorry that I couldn't—" The rest of her apology was lost as coughing filled her lungs. Struggling for breath, she braced her hands against the stone, feeling its cold exterior. Her gaze landed hazily on the symbol carved along the top as panicked thoughts flew through her head. She closed her eyes to block out the sight of it while she gradually calmed again and waited for the moment to pass.

21

The envelope was postmarked November 8th, its return address from a hospital near Bridgeport.

Mariah tore the flap open, ignoring those who brushed past her to the post office door. A single sheet of stationary was tucked inside, its front and back filled with handwriting she knew as well as her own. The words, however, might as well have come from a stranger, her lips forming each one soundlessly only to part in shock the further she read.

My faith is gone, Arthur confided at one point, *hidden from me in this madness that colors my every thought. Sleeping or waking, a field of death stretches always before me, the memory of smoke and blood and water. It is the water I wish to forget the most, along with the faces swallowed to its murky depths.*

I can feel the river choking their lungs, the heavy weight dragging their chests. The doctors say it is because the injury has weakened my lungs, but I feel as if this sensation will never again leave me. Neither will the memory of seeing one I loved as a brother—one who did more for me than any real brother could have been expected to do—curled alongside the others at the bottom of that muddy grave.

His features, so admired by all who knew him in life, are swollen and mottled. By now, the decay of the grave is claiming him, beneath waves instead of earth. Eyes empty of their former depth stare at nothing, turned away even from the light above. What light is there for those of us who grieve here below?

The Scripture that used to give me comfort seems hollow now, and the promise of heavenly reunion no match for the pain I feel day after day in this wretched place. My one hope—the only reason I'm alive, perhaps—is the thought of seeing you again, Mariah. I will be with you soon as may be possible in this terrible world. I cling to the belief that this letter will not be long in preceding that happy moment, if there is any way that such happiness can be.

She stared at the lines, re-reading the final paragraphs as if seeking to erase the despair in them. One of her hands clutched the porch banister for support, the other trembling as it held the paper with its painful lines.

Arthur was wounded—dying for all she knew. Broken in body and soul, his one hope the possibility of coming back to her, to the life they knew in his boyhood home. A home he wouldn't recognize if he saw it now, smoke rising in clouds of gray, the doors and windows of its homesteads shut tight against the omen of death.

Would he be safe here? The risk of infection seemed greater even than that of a hospital ward. She wanted to warn him from it even as she wanted to care for him with her own two hands. She had saved his life once before, but the thought of facing such a task again amidst everything she was already struggling with seemed overwhelming.

Lost in thought, her feet moved without direction. The street was nearly deserted, the few people who passed her giving just a brief nod in greeting. Some glanced with curiosity at the piece of mail she held, but the fear of infection was too strong these days for anyone to linger in the street for gossip.

Up ahead, the sharp *ping!* of the blacksmith's hammer told her another headstone was being readied. She wondered how many would bear that awful mark still painted across the town's doorways in crimson hue. A children's prank turned almost to prophecy, the hands that placed it there no doubt shaking with fear somewhere by now, if not stilled by the same illness that took so many others.

A woman, gray-haired and heavyset, was drawing water from the well into wooden buckets. She cast a sideways glance as the doctor grew closer, a frown lining her aged features.

Mariah's steps wavered as she passed the aged figure, glancing back at the woman for reasons she couldn't explain. Cart wheels clattered from a nearby lane. She staggered to the side as the breeze from its motion fanned her skirt. Someone shouted at her—the blacksmith, possibly—but their voice was more like a pounding inside her head.

Dizzy, she continued on, hand reaching for a hitching post when she began to sway. Her fingers missed, barely scraping the wood surface as she lost her balance, hands pressing soft, cool earth as she fell helpless to the ground.

છ૦કૃ

Someone was reading aloud from the Psalms. A voice thin and girlish, but not that of her mother's, as Mariah first imagined in her sleep-fogged state.

Instead, it was Nell Darrow who occupied the chair beside the doctor's bed. She stopped reading mid-Scripture as the figure before her began to stir. "Thank goodness," she said. "I've been worried. Your color looks so poor, and you slept so restless, talking under your breath."

Mariah didn't answer, pulling herself up slowly from the stack of pillows. She remembered now, being helped to the house, her arm slung around the blacksmith's shoulder. The family had laid her on top of the covers, wrapping her in a shawl for warmth against the growing chill. On the table beside her, a candle was lit, the light of day fading behind the muslin curtains.

"How long have I been this way?" she asked.

"Three hours," the girl replied, shutting the heavy Bible she had taken from Mariah's shelf. "Papa said you must be worn out from traveling so many miles these past days."

"Yes," she agreed, knowing this was only partly true. "There is a tiredness on me. It must have been too much, the extra miles I walked today."

Had the girl noticed the rash that crept just above her dress collar? She pulled the shawl closer around her, saying, "I should be able to care for myself now. Please tell your father I'm grateful for his help. It was only exhaustion, as he said, and shouldn't trouble me again if I rest."

"Yes, of course." Hesitating a moment, the younger woman pulled an envelope from beneath the book in her lap. "You dropped this—when you fell," she said, a blush spreading over her cheeks. "I hope that nothing in it was the cause for your fainting."

The way she bit her lip in quiet suspense told Mariah that she hadn't read its contents. Such restraint deserved no small amount of admiration and trust, considering her obvious devotion to the man who penned the words. She must have been in terrible suspense, having the news of his fate right before her, yet unable to grasp it without another's permission.

Taking it from her, Mariah stroked the paper gently between her fingers. "He's been wounded," she told her. "Shot during the skirmish a few weeks ago. Now, he writes the doctors' fear he may catch an infection from the other patients—" Her voice broke, her gaze lifting to meet Nell's eyes, already wide with fear. Swallowing, Mariah cleared her throat to regain some of her control. "I'm afraid for him," she said. "Afraid he may die there or even if he does come home, that I won't be able to help him."

Across from her, Nell's face had turned pale. Her hands trembled against the leather volume she still held, lips opened for a long time before any words came out. "Thank you for telling me," she said, at last. "Now I can pray for him with more understanding of the danger he faces. He's always been strong of faith."

Mariah shook her head. "Even that has been taken from him. The things he's seen...there's little to give him faith, he says. I don't blame him for thinking so," she added, bitterness lacing the tone.

"Neither do I," said Nell with surprising bluntness. "Although," she added in a gentler tone, "I hope it is only a temporary doubt that makes him feel this way. Perhaps he will come through this with a faith stronger than before."

She had not read the letter, of course. Mariah supposed her naivety was partly due to her youth, as well as her relative inexperience with life's hardships. "You can't understand," she told her. "He's seen men torn apart by artillery's blaze. Consumed by wildfires and waters deep. There's no healing for such a grief."

Across from her, Nell's gaze drifted down to the book in her hands. "I can understand a little. What happened to poor Charley, when he died..." She paused, voice faltering with the memory.

Neither of them had spoken of that night before, avoiding the subject for both their sakes. Now the doctor realized how terrifying it must have been for a girl who admitted to never witnessing a death before. A child's death, then, must have been especially shocking to behold.

"I had never seen anyone suffer that way," Nell continued, fingers stroking the Bible absently. "He was so desperate and scared. His hands reached out like they were trying to grasp the air and pull it inside him." Tears escaped her eyes. "I can only imagine how much worse the memory is that haunts Arthur's thoughts," she said. "It will take him a while—months perhaps—before he can feel the Savior's hand guiding him again."

"What makes you think he ever will?" Mariah wondered. "There is so much death and pain—even we've seen it around us for days now. How do you explain God's presence in all this? If He hears your pleas, He doesn't answer them."

"I think He provided for us in different ways. One way in particular." Looking up again, she said, "No one believed we would find a doctor—not a place this poor. Yet our need was met by one in equal want of a helping hand. He led us to you that day, something I believe this crisis proves more than ever."

"You think God uses *me* to accomplish His work?" Mariah laughed, breath threatening to turn into a cough. "An unbeliever to save the believing," she murmured. "That is not something I expected to hear from a person of your kind of faith."

The girl nodded, hand reaching to grasp Mariah's on the bedspread. "He must have known this trial would come to us and made sure we found the right person to see us through it. There was a reason He sent you to us, and I think it was for your sake as well as ours. There's a plan for you in this, I'm sure of it." When Mariah said nothing, Nell closed the Bible and set it on the bedside table. "You should take some water," she advised, studying the doctor with concern. "Or some tea. Let me bring some from the kitchen—"

"This will do fine," Mariah replied, indicating the half-empty tumbler on the bedside table. "I won't be taking any supper tonight but will try and rest instead. If anyone calls to see me or asks for medicine, you may come and wake me."

The girl rose and went to the door. Pausing, she turned and said, "Call out to me if you start feeling poorly. I'll be awake for several hours more in case any of our neighbors should need my help." She waited.

Mariah nodded.

Nell slipped out, shutting the door behind her.

Mariah stayed seated on the bed, the letter clasped between her hands. Its words came back to her with a heavy feeling, the weight in her chest growing the same as Arthur described in his own misery. Reaching to the bedside table, she found the vial of medicine she'd been dosing herself with these last few days. The bitter smell drifted from its depths when she uncorked it, bringing to mind the image of another sick chamber long ago. For this reason, she drank its dose as quickly as possible, coughing some of it back onto her sleeve. The vial was returned to the table, where it clinked softly against the tumbler. Beside them, placed there by Nell during their conversation, was the worn Bible.

The feel of its coarse leather inspired memories of a different sort from her childhood. She pulled it slowly into her lap, rustling the pages, as she thought of nights spent looking through it with her mother in the house where she grew up. "This is my greatest possession," her mother had told her. "Not the book itself, but the faith it stands for. I have it with me always, right here," she said, rocking the child in her arms closer to press their hand over the place where her heart beat.

Confusion wrinkled the young Mariah's brow as she studied the verses she couldn't yet read. "I thought faith was a feeling," she said, tracing the letters with a stubby finger. "You can't use feelings for anything real—can't make medicine with them," she added, thinking of her father's supply of vials and powders in the room below.

"Faith is stronger than any medicine," her mother said. "If we put our faith in God, He can use it to do anything. He can save people who are lost to all else."

Mariah frowned. "But Papa saves people, not God. I've seen him do it lots of times."

Sighing, her mother pressed a kiss to the braided hair. "Your papa helps many people," she agreed, "but his kind of medicine only makes them better for a little while. God's kind of healing lasts forever. It takes away the power of death by writing our names in the Book of Life."

"Your name's in this book," Mariah cried, eager to show off some of the only words she'd learned to recognize in her new school lessons. Flipping to the Bible's first page, she looked for the familiar name among the list of ancestral signatures. That of Jemima Harriet Moore came near the bottom, the most recent of the family to inherit the Holy volume. "See?" she said, jabbing excitedly at the signature. "Here's your name."

"Yes." Jemima laughed, squeezing her daughter affectionately. "My name is in this book, too—so is yours, and one day, your children's names will be there as well. An earthly sign of our devotion to the One who makes a place for us above."

They would read that way for many a night, until her mother could read no more. In her final weeks, her lips had struggled to form even a smile for Mariah, who sat at her bedside. Her mother's mind went somewhere else, concentrated on the pain that racked her body at all times.

Grown-up Mariah opened the volume's cover, seeing the same name inscribed there on the page, a little faded and smudged with the passage of time. She touched it, trailing fingers over her mother's handwriting, loops that dipped and curved in elegant formation.

Tears welled in her eyes, body trembling as she lowered her forehead to meet the words on the page. Her breath came harsh and loud against it, her words only a murmur. "Please..." she trailed off, struggling for more, some faint connection between her and this God who gave her mother such hope. "If You hear me...if You care at all—" She let out a sob, regaining her voice enough to say, "I need You to help me; show me what to do. There is nothing left to me, nowhere to turn. Please hear me, Lord. Tell me what I should do."

Exhaustion overtook her as she lay beside the open volume. Her thoughts grew faint and incoherent beneath the medicine's effect until at last she fell into a restless sort of sleep.

～～

Water, deep and wide, stretched away from her to an embankment surrounded by trees. It wasn't the spring in Crooked Wood, though, or any other place she'd been before in her life. A river stained murky green, cold and vast. Mariah stood in it up to her knees, shivering through her work dress and shawl.

She wasn't alone. Something rippled the water. A figure hunkered on the shore across from her. Gray hair straggled in long locks to curtain the face, a thick, squat form that was dressed in tattered garments. Their hands were submerged in the river, rising to the surface to wring out a soiled garment.

Crimson dotted the water, traveling in different directions like tentacles. She watched as a streak came towards her, winding snake-like through the water.

Slowly, the woman on shore raised her head, revealing a face of deep crevices, warts, and pock marks, eyes sad but wild-looking, when she glanced into the river's depths.

Mariah followed her gaze, saw plants crawling and dirt clouding beneath her pale reflection. A blink, and her features gave way to those of a stranger. A man, eyes bulging and face swollen as he looked up from the bottom of the river. There were more around him, their features puffy and turning blue. Bloodstained coats, brass buttons catching the light above. As if pulled by her gaze, they turned upwards, stiff fingers reaching blindly towards the surface.

A silent scream filled her throat. She shrank from

them, or tried to, but the water had risen to her waist without her even noticing. In a heartbeat, it rose to her shoulders, cold and slimy as it splashed her skin. She was stuck, frozen in place as the dead moved closer, closer, almost touching her as the waves came up to her chin—

Gasping, Mariah came awake, her body racked with hoarse coughs.

The candle on the table had burned down its wick, the growing daybreak her only source of light as it seeped through closed curtains. She sat up, fumbling for the medicine vial on the bedside table. Instead, her hand struck the tumbler in its haste, knocking the half-filled glass to shatter against the pine floor.

Mariah leaned past the side of the bed, watching as water trickled into the cracks between the boards. Water...yes, she had dreamed of water.

A river of death, ghostly figures in rotting gray uniforms.

The washerwoman crouched on the shore to prepare their burial garb, staining the water red.

Water. That was important—but why? She felt thirsty, her mouth parched, yet something else tugged her thoughts, like a word just out of reach from her tongue.

She pushed her hands through tangled hair, sweaty strands catching on her frustrated fingers, body rocking back and forth, as if willing the memory to push to the forefront of her thoughts. Her gaze fell on the open Bible, still turned to the page that bore her mother's handwriting.

The prayer she'd said hours ago came back to her, parts of it tangled up with the memory of her dream. This was her answer, perhaps, a sign that death had come for her, the same as it did her mother years ago. For Charley and the Lesleys, the teacher and others. The soldiers perished in a muddy grave at the cornfield, their life choked from the blood and water that stirred around them.

"The water," she mumbled, body ceasing to rock. "Water…yes, *water*. It must be—"

She sat forward, hand covering her mouth to hold back the wracking coughs. An idea was forming as if rising from the depths of her consciousness. Her gaze flitted to the stain on the floor, and then the desk piled with papers in the corner. She needed to write it down, capture the notion before another stupor came over her.

With a groan, Mariah pulled herself from the bed. Bare feet avoiding shards of glass, she stumbled the few feet to the desk, clutching the back of the chair as nausea swept over her. Her eyes closed briefly in a silent plea, trembling limbs easing her slowly into the chair's seat.

Shoving aside the stack of textbooks, she let them drop to the floor with a loud thud. Her hands scattered papers in every direction until she unearthed the daybook and pen she used for making her medical entries. Flipping to the first blank page, she pressed her quill against the paper, writing in a shaky script that barely resembled her own.

Perhaps the fever has already claimed my thoughts. I suppose it is possible, yet this feeling in me is so strong, I dare not ignore it. It is almost as if God had reached into the heart of my memory and plucked from it the very thought I searched for these many weeks. I cannot recall the name of the man or the medical journal which published his essay, but I have read before of a doctor's work in England where cholera outbreaks—

Pain stabbed through her. Her insides were being wrenched, twisted by an unseen hand. Crying out, Mariah dropped the pen, her knees hitting the floor alongside it. Her legs were too weak to stand, fingers scrabbling helplessly at the desk's edge. She tried to reach the daybook and pull it off, pleading for help under her breath when it proved impossible.

Exhausted, she leaned against the desk, eyes sinking closed. She was so close, just a sentence or two away from forming the answer she so desperately needed. Unless this was all a dream, a fevered imagining from a dying woman's brain.

How long she lay there she didn't know, her thoughts rambling from a prayer to the memory of sitting with her mother in the childhood nursery. A grown girl, years later in her father's study, surrounded by conversation and men's pipe smoke. Downstairs in the Darrow's parlor, Arthur's voice soft in her ear while his arms clasped tight around her waist.

These murmurs in her head gradually gave way to another voice, one calling from somewhere nearby. Mariah lifted her head, eyes struggling to open at the sound of the door hinges creaking. Footsteps pounded the floorboards, a woman's shape kneeling beside her to lift her weight.

"It's all right," Nell assured her, face gazing down with gentle concern. "Don't try to rise. Let me help you."

"Please," she said, voice a rasp in her throat. She needed to tell her, to let her know what had happened.

But her speech was as scattered as her thoughts, the other girl already shushing her attempts to explain. In another moment, she found herself returned to the sick bed, a shawl wrapped around her shoulders.

The daybook, with its unfinished thought, was left behind on the desk.

22

"That was it," Jenna said. "No explanation, no way to find out what happened next. Just that she knew of a medical case that resembled the town's illness. She wrote nothing else afterwards."

She sighed, frustrated as she balanced the tea cup in its saucer. Across from her, Josephine Maudell listened intently to the account of the doctor's struggle. Her great-great-grandfather's sweetheart, whose battle against the plague had proved as deadly as the combat Arthur and his fellow soldiers faced a hundred miles away.

"I never knew there was someone who had an answer for that supposed plague," Josephine said, gray head shaking in disbelief. "Those stories about the sickness had always seemed a lot of foolish superstition. Exaggerating the past and whatnot. To think, all those people were really dying that way— and most of it forgotten, until you took an interest."

They were sitting in a room that might have served as the Maudell's formal parlor at one time. The furniture had all been draped in sheets, except for the wingback chairs the hostess and her guest occupied, and a coffee table that held a silver tea service.

Josephine wore a dress that came from another era as well, with spread skirts and a high-necked collar that was pinned with a brooch. "I want you to find out what happened," she said, leaning forward in a motion that threatened to spill her tea. Placing it on the table with trembling hands, she insisted, "The past deserves its respect, something most around here don't know how to pay. You do, though. I can see that now." She ran a hand across the wrinkled mouth, smearing the dab of lipstick painted there. "Yes," she said, "the story must be finished. Then our ancestors will be remembered as they should. With the truth of what happened to them in those dark days."

A stab of anxiety went through Jenna with the woman's excitement, knowing she would have to crush it with her next words. "I don't know where to start," she admitted. "The courthouse fire took everything that might have recorded the doctor's findings. Death certificates, newspapers—all those things burned with the rest of the archives."

Triumph flickered briefly in the woman's gaze, shoulders straightening as she said, "My collection is far superior to anything the courthouse might have had. If there's a document of importance to the town's history, there will be a copy of it somewhere in my things. I made sure of that much when I still had a mind as sharp as yours." A chuckle accompanied this, Josephine raising her cup again for a thoughtful sip. "I have a doctor's visit tomorrow—bothersome, but it has to be done. We can start the day after that. The attic is the most likely place, though I kept a few things in my husband's study. Bless him, he didn't understand my hobby, but he never spoke against it."

"You would let me see your history collection?" Jenna was floored. She had assumed her presence was seen as a threat to the woman's territory, one tolerated only because of the compliment it paid to her ancestor's war service.

The lines softened in Josephine's face. "I believe you, of anyone I've known, could appreciate it. *You* know the past isn't dead," she insisted, "and isn't just a ghost story for parading around once a year. That's why I can show you what I've saved, because you understand how much it means."

Jenna nodded, eyes watering with the gesture of trust.

The woman's nurse seemed equally excited, penciling the date onto a calendar space next to the doctor's appointment. "All that stuff just sitting up there gathering dust," she said, "and now it's finally found its use. Mrs. Maudell's been hid away with it for so long, I can see it'll be a good change for her, too."

Jenna smiled, but the comment made her think of something else. The forgotten cemetery and Con, whose workshop was almost as hard to find amidst the wilderness landscape. Would it make a difference to him if she could discover the full meaning behind the stones? Somehow, she felt that it would, even though he'd never really said as much.

❧

Sage tumbled over the sides of the landscape boxes, vivid blue flowers that were destined to wither after the first hard freeze. Con ladled mulch out of a bucket, winterizing plants with a mixture of sawdust and wood chips. Less hearty varieties were potted for a season indoors, or else clipped to a stub and covered with a protective layer of soil.

He'd grown used to this after two winters of being the sole caretaker for the small herb garden. At times, it was almost therapeutic, more so than visiting a gravesite or staring at pictures that only skimmed the surface of the woman he knew.

This place had been rooted with Colleen's touch, imparting its scent to her skin and hair. He could breathe those memories without even trying, feeling for a while as if she kneeled beside him in the soft earth. When he couldn't pray—or wouldn't, as he knew was the case—the crushed fragrance of those same herbs gave him a sense of calm for sorting his thoughts and emotions.

Only it wasn't helping now as he faced the aftermath of that moment at the spring. He had not meant for it to happen, of that much he was certain. What surprised him was that he had *wanted* it to happen.

Closing his eyes, he felt again the touch of Jenna's hand. Her lips moving against his in kisses long and deep. The sense of not wanting to let go, even as he pulled back from the warmth of her arms.

Was it guilt that made him question it? A fear of somehow lessening his memories of Colleen by letting himself get close to another woman, perhaps. He had never pictured himself loving anyone as much as his wife, but then, it wasn't a theory he had ever put to the test before.

"When it's time, you move on, whether you want to or not."

Advice he once heard Mr. Sawyer give to a customer who was also a friend. The older stone carver had never remarried, of course, making Con wonder at the time how he could speak with such certainty. Not realizing until he was in the same position that "moving on" could mean anything from throwing out her junk mail to changing the message on the answering machine to just his own voice.

He reached for a pair of pruning shears by the fence, hand brushing one of the faded markers that rested there. These were headstones he was hired to duplicate, their original materials a kind that couldn't be recycled by the quarry. He had kept them, feeling it would be a shame for their beauty to be cast away unnoticed because of their damage. Scrubbing away the names from each surface, he had let them retire as garden ornaments, where visitors cast a wary eye until they noticed the sign above the workshop.

Jenna had looked at them differently, he noticed, with an eye for the details still faintly visible beneath the layers of rust. It was the same way she looked at him: past the rough exterior to the part she felt was still capable of making a difference. She thought he would help to bring the wooded cemetery out of the shadows, even though he was almost as forgotten as the crumbling stones.

A half-smile tugged his mouth for how optimistic she was, thinking answers could be found to mysteries other people gave up on years ago. That was her job, of course, but it seemed to be part of her nature as well.

Tonight she would be at the same place as almost everyone else in town: the *Ye Old Hallowed Days Festival*. Her camera in hand, no doubt, capturing the spectacle her research was supposed to change. Although, she had yet to find anything he could see standing up to the town's oldest legend.

Using the shears, he pruned the damaged vines of a rosemary plant until only the healthy parts remained. If he could do the same for his life, then maybe he wouldn't feel so helpless facing these changes. He would be able to see the reason he was drawn to Jenna, whether it was real or simply born out of loneliness for what he used to have.

Maybe it's not you who should do the pruning. His conscience was right; that Someone else was far better at recognizing his worst doubts and how to fix them. The same One stood by him when a call from the hospital shattered his life. Who gave him the promise of seeing his loved one again, in a place where death and pain had no power?

Already on his knees, he let his head bow, hands planted firmly against the soil. *You know what's on my mind, the questions I have. There's so many things I don't understand about this, least of all what I should do about it. Since You're the only One who knows where it's going, I'm asking You to lead me there. Tell me where to go from here.*

23

Jenna moved through the festival, snapping pictures with her camera. The whole downtown had been transformed to house a collection of booths and tents that featured a wide array of artisans. Music makers, craftsmen, cookery—it was all there, with a fireworks display scheduled to close the evening's entertainment.

Tying it all together was a strong sense of Celtic and Scottish folklore, particularly those related to All Hallow's Eve. Jenna felt her brows arch at the sight of women telling fortunes off a customer's lock of hair.

Another one predicted the gender of unborn babies while dangling a wedding band over the mother-to-be's open palm. "A girl," she cried as it swung in a circle over the beaming customer's hand. Back-and-forth motion signaled a boy, while a pause between different ones told of twins or possibly even future births.

Children in paper masks ran laughing as they scurried between displays of seller's wares.

Jenna stopped where a crowd had gathered to watch a silver-haired craftsman hollow out faces in gourds and turnips with a paring knife. Fiendish eyes appeared beneath the motion of his blade, a laughing mouth already cut below. The Celtic version of the pumpkin Jack o' Lantern.

Some that were finished had been lit with candles on the shelves behind him, ghoulish expressions and otherworldly scenes shining in the night with intricate detail.

"Makes it look easy, doesn't he?" Con was standing beside her, dressed in jeans and a white button-down shirt, the sleeves rolled almost to his elbows. Nodding to the lantern carver, he said, "It's not so different from stone carving, or woodworking when you think about it. We're all cut from the same cloth."

She stared, not realizing until now how much she had hoped he might show up.

He made it clear more than once that the festival wasn't in his plans. What had changed his mind?

"I didn't think you would come," she said at last.

"Neither did I." His expression grew somewhat awkward, a hand ruffling his dark hair. "I've, uh, been doing a lot of things I can't explain lately." There was no mistaking the meaning behind the words.

Jenna toyed with her camera strap, flustered with the recollection of their kiss just a day ago. It had been on her mind several times since then, a flash of emotion that came over her when she didn't expect it. To cover her nerves, she snapped a picture of the finished lantern, the craftsman holding it up while his audience applauded.

"You have a request?" he asked, scanning the faces around the booth. "Goblins, ghosts, witches—they're all within my reach, and more, besides." Suggestions were tossed out. The man took up his knife to carve a banshee's screaming face this time.

Jenna watched for a while and then drifted through the aisle again, Con falling in step beside her.

"You know," he said, "the lanterns were used for warding off spirits. If you put one in the window on Halloween, the dead won't cross the doorway."

"Then I wouldn't use one," she teased back, "because if the dead really could return—which they can't—I'd want to get their story. Then people could learn from their mistakes and experiences."

He smiled, a subtle turn of the mouth she felt was just a hint of the real emotion inside. At times, she would glimpse it, this part of him kept hidden beneath the serious demeanor. The reason his neighbors labeled him a recluse, perhaps.

They walked on, passing a band of musicians who coaxed ancient tones from pipes and drums.

She aimed her camera towards the spot where a woman in old-fashioned garb demonstrated the art of making corn husk dolls.

Con spoke. "Did you find anything? The other day you mentioned something about the doctor's notebook. I thought maybe it shed more light on the grave's connection with the plague."

"Yes—but not exactly," she admitted. "There was a problem with the end. Notably, that it didn't have one. At least not in that particular book." Forgetting they were part of a crowded festival, she began recounting the details of the doctor's final entries.

He raised his brows at the mention of the symbol as a prophecy mark and the doctor's speculation that she might know the cause of the dreaded plague.

With a laugh, Jenna's narrative ceased. "Sorry," she said. "That was probably more detail than you were looking for. I get carried away when someone asks me a question, since most people don't find dusty old manuscripts all that interesting."

"I can't see anyone not being interested in what you just told me." A trace of warmth was buried in the gravelly tones. "Whether you find the answer or not, I think your readers will care about those stories as much as you do."

"Really?" She wished she could know that for certain. It was the town's reaction she worried about most and whether they would accept anything but absolute proof that their legend was just that—a legend and nothing more. "As far as answers go," she said, "I may be closer to finding one than I hoped. Mrs. Maudell has agreed to let me see her famous stash of relics. In fact, I think she's more excited about the idea than I am, that the true story behind the legend has just been lying somewhere, forgotten."

He looked somewhat doubtful on this point. "Josephine's always been fairly protective of anything to do with the town's history," he said. "A lot of her stuff was on loan to the museum when it burned. It's made her hesitate to trust anyone else with it. People say she'll change her will and leave it to the historical society someday, although she doesn't think the younger generation looks after the collection properly."

"Maybe she's tired of keeping her distance," Jenna suggested. "The urge to share what she knows with others must still be there somewhere, deep down."

Con didn't say anything, his face angled away from hers in the glow of the clear lights.

From another part of the square, someone recited the lyrics to Robert Herrick's poem "The Hag", while a costumed figure pranced through the aisles, scaring children with their fake crooked nose and long nails. A fiddler had joined in with the pipes and drums, and cider was ladled into cups for eager customers outside a vendor's stand.

"Aren't you cold?" Jenna wondered, noticing the casual look that suited him, if not for the dropping temperatures.

He glanced down, as if forgetting he wore no extra layer over the long-sleeved shirt. Shrugging as he said, "My coats take a beating that doesn't exactly suit them for public appearances. Too many afternoons in the workshop or the garden. That's where I spent most of yesterday actually, winterizing the plants."

His wife's herb collection. The idea struck her as one he wouldn't want to talk about, based on their previous conversations.

"I think I'm starting to get the hang of it. At least, some of the plants bloomed this time instead of shriveling on the vine. Even the wildflowers looked better, so I'm making progress somewhere."

"I have a ficus tree in my living room," she said. "My neighbor waters it for me while I'm gone, but I think it prefers full-time company. I notice it perks up when I'm dictating a manuscript or playing the stereo..." She trailed off beneath his intent look, realizing how empty it made her home life sound. "I guess there's a lot of quiet to fill when I'm not on the road," she admitted. "Most of my friends juggle family with work, and my parents are a bus ride away in Annapolis. Which isn't a bad thing, really, since it helps me look to church for a sense of belonging."

"You're not one for subtle hints, are you?"

There was a gleam of humor in the remark, prompting Jenna to push it a little further. "Do you think you'll ever go back?" she asked. "Seek out any relationships with people again? Faith has been a comfort, you said. It could only help, having encouragement from others who share the walk."

"Well, I came to the festival, which didn't seem possible. I guess anything could happen, given enough time."

She stuffed her hands in her jacket pockets, wishing they were somewhere a little more private. It was hard to stay focused amidst the sights and sounds of Halloween mischief and old Celtic symbols.

But then, hadn't the same proved true of their wilderness hike? She kept returning to that moment, unable to shake the strong attraction that drew her towards him. Perhaps the same was true of his feelings, explaining why they found themselves in the same place tonight.

They turned the corner, Jenna letting out a cry of recognition for one of the artifacts displayed outside the historical society's booth. A coat and trousers dyed the color of ash, its wool fabric badly moth-eaten. "It's the soldier's uniform," she explained. "Mrs. Maudell said it would be here." She drew closer, studying the garment she had examined with such reverence at the woman's house.

The case reflected her image beside Con's, their hands almost touching as the crowd who went by pushed them closer together. "Thanks for being here," she said, her glance finding his in the glass. "I know you hate all this, with the crowds and the silly superstitions..."

"I don't hate it. There's a lot about it I would change, maybe, but other aspects have value. The sense of tradition, the craftsmanship. The knowledge of the past."

"Is that why you came?" She held her breath,

regretting the question. When he didn't answer, she started to apologize, only to feel a hand folding itself gently around hers.

"I'm sorry," he said, blue eyes seeking her gaze, this time face-to-face. "I might be a little rusty at this."

Warmth trickled through her from the unexpected touch. She smiled. "Me, too."

No other words seemed necessary, their fingers locked together as they moved slowly back into the crowd. *How can I feel so close to someone I just met?* She bit her lip, worried that her heart was getting ahead of her in the way her expectations did for certain projects. In this case, the two were linked, making it even more difficult to know how she should handle it.

"Have your palm read," called a woman in a tattered cloak and gray wig. "Learn your fortune in life and love," she said, with a small wink in Con's direction.

He merely smiled, pulling Jenna's hand towards another path. Their steps took them to a booth where lush, green plants spilled from hanging baskets and potted containers of all sizes. Behind the counter was the woman from the herb shop—Amelia, as her name tag reminded Jenna.

She wore a puzzled smile at the sight of their approach. "Well, this is a surprise," she said, nodding to Con. "I guess strange things *do* occur at Halloween. I haven't seen you at one of these events since…well, high school, at least."

"That long?" Jenna couldn't help the surprise in her voice. She had assumed he stopped attending it for the same reason as everything else. His wife's death apparently had nothing to do with this particular aversion for the town's celebration.

Leaning against the desk, he let his fingers slide free of her grasp. "I think training with Mr. Sawyer took some of the fun out of it for me," he said. "It made me see a lot of things differently—more seriously—and then I just never went back to how it was before."

"What about now?" the herbalist teased, nudging his arm. "Have you changed your mind about this town, or are you just being polite enough to show a guest around?"

The sound of a phone ringing cut off whatever reply he might've chosen to give.

Thinking it was her agent, Jenna reached for her knapsack, only to see Con pulling a phone from his pocket.

His gaze held an apology. "It's a local number— probably someone needing a headstone shipped or some onsite carving at the cemetery. I'll be right back."

She nodded, watching him stroll towards an open space beyond the noise of the vendor's booths.

Amelia followed her gaze, giving a small cough before she said, "So, you and Con. Are you seeing each other then?"

The question caught her off guard, even though she'd been holding his hand just a minute before. "Well, we only just met," she said, fumbling for a truthful answer. "I'm not sure it could be that serious yet."

"Of course—that was really nosy of me." The woman gave a hearty laugh, pulling a tray of plants from beneath the register. "I only asked because I've never seen him out with anyone. That, and he never came to the festival, even when it was Colleen helping me run the booth."

Jenna felt her eyes widen with this piece of

information. "Then he never does this sort of thing?" she asked. "Not even a dinner or two out?" It was something she should have guessed on her own, even though it made their sudden attachment seem all the more implausible.

"I never heard of him being with anyone," Amelia said, "but then, I didn't see him as much after he stopped coming to church or into town for anything other than a sack of groceries, for that matter."

Had he made an exception for her out of loneliness? The idea popped into her mind uninvited, poking holes in the romantic feelings she indulged earlier. Others quickly joined it, Jenna frowning as she tugged absently at the cross around her neck.

Amelia was busy with a customer by now, explaining the medicinal benefits of various herbs. A long line had formed by the time Con returned, looking distracted as he took Jenna by the shoulder to guide her to a quieter spot.

She wanted to ask him if he was sure about this—about anything related to the two of them. But there was no time, as he shared what had called him away those last few minutes.

"Jenna," he began, "the customer who called is one of Mrs. Maudell's relatives. They phoned because…well, Josephine passed away."

She gasped, a hand covering her mouth. "What? When? I just saw her," she said, trying to grasp the news. "Just yesterday we talked—"

"It happened this afternoon," he explained. "Apparently, her doctor noticed something was off in their visit this morning. He ran some tests and it turned out there was some bleeding in her brain. Jenna, I'm sorry—"

Tears engulfed her, escaping to run down her face. "I can't believe this," she said. "We were just getting to know each other. She was finally ready to do something for the town, to play her own part in its history."

It was too late for the answers or for anything else. The collection Josephine had been so proud of would probably be split among her different relatives, most of it to be sold or donated if they didn't share her interest. The uniform, the letters—all these things connected to the town's history would be lost to this place, along with the memory of the woman who had preserved them.

Jenna couldn't help the sobs that shook her. Strangers passed by, glancing their way. She covered her face, blocking out the sight of the festivities as Con wrapped a soothing arm around her.

24

Fireworks crackled on the night air, vibrant shades of blue and green winked out in a trail of sparks. Away from the cheering festival crowds, Jenna and Con rested against the stone wall at the corner. In the distance, the tall house with its pillars could be seen, the windows darkened.

"She was so eager to see her life's work finally realized in some way," Jenna said. "All that history she worked so hard to save...now it's too late." Her tears had finished drying earlier.

Con walked beside her in a silence that spoke more comfort than reassurance would have.

There was nothing to say, after all. She had failed, her best chance of finishing the town's story lost along with the wisdom of the soldier's descendant.

"I feel as if I let her down," she said, turning to face him beneath the glow of street lamps. "I wanted to find the truth for her as much as anyone. As a tribute to the history she tried to preserve."

"You could still do it," he pointed out. "Not for Josephine, but everyone else with family in the cemetery. She would want that. It would keep her legacy alive, which is the best kind of tribute, anyway."

She summoned a half-smile for this suggestion which paralleled his own work. They always came back to that somehow, Con always denying that his could make any real difference. Maybe that was why his words failed to inspire her now—because he never believed them himself.

"So. Now what?" he asked awkwardly. "You start the genealogy on the graves—"

"I leave." She watched the look of shock on his face melt into quiet disappointment. "It was only because of Josephine that my time here got extended," she explained. "Without her, there's no more answers to find—she *was* the history in this town."

"You're just giving up, then." He said it slowly, as if to let it sink in. "After all the research you did, tracking down the graves. That's it."

"There's nothing left I can do," she said. "I can't find answers without help, and even then, there's no guarantee the truth is still around to find. Even Josephine's collection might not have contained the answer." She could hear the frustration in her voice. Sadness more than anger, for the way things turned out. Not just with the cemetery, she knew, but the carver whose identity seemed linked to it in her mind for reasons she could never quite define.

The crowd in the square grew louder as red and gold fireworks whistled the tune to *Dixie*. "I'll still write about them," she said, watching the color stream down. "Tell their story, or as much of it as I know. Then, they won't be forgotten, no matter what happens with the cemetery."

He leaned closer, trying to be heard above the festivities. "Will you come back?" he asked, blue eyes finding hers with a look of quiet expectation.

Amelia's words floated in the back of her mind, stirring her own doubts for this sudden connection, a spark born as fast and bright as those which appeared overhead. Perhaps it would go out just as quickly. Ten days was a short time for any decision involving the heart.

"I don't know," she said, finally. "I just...I'm not sure it would work."

She could see the hurt flicker briefly in his glance. "Not that I'm saying you're wrong," he began. "But these last few days—I've only felt this way once before. I thought it must mean something."

Regret welled in her throat, an ache she fought back. "Maybe it does mean something. A sign that you're ready to move forward. Be part of the world again." She did not say with her. It seemed impossible to say after so short a time; to pin all his hopes of a future on a single person, whom he'd scarcely known, seemed wrong.

"You have a place in this community, same as everyone else here tonight," she said. "People who might appreciate your skill if you didn't hide it away."

He shook his head. "We've been over this. It's not that simple for me."

"Important choices seldom are." There was so much else she wanted to say, but none of it was coming out right. The more they spoke, the further apart they grew. Literally, even with Con standing to face the activity in the square.

"They don't even know what they're celebrating," he said. "An end to superstition? An imagined curse? An illness? It's just a made-up story at this point, to them and to everyone who comes here tonight."

She followed his glance, seeing the audience that was scattered across the roped-off downtown, watching the colored lights crackle above them. Kids in costumes or with painted faces were hoisted onto their parents' shoulders, pointing wildly to the bursts of color overhead.

Fluttering above, the banner with its Celtic symbols was faintly visible in the lamplight.

Jenna looked at Con to find his back was still turned to her. Quiet fell between them.

In the square, shouts and cheers went up for the lights that blazed across the sky.

∞∞

They hadn't really said good-bye, something that occurred to Jenna as she packed her bags later that night, folding clothes and sliding papers into a folder. Her camera, with its pictures from the last several days, rested back in its case. When she developed the film, there would be one of Con, his blue eyes staring back at her from the spring.

All she could picture now was the look on his face right before he left. The way he gently squeezed her arm, his parting words swallowed by the sound of the festival breaking apart. She had watched him disappear in the mass of strangers, wondering if she just made the worst mistake of her life.

Common sense told her it was the only choice to make. Her life was a road, after all, constant changes in the path to each new story she sought.

His was vulnerable and hurt, tucked away inside a wood that looped back on the past hundred years, unchanged by everything but neglect.

Morning brought an overcast sky, and rain that pattered against the windows of the historic inn. Jenna waited third in line at the desk, her room key in hand, along with her credit card. It took her a moment to recognize the woman in the sensible tweed skirt and flats who entered the lobby door.

Josephine Maudell's nurse, a relieved look on her face as she spotted the writer. "Looks like I caught you just in time," Mollie said, folding an umbrella to leave by the door.

Jenna smiled, moving to give the older woman a hug. "I'm so sorry about Josephine," she said.

"We all are, hon. It was coming on for a while now, but that doesn't make it easier." With a sniffle, she pulled back to look Jenna in the face. "You really brightened up her world those final days," she said. "Gave her a sense of purpose again, like when she still ran the society."

"I was looking forward to hearing more of her stories," Jenna said.

The woman chuckled. "She was looking forward to telling them. In fact," she said, rooting through the bag she carried, "she found something to give you that day if things had worked out. She meant to do it before, but said it went clean out of her mind—her memory wasn't as good lately, you know."

She handed Jenna a small leather book, a size that might easily fit in a pocket. The binding was cracked in several places, no print of any kind on the cover or spine.

"What is it?" she asked, a strange tingle passing through her with the book's ancient appearance.

"A diary from one of her kinfolk—well, the kind with several 'greats' in their name." She laughed. "She said which one, but I've clean forgotten the name. The handwriting looks a little hard on the eyes. I guess you'll know what to do with it, though."

"Should I take this?" she asked. "It must belong to someone else now—some relative—"

The nurse shook her head. "None of them would appreciate it half as much as you," she said. "She wanted you to have it. To remember her by, if nothing else."

"Thank you," Jenna said. She opened the cover. No date or name was inscribed to give her a clue how it related to her work. Still, Josephine must have thought it would be helpful. That was reason enough to look through it, and to cherish it in the memory of the history-driven figure who was so thrilled by her research.

"Are you ready to check out?" The clerk was peering expectantly at her over the cash register.

Mollie gave her a last hug. "Good luck, hon. I'll be looking for your book to come out."

Was it coincidence? Jenna kept the book in her hand as she checked out, feeling the leather that was rough, but fragile at the same time. Instead of exiting, she took her bag to one of the chairs in the small sitting room. She stared out the window, the book resting on her lap. Her agent expected her to be in Louisiana by nightfall, already booking a room for her at a local hotel. She should save this for later, yet she didn't move.

Why couldn't she let this go? All the other cemeteries had loose ends, with graves she couldn't identify. This place had been special, somehow. Personal in a way that none of her research projects ever were before.

She looked down at the book she held, afraid to open it and find another glimpse of the truth that always managed to evade her. Steeling herself for disappointment, she flipped past brittle pages, where handwriting was crammed to fit the space in small loops.

A woman's hand, but not as elegant as the doctor's had been. She scanned the page for clues to its author, breath catching when she saw the year noted at the beginning of each entry.

Eighteen sixty-two: the same year as the epidemic, and Arthur's enlistment in the Confederacy.

Its narrative, though plain, gave a vivid sketch of the one who wrote it down. Jenna pictured a girl on the verge of womanhood, shy and modest by nature. A heart that felt deep devotion for its Creator, and for the family that was split apart when the war claimed her brother's service in arms.

Summer gave way to fall with a flip of the pages. On November 1st came a brief account of the Mischief Night prank, the journal's owner writing:

This symbol is not familiar to my own eyes, but Granny Clare saw it once on a grave in the Highlands. I don't much care for the look of it. The dye the children used is almost the same color as blood, and I wish someone would scrub it off. No one does, though, so I must get used to it, I suppose.

Jenna paused. This was familiar to her; not just the phrases, but something about the writing itself. She felt as if it was tugging at her sleeve, some remembrance just beyond her reach.

She turned the page. Further down, she noted the first signs of the epidemic. The boy Charley's death, the school teacher, and another name she recognized from the gravestone rubbings she had made. The words were tumbling into her mind faster now as she read them.

November 16th 1862: They found Mr. Roan today. Two

boys peeked through his window on a dare, and saw the poor body lying on the floor. I heard they buried him in the grove where his family rests, and that someone has cut that same mark into the stone that Papa uses for those in the cemetery. No one seems to grieve his loss, but I feel sorry for Mr. Roan that he left no friend to mourn him.

Jenna continued on, forgetting to breathe as she read.

Many come to see the doctor or to stick a note under the door asking for medicine. It is terrible to see how she wears herself out, hardly sleeping or eating between the work she does. I help her as best I can, but there is little for it except to pray this illness will soon leave our midst.

Jenna leaned closer, silently mouthing the words preserved in the long-ago journal. Other guests who passed by offered her strange looks, but she didn't care. Her only concern was for the hundred and fifty year old secret that might be buried somewhere in the faded binding. Not knowing what to expect, she turned another page.

25

The doctor took ill last night.

Nell's pencil hovered above the page, hesitant to finish this painful thought. She blinked back tears, fighting the urge to give in to her emotions—a mixture of sadness and, strangely enough, hope, despite all that had transpired.

Hours before, she had left the doctor resting upstairs, the letter from Arthur clasped between her hands. The awful news it bore made Nell wonder if either of them would ever see him again. She could not help thinking of him dying in a crowded hospital corridor miles from home. It was a pain that paled only when compared to the loss of faith he described so bitterly according to Mariah's words.

Nell tried to write him, crouched over a candle's flame at the parlor's desk. All the words of comfort seemed stale, so she laid her pen down mid-sentence to stare at the dying embers in the hearth. Eyes drifting closed in silent prayer, she pictured a dark-haired youth in a hospital bed, his features battered and weary. He was lost right now, scarred in ways other than physical injury. She believed his faith was deep rooted, though, too long entrenched to simply die without a fight. *Let him see Your hand guiding him*, she thought. Leaning her head against the desk, she let the hair fall across her face, blocking the dim view of the parlor.

She woke in early morning to the sound of a heavy thud upstairs. Half-asleep, she imagined it was Henry rising—only there was no Henry, not upstairs anyway. With this realization, she was awake again, listening. The sound of movement was coming from Henry's old room, the doctor's quarters.

Nell took the stairs with haste. Pushing open the door to the doctor's room, she found Mariah sprawled beside the writing desk.

"Please," Mariah said weakly, glancing up at her. "The daybook. I need to write—"

"You need to rest," Nell corrected. Gently, she pulled the sick woman to a sitting position, supporting her slender frame. She wondered whether to call for her father's help. He would be in the barn already, tending the livestock before his ride to the smithy forge. Her mother would be with him. Granny Clare still asleep in the bedroom downstairs, where the heavy quilts were her best defense against rheumatism on winter mornings.

"Hold onto me," she instructed, draping the doctor's arm around her own small shoulders. Staggering upward, she pulled them both to a standing position and moved to the bed, where the covers had been left in disarray. Tangled up with a shawl was a large volume that Nell quickly placed aside as she eased the doctor against a stack of pillows. "Let me fetch the others from the barn—"

"No, wait." A hand gripped her arm, pleading with her to stay. "There is something I must tell you, before I have not the strength left. This fever muddles my thoughts, but I am certain that what happened— what I saw—was more than imagination."

"What did you see?" Nell asked, troubled from the intensity in her gaze. The boy, Charley, had been the same, she realized. His mind wandered to other times and places while she clasped his hand beside the bed.

"It was a dream," Mariah said. "But a sign, as well, I think. An answer to prayer."

Had she misheard? Nell could think of no response, her glance falling on the leather volume still open on the bed. The Bible she read aloud from the night before and then placed on the side table when she left. Meaning Mariah had opened it again later that night, despite the doubt she expressed when they talked.

"I prayed He would guide me," Mariah said, words coming fast between breaths, "and then I had such a strange dream. Of a river with soldiers drowned below, and a washerwoman on the shore to clean the burial clothes."

This reference to the *bean nighe* made Nell shiver, as if talk of superstition from the doctor's lips confirmed her fears.

The doctor looked as if she might faint with the recollection of her dream. "They died in the water," she gasped, "water stained with crimson—"

"This is too distressing for you," Nell interrupted, wishing she would let her go for help. The hand clinging to her was so desperate, though, she couldn't leave even to call for help from a window.

"When I woke, I knew." Mariah's voice was hoarse. "Knew the water has caused our suffering these past weeks."

"The water," Nell repeated, not understanding the claim. "We have always drank from the spring, and never had trouble."

The doctor shook her head. Her fingers clutched at the girl's sleeve, drawing her close.

"Contaminated. It has been contaminated," she said, slowly. "I read of it long ago in a medical journal...but somehow forgot. The water, not the air, is what makes us sick." Her words thickened, stumbling over themselves as she spoke.

To Nell's ear this seemed nonsense; but then she knew too little of science to doubt it as others might. "What can be done?" she asked "Many have no other means of water aside from the spring. It is only a few that have a different source, and they are so far away, on the edges of town—"

"There can be no water consumed from the spring that has not been boiled first," the doctor replied. "Your grandmother saved you all. She made tea because she loved it more than fresh water...even from the pump. I took her tea at mealtimes but drank the pump's water at the homesteads. That's why...why I am sick."

Nell sank onto the bed. Taking the doctor's hand, she found its skin to be callused as her own. "You say this answer comes from God," she said, softly, "yet I have heard you speak many times of His indifference to our troubles. Why do you think He has told you this? Why do you believe it?" She had to know the answer. Not just for the sake of explaining to others that the doctor condemned their water supply, but because the woman lying before her was a friend.

"Many things have changed my mind," Mariah answered slowly. "Some of them from my life here and others from the life I knew as a girl." She closed her eyes and drew a clearer breath. The cough in her chest was momentarily gone, it seemed, her hand remaining in Nell's clasp. "My mother's faith is what I remember most about her, even more so than the illness that took her from me. You have often spoken of things she believed, things she wanted *me* to believe." Drawing another breath, she continued, "My doubt had been sealed with her death, my child's mind thinking she was misguided those times when she spoke of God's healing. It was despair that drove me to seek His aid last night, though I had wished for it many other times, but—but I did not know how—"

Nell let her talk without interruption, pressing her fingers in reassurance. Forgiveness was all she lacked it seemed, for the heart to make itself right.

"It is difficult," she said, face still damp from crying. "The prayer I knew from childhood seems too simple for such a request."

"Since we must believe as children do, nothing is wrong in such a prayer," Nell answered. "If you wish to say it now, I will help. I will help in any way that I can."

Gratitude flitted briefly over the doctor's worn features. They were so altered in such little time, Nell realized, from those of the young woman who had been waiting at the station. Pain and fatigue had made them older, yet this moment of confession had begun to ease those lines.

After a moment, Mariah closed her eyes again. Bowing her head, her lips moved to find the words of repentance. "My life I give to Your keeping—do with it as You see fit." This whisper at the close of the prayer faltered, its words as quiet as the ones Nell had heard softly, brokenly spoken in the seconds before.

Tears escaped Nell's eyes. She let them fall unchecked, relief outweighing the sadness that led to this moment.

When Mariah had grown quiet after her prayer, they sat in silence, the clock chiming the hour from downstairs.

Five in the morning. Her family would return in another hour expecting to find breakfast ready. Across from her, the doctor leaned her head back against the pillows. "I can rest now," Mariah spoke again, this time to Nell. She let go of the girl's hand with a faint smile. "Find Mr. Darrow. Tell him about the spring. He will know how best to tell others."

Nell nodded. "After that, I will come back and sit with you," she promised. The ashen features beneath the curls worried her, even with the doctor's expression once again calm. "There must be something more I can do to help. Something to bring down the fever." She looked towards the vials of medicine on the nearby table.

"All that can be done for me has been," Mariah said. She wasn't looking at the table, but the Bible tumbled open on the blankets. She closed the cover, fingers resting there.

She was no better when Nell returned.

Mariah did rest for a time, but her sleep was broken with bouts of sickness. Coughing left her unable to speak, the medicine Nell gave her impossible to keep down.

Nell bathed her brow, pushing back the curls she had sometimes envied.

Granny Clare brewed her healing tea, while Mrs. Darrow heated bricks and wrapped them in rags to warm the foot of the bed.

Mariah seemed not to notice these attempts at soothing, her mind roaming as freely as the gaze that searched the four pine walls. Mostly, she looked for Arthur, his name escaping her lips more than once as she woke from sleep. Other times, she called for her mother. There was no distress in her voice to Nell's ear, her tone hopeful as she peered at the growing light from the window. The clock chimed the hour of six, then seven. Five minutes to eight, the hands were stopped to mark the moment her struggle ceased.

Mirrors were covered, the curtains drawn so that candles burned at mid-morning. Granny Clare rang the hand bell from the old country twenty-one times in reference to the doctor's short life. Its mournful sound carried through the house, reaching Nell's ears as she stretched a sheet across the lifeless form.

Papa has agreed to speak in Mariah's stead at the town meeting this afternoon. He and mama set off directly after lunch, and I sit alone in the parlor, since Granny has retired for a nap. Never has the house felt so still, with the doctor's poor body lying upstairs.

Tomorrow, we prepare her for burial, a task I can bear only by knowing she found her faith those final hours. It amazes me still how she let the Savior guide her to the solution for our troubles. This dream of water she described, and her realization that our wooded spring has caused this sickness among us, is the closest thing to a miracle I have witnessed my entire life.

Even now, she could hardly believe such a thing had happened in this place, and to people that she knew and cared about. She tried to imagine what the doctor's mind understood so readily from the vision of the dead beneath the water and found nothing except pain in the picture.

What if no one believed Mariah's final piece of advice? Superstition ran strong in these parts, the wandering spirit of the plat-eye more likely to gain credence than a young woman's theory of water being polluted. What if nothing was found, or could ever be found to prove it was so? Would people keep drinking the water and dying?

Anxious, she glanced to the window. It was a pointless gesture since the curtains were drawn and blocked the outside view. Her parents had been gone for roughly an hour, long enough to deliver their news to those who gathered at the meeting in town.

It is useless to worry, I know, when already God has seen fit to reveal this piece of information. He worked in the heart of a skeptic, a woman as firm in her disbelief as my own heart has been in its faith all this time. Yet I continue to question His ability to implement His Will—to believe He will make a way for our neighbors to receive this message that even Mariah herself accepted without delay. I must shake this doubt, and learn to trust no matter the outcome of this crisis we face.

The sound of the front door banging shut made her push away from the desk and her half-finished journal entry. Her family had returned from the meeting, and with them brought the answer she wrestled with even now. Bracing herself for what might be said, she passed quickly through the hall, where a tall shadow was cast from the person standing in the entryway.

She was almost upon them when she saw her mistake.

The figure that lingered in the hall was not her

father, or, for that matter, any other member of the Darrow household.

It was someone Nell did not recognize at all.

26

A ragged youth clutched the wooden bench by the door, face half-hidden by a dingy hat. His jaw was unshaved, his clothes far too big for the scarecrow frame beneath. A cloth bundle rested on his back, a knife sheathed in the belt looped through his trousers.

Nell's thoughts flew to stories of deserters and enemy soldiers who broke into homes in search of food and other goods. Scream frozen in her lungs, she stumbled backwards, accidentally knocking a candlestick from the hall table.

At the sound, a pair of eyes—coal black and instantly familiar—rose to meet hers.

"*Arthur*," she said, breathless with the realization. Frozen, she stared as if a phantom of the convict hung in Crooked Wood, who used to haunt her dreams, had materialized—the plat-eye or the washerwoman from tales of old. After a moment, her common sense returned to the soldier's obvious distress.

Taking his arm, she helped him to the bench, seeing he all but clung to the nearest support to hold himself upright. "You are here," she cried in disbelief. She sank down beside him, still holding onto him. "We thought—that is, I was so afraid you would not come back to us. That you would stay at the hospital or—"

He shook his head, returning the touch with gentle pressure from his calloused fingers. "Nothing could keep me from leaving that place," he said, voice hoarse with exhaustion. "Even if I had not been given a furlough, I would have come home." This was said with a colder manner. Eyes narrowing, he asked, "Do you think it wrong of me to admit it?"

"I think all that matters is you are here now," she said, faltering under the bitterness in his tone. Clearly, he expected her to scold him; perhaps he even wanted her to, knowing deep down that such a sentiment was mistaken.

She noticed the stain on his shirt, the mark of an open sore. "Your wound should be tended," she said. "There are bandages and also some of Granny's herbs that I can mix into a poultice."

"The stain is an old one," he assured her, pulling at the fabric with a thoughtful expression. "It is still painful, of course, and slows me down a little, as you see. None of that is important, though. Not when I have a proper physician to look after it for me."

Fear trickled through her at the thought of telling him something so painful. "You should at least take something to eat after your journey," she said, starting to rise. "It seems there was a little bread and pork left from last night's supper—"

"Where is she, Nell?" He gripped her arm with a force that scarcely seemed possible from the starving frame. "They told me people have been sick here. Dying, even. Mariah has cared for them. She is in danger, perhaps." He ran a hand through tangled curls, the frayed hat balanced on his knees. "Has she called at a patient's house? I can go to her on foot if it is not too far. Otherwise, I should have to trouble your father for his second-best mare."

"Rest awhile," Nell encouraged, avoiding both his question and his glance as she spoke. "Your injury shouldn't be tested this way. I am sure the doctor would agree."

"Forget my injury," he snapped, pushing away the hand that encouraged him to stay seated. "Mariah can advise me after we are reunited. That is all I care about and feel I will go mad with waiting. Surely *that* can do my health no good." This was said with a spark of the old humor, sending a pang through her conscience.

Sitting beside him again, Nell placed her fingers firmly over his hand. "It is true there has been much sickness and death here these past weeks." She bit her lip, searching for any way to lessen the blow. "Mariah cared for all who would let her," she began softly, "sometimes going without sleep or food for days. She grew ill, but continued to work, with no thought for herself. I don't know how she did it, how anyone could have unless God Himself gave them the strength."

"Stop," he said, voice cold with warning. "Don't talk this way. Tell me what has happened to her, where to find her."

Nell sobbed, unable to hold it back any longer. "She is gone from us. This morning, she succumbed to the illness. I was with her and held her hand." Her tears were coming freely now, for she could not stop them. Before her vision blurred, she saw the pain in Arthur's hollow face.

"It isn't true." Disbelief flared in the coal eyes. "After what I've gone through, everything I've lost...it can't be. It can't." His words died away in a whisper of despair, hands clutching his head.

She reached to comfort him, feeling him shrug away from her.

He struggled to his feet, his steps lost for direction. "I have nothing left," he said. "My faith, my dearest friend, the girl I loved—all taken from me. There can be no reason, no possible good to come from such loss."

"You have friends, still," she reminded him gently. "You have parents who love you, and a God Who never forsakes you, whatever your heart says right now."

There was no response to this, except a faint groan. He moved to the parlor, hands resting against the desk where Mariah used to conduct her business. Shoulders stooped, he hung his head in something that resembled defeat more than a prayer.

Nothing she said at this time would be heard— that much Nell realized from her own experience with grief. For this reason she, too, rose.

"I will make you something to eat," she said, gently. "Sit down and rest. You need your strength— Mariah would want you to take care of yourself." With that, she went to the kitchen, preparing what few comforts she could offer Arthur, who mourned his love. Maybe when he was ready, he would find her there, and agree to hear the truth of Mariah's sacrifice.

❧

Arthur had left the hospital in a farmer's cart, his tattered soldier's coat rolled inside a blanket on his lap. The plain cotton shirt in its place made him look like a farmer's son again, with no brass buttons or kepi hat to reference his service.

Eighty miles, then sixty lay between him and the place he called home. Two strangers from different towns provided his transportation, the second one a photographer on his way to the bigger town of

Woolwich.

"Sad country out this way," he told Arthur with a shake of the head for scrappy fields and lean-to sheds along the road. "Most folks poor as the dirt on their boots—those that has any boots, that is."

"They do what they can," Arthur replied, clutching the bundle of fabric that held his tattered pride. His home was a poor one compared to fine houses in cities, but no part of him wished to disown it, with the wound burning beneath his shirt to remind him what he sacrificed to protect it these past months.

Smoke curled on the horizon as they drew close to town. Arthur clutched the side of the buggy, straining for a view of the shops and sites of old. What he saw on closer inspection left him more puzzled than comforted, though.

Houses were shuttered, curtains closed against the mid-day sun. Upon more than one door, he spied a crudely painted symbol that struck him as almost pagan-like in appearance, the vivid red drawing his eye.

More troubling still was the black crepe paper strung through some of the door handles. They weren't among the homes that sent a soldier to war, making him wonder even more for the nature of their loss.

"Spot of trouble here," the photographer guessed, a flick of the reins slowing the horse's pace as they drew near the business street. Closed signs were placed on doors that should read as open, the dry goods store the only place to boast a welcome message to visitors.

Arthur shouldered his bundle, climbing to the dusty lane below. Before he could fish a coin from his pocket, the photographer had urged his horses in another direction. A hand raised in farewell, he called, "Good luck to you, son," in a voice that implied the soldier would need it in such a place.

He could use his soldier's pay to buy a new coat, and maybe a razor to replace the one he lost with his haversack. To see Mariah was his first wish—his strongest wish—but he dreaded meeting her this way, shabby and defeated, the same figure that strangers shrank from whenever the regiment had passed through towns for supplies.

The store's manager, Harold Girvin, peered at him through a veil of pipe smoke. "Passing through?" he asked, taking a moment to recognize the boy who used to buy penny candy from his shelves. When he did, astonishment dawned on his face—for a moment, Arthur believed he saw the glint of tears in the man's eyes.

"So you've come back to us," he said, offering a warm handshake. "It's good to see a body come back alive. Mighty good. We heard such different tellings of that event as to make it more a fable from the old country."

"I wish that is all it were." He turned the subject to the strange sights that greeted him, asking, "Where is everyone? All the shops are closed but yours. Is trade so bad these days?"

The man's face darkened. "You've not heard of our troubles, have you?"

It was then Arthur learned the reason for the black crepe on the door handles. Of Mariah, the manager could give no account, expect that she spent her days traveling the lanes in Crooked Wood. "That's where the trouble started, they say. A stench in the air that makes the fog last 'til afternoon."

He left the shop on foot, meeting not another soul on the road to the house where she boarded. Haste made him forgo a knock on the door, pushing it open as he nearly collapsed. It was then that Nell appeared, and even then, in her face, he could read the sorrow beneath her surprise.

It was all for nothing, his journey; the time he spent treating the wound in his shoulder, face scrunched in pain as he wrapped the makeshift bandage back in place. He had clung to life just to end with more grief, a blow even greater than the one delivered to him on the battlefield. This was what ran through his head, sitting alone in the Darrow's parlor. In this place, he'd spoken to Mariah for the first time, had first felt the warmth of her touch.

If not for his faith, he would have married her. Even if it was only for a few days, they would have been together as man and wife. He felt cheated of that happiness, anger boiling inside him for the God Who made him question the wisdom of their union.

No sobs came, only hatred more intense than anything he'd known in a while. Time slipped past, unmarked by the clock in the hall as Arthur gave himself over to the despair building inside him. The numb sensation he'd come to know from weeks of lying in a hospital bed would follow, as it always did when he felt the surge of pain and anger.

Noises from the other room pulled him from his thoughts. With it came the awareness that he was hungry, his mouth dry from breathing in the dust on the road. He felt almost ashamed that basic human needs should trump his grief, pulling him back into the living world again. Slowly, he moved towards the kitchen, where Nell was busy stirring something into a kettle.

A lamp burned on the table, illuminating her small form in its calico dress. She hadn't noticed his presence yet, intent on her work until he pulled out a chair. When she glanced up, strands of hair escaped its bun to frame the suntanned face.

They were friends of old, but part of him felt a stranger before her in the kitchen he'd visited dozens of times growing up. She had changed in some way. She'd grown older, as if grief and human struggle had worked the same changes in her as the war had wrought in him.

"This will do you good," she said, setting a cup of tea before him. There was one at her place as well, her hands cradling it when she sat.

Both were quiet, Arthur tasting his drink with a grimace for its strong herbal flavor. Reaching past the kettle, the girl offered him a plate with a napkin covering it. "You have not been fed proper for a while," she guessed. "It is not much, but the pork should taste better than the cornmeal Henry described."

"He is safe—your brother," Arthur said, uncovering the plate to find a slice of meat and some cold potatoes nestled beneath. Despite himself, his mouth watered with longing for the tastes denied him so long in camp. "Of course, you knew his fate already," he said, "or you would have asked me about it."

She smiled faintly. "We were all relieved to hear from Henry. I only wish he had mentioned your condition in the brief note he sent. Or that he had told us of poor Wray." That was all she said, letting the silence return as he halfheartedly continued eating from the plate of leftovers.

When he had almost finished, Nell spoke again. "There is something I need to tell you. Something I think you will be glad to hear."

Arthur could think of nothing that would make him glad in these circumstances. Nudging his cup aside, he said, "This brew isn't to my liking. Something pure from the spring would be welcome, given the parched feeling in my throat."

"I am afraid this is all we can drink," Nell replied. "For now at least, it is all that is safe."

"Safe?" He stared at her, not sure he heard correctly, so tired from everything, he would not be surprised if his mind were playing tricks on him.

She took a deep breath, plunging forward nervously. "Before she died, Mariah spoke to me of something in her mind. A conviction that she had found the cause of our epidemic."

With surprise, he listened as Nell recounted all that his sweetheart supposedly said in those final breaths. "She could not have been thinking clearly," he decided. "There was no faith in Mariah. She told me that many times."

"Yet I saw it," Nell replied. "I heard the sinner's prayer from her lips."

He frowned. "If you say this because you think it will give me comfort—"

"I say it because it is true." She gripped his hand, small fingers locking his own in place. "Mariah did find her way in the end. She had wanted to for much longer than that, had felt the Savior calling to her. It was the reason she cried out for Him when everything else failed her. And He gave her the answer to save the rest of us from sickness."

The press of her fingers pleaded with him to agree, but he couldn't. "There is no comfort for me in hearing this. Not when my heart is hardened against Him. Not after everything I have seen."

"We will find a way to soften it, then," she said. "For Mariah would want that, too."

27

Nell could see the stubborn hurt in his gaze, the lamplight making it darker than ever.

Arthur did not believe her.

His lips parted, saying, "I saw my faith chipping away more each month. Every time I reached for Him, something else would deepen the chasm. As if He rewarded my efforts to find Him with further indifference."

"There have been times I doubted as well," she said. "Especially with the plague bearing down upon us. It is not wrong to doubt, you know—only to give up hope of ever understanding."

"How can I understand such pain? My death would have been easier to suffer than what I have lost." Sighing, he continued, "You never loved as I did, Nell. Never felt the pull of another's heart so deep you could only be happy if they felt the same."

She had, although he did not know it. "Many hearts feel that way, with no chance of it being returned. Perhaps you were blessed to find one who shared your love, even for just a short time."

"Six weeks," he said. "That is all I had with her. Letters were a poor substitute for the time we might have shared. Had I known—" he shook his head, letting the rest go unspoken. His face was proof enough that he blamed himself, as well as God, for this misery.

"You can have no reason to regret such tenderness," Nell said. "Not when Mariah's prayer has made it possible to meet her again one day. That is something to be grateful for, at least."

His answer was slow to form, brow wrinkled in deep concentration.

"Think of her faith," she urged. "It was all you would have asked of her when you—when you wanted her to marry you. You cannot want to mock her final moments by denying them. Not when you loved her so much."

She could see him struggle to hold back tears, his tone softening when he said, "I think...it seems there is truth in what you say. You see things more clearly than I would. Even in childhood, you had the best judgment of anyone I knew."

She wished to avoid such praise, but there was no time, Arthur gently returning the touch of her fingers. "You must think me selfish, indulging this grief as if it belonged to me alone. I forget that you, and others we know, have suffered badly."

This mood would be challenged, she knew, and changed every few moments over the coming days. The challenges which lay ahead would provide more pain—not the least among these would be Mariah's burial, an event they must all face in the following day.

"I can make no promise to change my unbelief," he said.

"I would not ask it. Not unless it was sincere. You know that, Arthur."

He swallowed. "I would not object to trying. Were you to help me, Nell, it would be a great comfort. If I could lean on your faith until I...until I am more sure of myself."

"Of course," she said. "When you are ready."

Slowly, he brought their clasped hands to rest against his forehead. She felt her fingers against his face for the first time and trembled in response. Shaky breaths escaped his frame, filling her with pity for his pain. Even if she had not loved him so deeply, she would feel it. They would always be friends—and fellow believers, too, when this time of doubt someday passed for the young man before her.

"I can think of nothing but questions." With a deep breath he asked, "Will you pray with me, Nell? Pray for the answers. For whatever good can come out of all our pain."

"I will," she replied, closing her eyes at the same moment as Arthur did, their heads bowed together to seek the answers.

ॐ

March 22nd, 1863: Today a few people gathered in town to honor those who were taken from us, and our delivery from the illness trial we endured. A simple prayer was spoken, a hymn was sung, and a bell was rung in the old manner of bidding farewell to the departed souls one has loved.

There are many kinds of love, I believe. Some come without warning, a thunderbolt in the blue sky. Others take a slower path to find us. My own has mostly been the latter kind, I suppose, with years of happy and painful moments alike to forge the bond. Dearest Arthur was always in my heart, and I am glad to find there is still room for me in his. For he has told me that he has come to love me—not as a friend, but as something more.

Neither of us will ever forget Mariah, even in our love.

Because of her willingness to hear God's counsel, there were no more stones added to the northern part of the cemetery to bear that awful sign of plague. We have reason every day to be grateful that she led us to the source of our suffering.

Some people—those who still believe there was a curse at work among us—say we must find a new burial ground. They feel trouble may come to those who set foot on the resting place of a plague victim. I can only sigh and shake my head for such talk, since I suffer nothing but bittersweet memories when I carry flowers there every week for those who rest there. But others—rightly so—argue there is so little room left in the cemetery that only a few graves can join those we loved and lost.

Perhaps a time will come when less talk is made of the curse, and more about God's way of showing us what really happened, if we will remember that a careless prank on a night for making mischief led to a very real kind of terror. Even with proof, though, some will never believe. But I will always know and be thankful.

It was the last entry in a journal that had only one more piece of the past to offer. A folded newspaper clipping from the *Woolwich County Times* was slid inside the book's trough. Its edges crumbled as Jenna unfolded it to read the headline: "Farmer's Bull Found in Spring after Mischief Night Fun.".

Dated a week after Mariah Moore's death, the story detailed how a bull's carcass had been discovered in the community's fresh water supply, upstream from the pump site. Already quite old for its breed, the animal was thought to have escaped from its field and passed away naturally while living among the stretch of woods along the spring, where its body inspired a group of older boys to roll it into the water near the boggy shores.

Its fur had still born traces of the dye the children had used to paint it as a mythical beast for scaring people, the symbol from the doors. Two broken, twisted tree limbs were tied to its head like vast antlers spiraling above the skull. It had been dragged from the water by local men and burned.

No mention was made of the doctor or her theory about contaminated water—only that the carcass was responsible for a terrible stench in the woods that some people had blamed for causing sickness. And that children had spotted the body sometimes in the twilight and believed it to be the plat-eye of old stories, a huge shape crouching in the water. No doubt, both the smell and the rumors were consequences intended by the pranksters, who had not known what kind of horrors existed in contaminated streams.

Jenna stared at this fragment of paper, amazed that in her hand, she held the long lost secret to Sylvan Spring's curse. She could no longer recall what she expected to find, but certainly nothing as strange as a rotting carcass painted as a folklore monster.

But it was the loneliness of three graves in the wooded cemetery that haunted her most. Especially that of the doctor, who died saving the others. Beside it lay the soldier and his childhood friend, who came to mean even more to him when he rose from his grief.

Would the town's modern-day residents feel the same? The festival crowd had kept alive the memory of those superstitions for years without even knowing why their ancestors believed them. Would they find the true story, one of faith and science, equally fascinating? Or disappointing?

There was one person she knew for certain would

understand. To share this with him was her first impulse; her second would be to apologize for the way she fell apart the night before. She had pushed away the possibility of a relationship based on hesitation and caution for his feelings. It was a reaction she wished she could take back more than anything.

Outside, the rain still fell, spattering the banner from last night's celebration. It flapped in the breeze as her car passed beneath, her hand flicking the turn signal for the direction that would take her to the outskirts of town.

Gradually, the buildings gave way to fields and trees. Jenna turned the car onto the narrow dirt road, fingers gripping the wheel with a mixture of nervous excitement. As she turned the corner, windshield wipers swept a path to show the farmhouse and workshop, the battered monuments leaning against the garden fence.

"Con?" She rapped against the workshop's storm door, rain cascading off the awning behind her. "It's Jenna," she called, knocking again. "I found something—and I really need to talk with you."

No answer. Turning around, she looked to the farmhouse to find its windows darkened. The truck was gone from the driveway, Con apparently choosing today for one of his rare trips away from the workshop.

Tears burned her eyes, telling her how badly she had wanted him to be there. For a while, she stayed huddled under the awning, listening for the sound of his truck's engine above the downpour.

Maybe this was more than bad timing. If her heart was wrong...well, maybe it was God's gentle way of telling her it wasn't meant to be. She wished she could be sure what He planned by letting her meet Con Taggart. Their time together was so brief—yet the connection forged between them so deep. She could not escape the feeling that something must come of it for one or both of their lives.

Is this a missed opportunity—or did we already share whatever was meant between us? I can't see how we'll meet again, unless You intend it...so please, tell me what I should do.

She waited longer. The rain had become cold, soaking through her clothes. Puddles formed in the truck's tire ruts in the driveway, turning into muddy rivers overflowing with water.

Joyce was counting on her to go to the next assignment. Her book had deadlines and responsibilities attached to it. And she had no idea when—or if—Con would come home before those obligations swept her away again.

With a sigh, she gathered her bag and ventured into the rain to leave.

29

Ten Months Later

The package came while Jenna was finishing up breakfast. Scraping bits of egg from a frying pan, she paused at the sound of the door buzzer for her Maryland apartment.

When she saw it, she knew what it had to be. Full of anticipation, she cleared a spot among the papers on her desk. Ripping tape from the box's top, she pulled back cardboard flaps to reveal six glossy hardbacks among the packing materials.

Advance author copies for her latest book, still a month away from being released. Slowly, she pulled one from the depths, studying the title splayed across the cover. *Stories Behind the Stones: A Tour of the Deep South's Forgotten Cemeteries.*

Flipping open the cover, she read the dedication printed inside.

> *To the real 'ghosts',*
> *Who never fade as long as we remember them,*
> *and*
> *To those who dedicate their time and talent to keeping*
> *those memories alive.*

She flipped the pages, watching sections go by for places in Georgia and Mississippi, Louisiana and

Tennessee. Slave cemeteries left to sink in the swamps; private family graves forgotten behind a rotting plantation.

Reaching the section for Alabama, she paused where a set of images had been inserted. Pictures of graves that all bore the same carving of an inverted half-moon, its shape pierced through with a broken arrow. She touched the picture, her eyes closing in a memory.

The feel of her fingers tracing a beveled edge in a piece of rough-hewn stone. Bits of dust and sand clinging to it in the trailing touch. Strong hands closing around her own, guiding them to form a shallow curve in a piece of slate, hammer and chisel beating a steady rhythm.

"You should celebrate," her agent said, calling to congratulate her for the critic's favorable reviews. Quotes from some of these were displayed on the back of the book, dubbing it *achingly romantic*, and *haunting, down to the last page*. According to Joyce, such lofty praise called for a night on the town with friends, or someone even more special.

"Actually, I already have plans for how to celebrate," Jenna said. Her gaze returned to the page where the Celtic V-rod peered back at her from beneath the layers of rust and grime.

∞

Dust rolled off the wheels of the rental car as Jenna steered it down the dirt lane. Her knapsack lay in the passenger seat, a bouquet of violets tucked carefully beside it. There had been two others of a different kind, which she left at the cemetery in town: roses for

Josephine Maudell's headstone and a mix of flowering herbs for Colleen Taggart's marker with the ivy pattern carved around its edges.

She had stood in front of this one the longest. As her hand rested against the chiseled slab, her mind wandered back to conversations with the man who fashioned it.

The peace she felt was unexpected, no guilt or self-doubt rising to twist her heart. It was as if she was forging a connection with the woman whose body was sleeping here, although she knew no ghosts or souls lingered in this peaceful grave. When she left, it seemed a clearer purpose drove her towards the cluster of woods by the spring.

The sign was the first thing she noticed. It was metal, with an arrow pointing in the direction of the cemetery's hiding place with the words *Historic Crooked Wood Cemetery, 1.5 Miles* painted in white lettering. She looked back at it in the rear view mirror, not at all sure she hadn't imagined it.

Had the county put it up from mere formality? The possibility had to be considered, though part of her couldn't help wishing another reason—another person—was behind the change of scenery. By the time she parked, her hands shook so much they nearly dropped the violets as she climbed from the car.

Gravel crunched beneath her feet, the path altered since she last took it months ago. Her steps were quick until she came upon the actual destination. Pulling off her sunglasses, she stared in disbelief at the scene before her.

A wrought iron fence surrounded the graveyard's perimeter. Inside, rows of headstones reflected the morning sun, free of the stains and cracks that marred them before. A few bore wreaths and flowers, decorative ribbons fluttering in the breeze.

Slowly, she pushed against the gate. It swung open without a sound, her steps muffled in the woodland ground cover. She passed through the yard, fingers trailing over the fully restored monuments with wonder. When she reached the three which sat beneath the sycamore, she crouched to study them with tears in her eyes.

They were just as she remembered, except the doctor's had been cleaned of the rust that tried to engulf its lettering. She reached out, tracing the name and then the symbol, with its eerie connotation, smiling ever so slightly when she thought how death's power was defied in the final brave gesture from the woman whose tomb it graced.

Beside it were the graves of the soldier and his wife, loyal to their friend even in death. Three hearts with the same faith to save them from a living nightmare, even as the shadow of those events had managed to survive over a hundred and fifty years of time.

She placed the bouquet of violets before the group of stones, still lost in the memory of their story when she heard a footfall in the grass behind her. Heart racing, she turned to face them and found Con standing there.

He stood on the path behind her, a look of shock in the blue gaze. It was as if he saw a ghost from one of the graves instead of the woman who found them by accident one rainy afternoon. "It's you," he said. "I thought I was seeing things. Wishful thinking."

This was her exact sentiment. "You did this," she said. "After what happened, the way we left it…in boxes, with labels..." She shook her head, struggling for a way to finish. "I thought you weren't ready to move on."

Con's face had softened as she spoke. He stepped closer. "It wasn't just me. The heritage society raised money for the fence, and sent volunteers out for the cleanup. So did one of the churches." He cleared his throat. "I, uh, started going there again. The church. You were right—it was time. Past time, actually, for me to be part of something again."

Jenna could feel herself trembling with the unexpected words. It was an outcome she had imagined countless times but never expected to find as reality when she finally summoned the courage to come back.

"I brought you something," she said, digging through her knapsack. "It's not the same as what you did here—" with another glance at the newly restored cemetery "—but I hope you'll like it."

Handing him one of the hardbacks, she watched him study its cover with a long look. When he read the dedication inside, a half-smile appeared on his quiet features. His gaze rose to meet hers, full of an emotion she recognized from her own barely contained feelings.

"I missed you," he said. "It's different from missing Colleen. Because you're still here, there's still a chance we could be together. Which makes it worse, somehow, when I think how it might not work out."

"But it might." Something inside her came undone with the words. Thoughts and emotions bottled up since they last spoke came tumbling out, with barely a breath in between. "That's why I had to come back," she said. "To see you again, to see if you still felt the same. I kept thinking of our time together, even though it was just a few days and that—" She stopped, drawing a breath. "That must mean something."

Across from her, Con grew still. "Then you feel it, too," he said. "I kept hoping you would. Praying I wasn't the only one who thought we could have a future together."

"We'll see it through this time," she promised. "We won't let it go just because it seems impossible. This time, we'll let faith guide us instead of doubts."

Tentatively, he took her fingers, drawing her closer to him as he searched her face with a tender look. "I never thought this could happen again," he murmured. "But it's real. That much I'm sure of. "

Jenna reached for him, stroking his jaw before they shared a kiss more tender than their first. She had wanted this to happen again since that day in the spring, when she hoped it was more than just a rash moment between two uncertain hearts.

When they pulled apart, she rested her forehead against his shoulder. "Thank you for looking after this place. Even though you weren't sure I'd ever see it."

"I'm glad you did," he said.

A breeze ruffled her hair, goose bumps traveling over her skin. With his arm curved around her, they moved slowly towards the gate, Jenna glancing back for a last look at the three graves nestled beneath the sycamore's tall shadow.